I0660162

THE CHEMIST

BOOK OF SIN
BOOK 4

MATTHEW DANTE

Book of Sin- Book 4- The Chemist

Copyright ©2025 Matthew Dante

All rights reserved.
Cover by **The Ravens Touch** @the.ravens.touch
Edited by Steph White (Kat's Literary Services)

No part of this publication may be reproduced, stored in a retrieval system, or transmitted in any form or by any means—electronic, mechanical, photocopying, recording or otherwise—without prior written permission from the author. The exception would be brief passages by a reviewer in a newspaper or magazine or online. To perform any of the above is an infringement of copyright law.

This book is a work of fiction. Names, characters, places, and incidents either are products of the author's imagination or are used fictitiously. Any resemblance to actual persons, living or dead, events, or locales is entirely coincidental.

Warning: This book contains scenes that may be considered triggering events for some involving extreme violence, murder, kidnapping, and torture.

ISBN eBook: 978-1-0689041-2-7

Paperback: 978-1-0689041-1-0

CONTENTS

Prologue   v

1. Diesel   1
2. Diesel   12
3. Zero   19
4. Diesel   28
5. Diesel   39
6. Diesel   46
7. Zero   53
8. Diesel   59
9. Diesel   66
10. Diesel   76
11. Diesel   85
12. Zero   91
13. Zero   96
14. Diesel   106
15. Diesel   112
16. Diesel   122
17. Zero   128
18. Diesel   137
19. Diesel   146
20. Zero   154
21. Zero   162
22. Zero   172
23. Diesel   179
24. Diesel   185
25. Diesel   195
26. Diesel   202
27. Zero   208

28. Diesel   217
29. Zero   224
30. Diesel   234
31. Diesel   243
32. Zero   248
33. Diesel   256
34. Zero   265
35. Zero   271
36. Diesel   278
37. Zero   290
38. Diesel   306
39. Zero   314
40. Zero   320
41. Diesel   335
42. Diesel   344
43. Zero   351
   Epilogue   360

   About the Author   373
   Acknowledgments   375
   Also by Matthew Dante   377

PROLOGUE

Profile #18
    Name: Nicolaus Baasch (a.k.a. The Chemist)
    Age: 52
    Marital Status: Single
    Net Worth: 3.5 Million Euro
    Bio:

- Scientist.
- Narcissist.
- Suspected kidnapper.

Unique Identifiers:

- Blind in left eye. Missing left finger.
- Has a thing for being in control and docile young men.

The large metal door beeped before being pushed open by a man holding a machine gun. The armed guard didn't make eye contact; he simply held open the door and waited for his employer to make his way through.

Good. It was nice to see that his simpleton guards knew their place. They may have been hired because of their physical strength and ability to follow orders, but the true show of power here was all about intelligence. Knowing what to ingest, what to avoid, and what didn't mix well with others. This was a place of experimentation. Of making hypotheses, testing out theories, and determining what worked best in which situations.

And of course... there was the other thing. The thing that paid the bills and made sure that his research and advancements could continue for decades to come. This other thing was also the reason that he had men with machine guns guarding the facility. There was too much at stake to just allow anyone to enter or leave... the facility.

Walking down the long corridor, Dr. Nicolaus Baasch ignored every person he passed, not stopping until he came to a door marked "DO NOT ENTER."

"Evening," Dr. Baasch muttered, giving the guards a slight nod with his head.

Both men returned his nod before lowering their weapons. The guard on the right of the door punched a code into the keypad, then pushed the door open once he heard the buzzer ring.

Without a word, the doctor walked through the door.

Fluorescent lights and flickering screens welcomed him, as well as a shit ton of electronic equipment, most of which were used for high-definition streaming and surveillance.

He walked to the center of the room, where a man wearing small, thin-framed glasses sat staring at a computer screen.

"How are we looking?" the doctor asked, stopping behind the man and placing a hand on the back of his chair.

"Right on schedule. The subjects are primed and ready to go."

Perfect. Dr. Baasch didn't like delays... or problems. He preferred numbers and timetables and everything running problem-free. This was also one of the reasons he quit working at the university years ago. He hated having to work with people and having them make last-minute changes or demands on progress.

"And Subject A?" the doctor asked.

The technician in front of him pressed a few keys on his laptop until a large monitor next to them lit up with the face of a woman in the center.

"Subject A has been given a sample of LX5 and is currently placed in the center of the grid."

They both watched as a young brunette, no older than twenty-five, struggled to get to her feet. Her hair was messy and fell chaotically over her face. When she managed to finally get both feet under her, she swayed as she concentrated on remaining upright.

"And her vitals?" Tracking his subjects' vitals was crucial

to his little experiment. He needed to know the effects of LX5 on the subjects and any possible side effects that may be present. Also, he didn't want his subjects to die too quickly. That was never good for business.

"Her heart rate is elevated, which is to be expected. And it appears that her hallucinations have just begun manifesting themselves." The technician pointed to the woman, who appeared to be swatting her hand at nothing in particular.

The doctor smiled. Right on schedule.

"And Subject B?"

The technician pressed a few more keys before a screen to their left went live, displaying the image of a dark-haired man growling and holding a metal pipe in his hands.

"Subject B was injected with LX3 and appears to be exhibiting the same heightened aggression and paranoia as our previous test subjects. Not sure where he got the pipe from, but it should make for an interesting show."

Glancing between both screens, the mad scientist marveled at his creations. He had spent the last three years designing his LX series of narcotics and was now busy studying the effects of the drugs on humans. It was all part of the experimental process. First, you theorize, then you design, test and observe the effects. Then you modify and adjust as needed. When this series is perfected, it will change the way we handle fear and paranoia.

Then he nodded toward the large screen hanging at the far side of the room. "And them?" Thick red numbers counted down from sixty.

"Right on schedule."

Perfect. Everything was going to plan.

"It's time to begin."

The doctor waited until the numbers reached zero before pressing the enter button on the technician's laptop and watched as the horrors began to unfold on the screens.

1

DIESEL

Straightening himself, Diesel ran his fingers under his nose, removing any evidence of the white powered residue that might be lingering before leaning forward and checking himself out in the mirror.

His eyes took a moment to focus as the effects of the last two bumps he had just done began their journey through his body. Warmth, followed by a tingling sensation, followed by a feeling of being pulled away, all added to the euphoric bliss sweeping across his body. He loved this part.

Smiling, Diesel leaned closer to the mirror to make sure that there were no traces of the powdery substance clinging to his nostrils. Not that he was ashamed for doing a line of coke, but rather he didn't think Matteo would appreciate his dancers strutting around onstage with a nose full of cocaine on full display. That didn't exactly scream "classy"—more like *five-euro hooker who will blow you in a back alley if you ask them nicely.*

Loads of clubs in Europe offered that sort of thing—naked young men, eyes glossy as fuck, with traces of drugs on their faces or needle tracks in their arms. But not here. Not at *La Maison de M*.

Here, at this club, Matteo and his boys offered nothing but class and luxury. A mix of high-end elegance and sinful debauchery.

Watching as his reflection came into focus, he scanned his features carefully.

Good. Nothing on his face and no evidence of his extracurricular activities. Matteo wouldn't freak the fuck out.

Lifting his hood over his head, he gave his cock a few extra tugs. In the mirror, he watched as the blood rushed to his cock, causing his meat to thicken in his boxer briefs. His cock always looked good when it was sitting low against the material—like a sleeping anaconda just waiting to wrap itself around its next victim.

Admiring the thickness of his shaft, he thought about all the men... and a few women who lost themselves in the pleasure of his beast. Remembering the way their eyes rolled back in their heads or the way their bodies quivered beneath him was... *fuck*, those memories were making him horny.

He needed to get laid. Not just shoot his load because someone was paying him to, but actually enjoy himself, connect with somebody...

Connect with somebody? Ha! Who are you kidding?

Diesel's jaw tightened as he stared at his reflection once again.

Who was he trying to kid?

Giving himself one last scan, he adjusted the waistband of his briefs, then adjusted the hoodie he was wearing. The zipper was undone, and his chiseled chest was on full display. He was going for that stoner-fuckboy look that always made men hard in their pants. It was that combination of not giving a shit and always being down to party that seemed to resonate with his client base.

Damn, he looked good. Even he would fuck himself. It was time.

Turning, he made his way down the short corridor from the guy's dressing room to the theatre's stage. Diesel nodded to a few of the crew members as he strutted past them.

He couldn't exactly remember their names, but one guy liked to smoke pot out behind the maintenance garage, while the other guy liked to get his dick sucked by the dancers on the DL. Always on the down low, these straight, questioning, sometimes-married straight guys... if you can call someone straight who enjoys having their knob worked over before coming down a man's throat in the darkness of a secluded maintenance area.

Diesel didn't judge. Every guy's secrets were his own.

So long as no one was getting hurt, he didn't care who got their dick sucked, when, where, or by whom.

"You ready, brother?" a familiar voice asked over his shoulder as a large warm hand landed on the back of his neck.

"Always. You want to take the lead? Or should I?" Diesel asked Jared as he stepped up beside him. He already knew the answer.

He and Jared had been best friends since they both started working at *La Maison* several years ago. Jared was a good guy. Caring, passionate, loyal to a fault. The kind of guy you would do anything for to keep around and in your life—even share him with a certain blue-haired, attention-deficit little shit who liked to play pranks and had the loudest freakin' orgasms Diesel had ever heard.

Glancing down at Jared's package, he wondered if perhaps Isaac's orgasmic screams had more to do with the size of Jared's rod and not the need to rub it in everyone's faces that he was getting dicked down on the regular.

No, Diesel wasn't jealous. Well, yes, okay. He was a tad jealous that he wasn't bustin' a nut as often as his best friend and his best friend's fuck-hole—a.k.a. Isaac. But, no, he was not jealous of the disgustingly sweet *relationship* that the two of them had been sharing for almost a year now.

Nope. Not jealous. Not even a bit.

"I'll lead," Jared noted with a wink of his eye.

Like there was ever a question. Always the top in the relationship.

That boy's butthole was probably so tight that it could make diamonds if sand ever got caught between his butt cheeks and left there for an extended period of time.

Actually, that was kind of gross. But the point was that Jared—who was gay—was one of those "strictly top" kind of guys. How boring.

We get it. You're a control freak and tough and like to act like the hero in the bedroom.

But in actuality, it was the guys who flipped who controlled all the power between the sheets. They were the dominators and the submissives. They were the ones who were able to give power as well as take it away. If one was bottoming and not getting what they wanted from their top, they could easily take control and seize power over their partner.

Kind of like him.

Diesel was one of those guys who liked to switch-hit. He liked to top, bottom, lead the train, onload/offload passengers... you name it. Diesel enjoyed doing it. He even played with titties from time to time. While pussy was not Diesel's meal of choice, he didn't mind having a bite here and there, especially when a questioning young dude was involved in the meal.

Pulling the curtain back, Diesel slapped his best friend's ass as Jared hopped up onstage to the sound of cheering, horny, rich men. *God, he loved that sound.*

Smiling, Diesel joined his buddy and let the music and cheers and cocaine take control of his body.

He loved the feeling. He was happy, confident, a tad arrogant, and horny as fuck. Perfect for getting down and frisky with a room full of cash-loaded, horny dudes who all wanted to shower him with attention and alcohol.

It was great being wanted.

Out onstage, Diesel pumped his arms to get the crowd going. They screamed and cheered while others threw cash on the stage at their feet. Diesel loved the feeling of power and control, knowing that it was up to him to decide how much or how little he showed these men. That their lustful eyes pleaded for mercy, begging him to show them more.

And he would... for a price.

Running his fingers slowly across his bare chest, he teased the rows of salivating men, no doubt wishing that they were onstage, licking every exposed piece of flesh that he allowed them to see.

Power was addictive.

Behind him, Jared removed Diesel's hoodie and tossed it over his shoulder. Next, Jared moved in close, wrapping his arm possessively around Diesel's body and began slowly licking the side of Diesel's neck.

To the casual observer, the act was hot as fuck. Sinful, sensual, and boner inducing.

To Diesel, it was torture. He tried his best not to laugh or twist away from the fiendish succubus currently trying to make love to the side of his neck!

How could one man's tongue be so fucking ticklish?

Across the room, Diesel spotted Isaac quietly giggling, knowing just how ticklish Diesel was whenever someone tried to suck on his neck.

Bastards.

Both of them.

Deciding he needed to break from Satan's tongue, Diesel bent over, being sure to press his butt back onto Jared's junk.

Let's see how funny you find this. Diesel smirked, stealing a glance over at Isaac.

Isaac was no longer giggling.

Enjoy this, you little giggling bastard. Yes, Diesel could be an asshole like that.

Grinding his ass deeper into Jared's lap, he winked at a handsome Filipino man who was waving a hundred-euro note up in the air.

Yeah, you want us, don't you?

Diesel and Jared had been doing a joint strip routine for the past two years. At first, it was a bit awkward. Jared, being the tight-ass alpha male that he was, had trouble relaxing and letting Diesel take control from time to time. But as they got to know each other and their friendship developed, Jared began to relax and let Diesel take the reins... once in a while. And their routines became f'ing hot!

No. There was nothing sexual going on between them. No matter how much it looked like they wanted to fuck each other onstage or how much he played with Jared's boner—hey, it was part of the job!—Diesel had no desire to stick any part of Jared's body in his mouth or up his ass.

It took a certain blue-haired little freak a few months to learn that fact when he first moved into the mansion—poor guy had the biggest hard-on for Jared, even though he refused to admit it to himself. Eventually, Isaac began to see that Jared was basically just a brother to Diesel. Okay, perhaps a frat brother—*ew.* He couldn't believe he compared himself to a beer-guzzling, brainless muscle pod. *What the fuck was wrong with him?*

They were performers.

They created fantasies when onstage. Fantasies that gave

them access to their clients' wallets and handfuls of cash stuffed into their underwear.

No. Diesel was not too proud to take his pants off and suck a dick for money. He was young, hung, and always up for a good time. Those that said otherwise were just jealous because their dick was too small to use to get what they wanted.

His dick was like a magical wand. He waved it around, and people became hypnotized by its power. He might not be the smartest man in the room or the best looking, but when it came to dicks, his commanded attention.

Moving in sync with the music, Diesel and Jared groped and ground and played with each other's bodies—all to the encouraging whistles and cheers of the rich and powerful men who came to *La Maison* searching for a good time.

After their three songs were done, Jared and Diesel joined their fellow brethren down on the floor, drinking and flirting with any horny guest who happened to make eye contact—or in Diesel's case—stared at his dick for way too long.

Yes, his dick was big, but Diesel never considered it weapon-status worthy. Although, sometimes, it did inflict a lot of pain... especially on those who weren't as "experienced" as they claimed to be.

"Your turn," Diesel announced, giving the Hungarian politician sitting next to him a devilish grin.

They were heavily engaged in a game of "Never Have I Ever," to which Diesel was painfully winning. Every friggin' question the man asked, Diesel had done.

Never have I ever... had a foursome.

Drink.

Never have I ever... been caught fucking outdoors on a motorcycle.

Drink.

Never have I ever... fucked a dude, then fucked his girlfriend right after.

That one had been a funny story.

One Halloween, he had been partying hard with some dude and his girlfriend, doing lines of coke and taking shots of whiskey, when his girlfriend decided she needed to run to the corner store to buy some more smokes. The second the bitch left the apartment, he pulled out his cock, and her boyfriend went for the ride of his life. He wasn't sure how long the girlfriend had been standing there, but the moment her boyfriend came, she announced it was her turn and practically pushed her man off Diesel's dick so that she could hop on and experience the ride herself.

Drink.

"I think you won this game," Diesel said, sliding his hand down the Hungarian's chest and grabbing the bulge jutting out from the man's dress pants. "Or perhaps I'm the winner after all."

Smiling, the man took a sip of his whiskey and let Diesel play with his cock.

Teasing and flirting. It was all part of the game.

Diesel would get the man nice and close, then stop, claiming he was getting thirsty. The man would either buy him a drink or ask him for a private show. That was the point at which Diesel would "finish the job"—for a fee, of course.

Onstage, the music shifted to some Euro fast-moving beat that Diesel and his untalented white ass could never hope to dance to. Somehow, Gunnar and Anders made it look so simple... and sexy.

Leave it to the six-foot-two, blond, blue-eyed Scandinavian brothers to make dancing to this crap somehow look like they were making a porn video onstage.

Whatever.

Two tables over, Isaac and Jared were having drinks with three strapping gentlemen who appeared to be from Bulgaria. Two didn't speak English, while the third seemed to be translating for them.

Do translators provide translation services in the bedroom as well? That might make for an interesting encounter.

Watching his best friend and his boyfriend work together, Diesel almost felt jealous. *Almost.*

Adjusting his grip on the Hungarian's thick piece of meat, Diesel glanced across the room to where Chase was sitting on a barstool chatting with Levi—his fiancé. Another case of love sickness striking hard at *La Maison.*

Diesel didn't exactly hate love... he just didn't trust it. Love was an emotion that made smart people stupid and kind people into monsters. It was crazy how many people Diesel knew who were willing to stab someone in the head if they so much as looked at their partner. *See?* Crazy.

Finally, Diesel's eyes fell on Matteo. The one man he owed everything to. The one man who cared if he lived or if he died.

Even Matteo, the man who swore off love so many years

ago, was sitting at the bar staring lovingly into his partner Ares's eyes.

How does that even happen? One day, Matteo was ready to stab the man in the eye just for breathing near him. The next, he was letting the man rub his belly and shower him with kisses.

See? Smart man, stupid.

There was no denying that his boss and mentor loved the crazy Russian. Romanian? German? Whatever the sneaky gun man was. Matteo had apparently gotten over his aversion to love and joined the other cultists as they polished off their crazy juice.

Then there was himself. The perfect reminder that all he had going for him was sex, drugs, and alcohol. All around him, he was surrounded by people who claimed to be his—his family. Yes, they all loved him and would always be there if he needed them. But in the end, they all had their own lives, and like everyone else in his life, they would all eventually leave him.

Alone.

In the end, that was all he was.

Letting go of Mr. Hungarian's throbbing cock, Diesel downed the last of his drink, then signaled for their server to bring them another round.

He wasn't drunk enough yet.

2

DIESEL

"What the holy hell?" Diesel mumbled as he stepped out onto the deck of the pool. His eyes were assaulted by a stream of red and white as far as the eye could see.

He was used to Matteo and the guys throwing some pretty out-there parties, and usually, they involved leather or lace or glitter.

Glitter.

Diesel shivered.

Whoever invented Satan's *fairy dust* should have been shot, quartered, and forced to listen to hours of boy bands singing on a loop—the same three songs, over and over and over.

Another shudder.

"Happy Canada Day!" a cheery Chase shouted, slapping Diesel on the back as he walked past him carrying a tray filled with what looked like fries drowning in gravy and cheese curds.

Confused by what he was seeing, Diesel watched Chase's chunky man-ass jiggle as he walked in the tightest f'ing Speedo Diesel had ever laid his eyes on. No doubt that thoughtful gift came from a certain love-struck fiancé of his.

Keeping in line with the party's theme, "O Canada," Chase strutted his stuff, wearing a red-and-white bathing suit with a large Canadian flag plastered across his ass.

Chase was not a dancer at *La Maison de M*, nor did he work at the exclusive gentlemen's club. Chase had come to *La Maison* last summer, undercover, to look into a mysterious journal that contained names of powerful and wealthy men who, according to the journal, had committed unspeakable crimes. Unfortunately for Chase, he never intended to meet and fall in love with Levi, one of the dancers working at *La Maison*. Ever since that fateful day, Chase has been chained to the boy by an invisible tether to his heart. He's still investigating and hunting down the monsters listed in that journal, but he now resides permanently in Levi's bedroom.

"Scary, isn't it?" Jared asked, stepping up next to Diesel.

The two watched as Mr. Canada placed his tray of heart disease down on the large buffet that had been set up in today's honor.

"What? Watching that material stretch to its limits across the guy's meaty man-ass? Or watching how a man who used to have balls is now strutting around the pool, playing

Martha Stewart?" Diesel asked, still trying to understand what it was that he was witnessing.

Jared chuckled.

"Let our boy have his day. I think he's feeling a little homesick."

"You bitches better not be talking smack about my man-beast," Levi noted, stepping up next to Jared. He, too, was wearing a matching red-and-white Speedo, but instead of a flag plastered across his ass, he had several little maple leaves peppering his tight little twinky ass.

Jared wrapped an arm around Levi's shoulders.

"No, we were saying how scary it is seeing Chase so... happy. What happened to the growly ex-cop who beat the shit out of an old man just because he wouldn't answer his questions?" Jared asked, eyes still glued on the cheery Canadian rearranging the assortment of food being laid out.

"First off, that 'old man' kidnapped me and held me and others captive in his creepy old-man stalker cells for days. Secondly, that happy look is what happens when you get your balls drained three times a day," Levi said, stepping out from under Jared's arm and swaying his hips as he made his way toward his sexy man-beast. "You and Isaac should try it sometime."

Diesel couldn't help but chuckle. "The dude's got a point."

Next to him, Jared snarled. "That blue-haired sex demon of mine gets his daily dose of dick often enough. Any more, and I'm going to have to get the boy crutches."

Diesel couldn't contain himself. He let out an uncontrollable laugh that sent pains through his side.

That, right there, was why Jared and he were best friends. They both had a fucked-up sense of humor.

Adjusting the skintight swim trunks he was wearing—no doubt a purchase made by his fiancé Isaac—Jared gave Diesel a weird look. "What? Do you think it's easy taking this cruise missile on the regular?"

Still laughing, Diesel shook his head. "Coming from someone who's actually had a cock shoved up his ass, no, I'd say that you have to be crazy to want to have that thing inside you more than once."

"Damn straight," Jared responded with a cocky grin plastered to his face. "Now, where is my little pain-in-the-ass sidekick? Time to see if he's ready to take his vitamin D."

"Have fun." Diesel nodded as Jared went off in search of his mate.

Deciding it was time to check out this foreign holiday that had suddenly manifested itself within the majestic confines of Paris's welcoming lands, Diesel made his way toward the cheery Canadian.

Several of the *Maison's* guests were crowded around the tables set up, some in barely there swimsuits, others just wrapped in a towel. All seemed to be having a good time.

"So, what do we have here?" Diesel asked, passing his eyes over the hordes of food.

Smiling, Chase turned, holding a beer out to his friend.

"Here, try this!" He shoved the bottle into Diesel's hand before picking one up for himself.

There was a large maple leaf plastered to the label, no doubt a way to remind Canadians that they were actually Canadian. Kind of like how Americans hang American flags on every single property that they own. Civic pride? Or mass amnesia?

Diesel didn't need a reminder that he was English. Born and raised in Essex, he struggled against the poverties of society and managed to claw his way out of the slummiest parts of London before ending up on Matteo's doorstep. That was enough of a reminder for him.

"Cheers."

They both raised their bottles before taking a sip together. Brotherhood at its finest.

The taste was smooth, with a slight sweetness that captured your tongue at the end. It wasn't bad. It was just... different. Diesel was mostly a whiskey drinker, but when he dabbled in the beers, he usually stuck with the European brands. But, hey, this was a special occasion, and he needed to support his Canadian brother.

"Good, right?"

"Yeah. I can feel the hockey flowing through my veins as we speak."

Speaking of hockey, their attention was temporarily diverted to the group of angry men shouting insults and death threats at one another while they slashed at a rubber ball with hockey sticks they angrily gripped in their hands.

Down on the lawn, a ball hockey rink had been set up, complete with homemade hockey nets and paint outlines on the grass.

"Nothing says Canada like a bit of hockey," Chase explained with a gigantic smile on his face.

"Hmm, drunk CEOs with hockey sticks sounds like a great idea." Diesel was always the enthusiast. "Now, back to the food."

"Yes! Over here, we have Montreal-style smoked meat. Fucking delicious when you put it in a brisket with a pickle." Chase kissed his fingers like he was some sort of Italian master chef. "Next, we got poutine, the best friggin' fries you'll ever eat."

The man continued down the buffet, shoving samples of food into Diesel's mouth, sometimes not even waiting for him to swallow in between dishes.

Was this how Italian kids felt when they visited Nonna's house? Being force-fed spoonful after spoonful of delicious, heavenly food.

Seeing Chase so excited was just so... unnerving.

The rest of the afternoon was spent sipping Canadian beers by the pool, chatting up men, and trying to avoid offers to join in a friendly game of something called "lacrosse."

Sometime around three or four in the afternoon—his memory was getting a bit hazy thanks to all the celebratory drinks—the ball hockey game morphed into something somewhat different. The hockey sticks were suddenly swapped out for sticks with nets attached to their ends, and suddenly, the goal was to keep the rubber ball in the air instead of on the ground. It was like Canada had a flip side to it.

As it turned out, Canada apparently had two national

sports—ice hockey in the winter and lacrosse in the summer —although if you ask most Canadians, they will only recognize the one game played on slivers of blades. Gorillas on ice?

Both games looked violent as shit, and both involved running back and forth chasing a piece of rubber. Diesel had no interest in playing either.

Floating on his giant inflatable unicorn, Diesel watched his friends around him enjoying the day with their fiancés and significant others. Levi had Chase, Isaac had Jared, and even Matteo now had Ares. Slowly, everyone was coupling up. Everyone but Diesel.

Raising his glass of whiskey—yes, he finally switched to something that might actually get his ass drunk—he downed the remainder of the amber liquid.

"You look bored as shit."

Diesel turned his attention to the handsome gentleman swimming beside him.

"Yeah, this party is getting kind of stale."

"Want to take this party someplace more private? I got a little something that will help fix the mood." The man slid his finger discreetly across his nose, indicating that he had some blow to share.

Guests who came to party at *La Maison* usually had the good stuff on them. Hey, if he was going to get high, he may as well do it with someone who's got the good stuff.

"Sure, sounds like fun," Diesel said, sliding off the majestic beast and following his new friend out of the pool.

3

ZERO

Six Months Ago

V oices filled the evening air, children complaining that they were cold while their parents scolded them for not wearing their mittens properly. Others laughed and cheered, taking in all the sights that New York had to offer in mid-January. In the city that never sleeps, there was always something going on. Some show to be seen, some food to be tasted, some music to be danced to.

That was the fun side of New York.

The other, much darker side was not so cheery and welcoming. It was in the dangers of the shadows where the more questionable deeds were done. Junkies turned to their dealers, hoping to score more crank, gangs walked the streets flexing their muscles and wreaking havoc on those that got in their way.

This was the side of New York that tourists feared to tread. With every great city comes a darker, more dangerous side to it. It was in this part of New York where Zero spent most of his life, honing his skills and learning tough life lessons. He had his father to thank for that.

"Who's next?" Zero called out, looking up from his table into the smiling faces of tourists all around him. "Test your skills. Show me what you got! It's easy. Follow the balls with your eyes, and if you can guess what cup the ball is under, you win! Only twenty dollars to play!"

Staring out at the faces, he watched the gamblers as they assessed their odds. There were three cups, all upside down. One ball that they had to follow as he shuffled the cups around. It wasn't hard. You just had to be quick with your eyes.

"So, who do we got? Who's got the balls and the talent to beat me at this game?" He knew that egging the gamblers on would give them the push that they needed to step forward and give him their money. With hardcore gamblers, it was their sense of pride that was always their undoing. Whenever they lost at a casino or card game, it was their wounded pride that always kept them betting more or pulling that lever one... last... time.

Yes, Zero knew how to work a man. Play on their weakness, stroke their ego, gain their confidence. He had his daddy to thank for that.

"Anyone?" Zero threw his hands up in the air, locking eyes with a cocky gentleman wearing a tanned trench coat and a five-thousand-dollar watch. "Does no one have the skills to challenge me and my swift hands?"

And there it was. That cocky smirk on the man's face that told Zero he was going down. About to be beaten by a man who was smarter, faster, and more successful than he.

Poor chump.

"I'll take you up on that," the cocky man said, taking a step through the crowd and stopping right before his table.

"Finally! A man willing to test his skills and prove to the world how truly gifted he really is." Zero gave him a wink as the cocky bastard smirked back at him.

The man pulled a twenty out of his wallet and handed it to Zero for safekeeping.

"You win this challenge, and you get back your twenty, plus twenty of my own," Zero explained, loving the confidence oozing out of this guy.

"You can do it, honey!" a pretty blonde shouted over his shoulder.

Of course it was a blonde. This guy was so cliché. Zero couldn't wait to beat this man and put him in his place.

He tucked the man's twenty into the stack of twenties he already had, then gave the guy a smile of his own.

Holding the tiny plastic ball up to the crowd, he raised his hand, encouraging cheers from those gathered around. The more they participated, the more excited they got and believed that they had a chance at winning this simple game.

He placed the ball under the center cup and pressed play on the music app on his phone. Dance music played as he began moving the cups around on the black velvet cloth he had laid out on the table just for show.

Left and right, and around and around, he moved the cups at varying speeds.

The crowd shouted, cheering the cocky man on. This was the part he loved. The audience and the player all thinking that the game was so easy and the win was guaranteed.

After a minute, he stopped moving the cups and took a step back.

"Now, dear sir, please tell me which cup the ball is under?"

With a confident smirk, the man pointed to the cup on the left.

"Are you sure?" Zero asked, giving the man one more chance to change his mind.

"Yes. It's under there, guaranteed."

"Okay, if that's your final guess." Zero stepped forward and lifted the cup. The tiny white ball sat still, staring up at the cocky man declaring his victory over the simpleton cup man.

"Told you so. Now hand me my money."

Saddened by his loss, Zero handed the man forty dollars.

"Hey, sometimes you win, sometimes you lose. Thanks for playin', man." Zero gave the man a wave as he walked off toward his wife.

"Told you that game was a cinch."

Turning back to the eager crowd, he cheerfully asked who was next.

Two other players won, with a third failing to guess the correct cup. It was getting late and time to wrap up the game before the police stopped by and raided his gig. He didn't exactly have a permit to be playing this little game out on the *street. It was always a gamble. Some nights, he got caught and lost his earnings, and other nights, he made off with thousands of dollars.*

He had played enough for tonight, and his take home was good enough.

"Okay, folks, it's time to wrap up this gig. Thanks for playing, and I hope to see you out again tomorrow night!"

He was just about to start collecting his cups when a young girl, perhaps nine or ten, stepped up to the table and held out a twenty.

"Excuse me, sir, but can I give it a try?"

The tiny girl was so sweet and innocent-looking. Her big brown eyes were shy and bashful. Her hair was tied back in a ponytail with some red ribbon, no doubt saved from her mother's sewing scraps.

Standing behind her, with a hand gently on the girl's shoulder, was her mother. Her clothes were ratty and torn, and her hair was tied back in a messy bun.

Zero had seen families like these roaming about. Usually begging for money and trying to sell whatever homemade item they could to the tourists. It was folks like these who tugged at Zero's heartstrings. They were the people who fell through the cracks of society, lost and abandoned. Not seen by those who had money and lives filled with busy schedules.

Glancing up at the young girl's mother, Zero gave her a smile and a gentle nod.

"Sure thing, sweety. Do you know how to play the game?" Zero asked, bending down and looking at the girl eye to eye.

She nodded before placing her money down on the table.

"Well, it appears that we have another contender!" Zero shouted, standing up high and gathering as much attention as he could for the child. He wanted her to experience the laughter and joy of winning a game that was rigged from the beginning.

The young girl smiled, giving a jump as she waited for the game to begin.

Zero placed the ball under the center cup, then began moving the cups at a much slower speed than the games prior. Hey, she was a little girl, and he wanted to make sure that she won the game.

All around them, people cheered on the little girl. He tried not to involve children whenever possible, but tonight, there was no escaping the little girl's request.

Slowing to a stop, Zero took a step back and motioned his hands over the cup.

"Now, brave child, can you tell me which of these cups is hiding the ball?"

Without hesitation, the girl pointed at the cup to the left. Zero smiled.

Slowly, he raised the cup and gasped in surprise.

"You won!" he cheered, glancing up at her mother with a bright smile. "I can't believe you beat me at my own game!" He pulled forty dollars from his stack of twenties and gave the little girl her winnings.

The look on her face was worth the twenty-dollar loss. At least the money would go to good use. Even with the last-minute loss, he still made quite a bit of cash these past few hours.

Twenty minutes later, he was all packed up and on his way home when he decided to make a stop at a pub and grab a quick pint.

Halfway through his beer, a man stopped at his booth and stared.

"*That was a pretty good show you put on earlier this evening.*"

Zero glanced up at the man and nodded his thanks.

"*Too bad I kept losing. At this rate, I'll be broke by next week.*" *Zero looked away and took another sip of his beer.*

"*Yes, you suck at winning that game, but winning is not really the point, is it?*"

Zero turned to face the man once again, watching him with suspicion. "*How am I supposed to make any money if losing costs me twenty bucks each time? Seems pretty stupid to me.*"

Nodding his head, the man slipped into the booth across from him and leaned forward to whisper.

"*But you and I both know that you didn't lose any money at all this evening, except perhaps to that kid. What was so special about that little kid?*"

Zero leaned back, getting a little uncomfortable with the stranger's line of questioning.

"*I don't know what you mean.*" *He studied the man carefully. He was around five foot eight, brown eyes with chestnut hair. There was an oddness about him, like he was calculating moves as they spoke. Was he a cop? But he didn't carry himself like an officer.*

Still, there was something about the man that he couldn't quite put his finger on.

"The game with the cups is just for show. The real con happens with the dealing out of winnings," the stranger said, eyes locked with his.

Zero remained silent. He wasn't about to give anything away. If this guy really was a cop, he would have to prove that he ripped those guys off on his own. If he was just another jerk-off looking to shake him down, he had a knife to the gut coming for him.

"For every person who won, you gave them their winnings from the top of your pile of cash. When the little girl won, you pulled her winnings from the bottom."

"So? What does that have to do with anything?" Zero asked, challenging the man to get to his point.

"While everyone was so busy looking at the cups and trying to figure out how they were going to beat you, they failed to notice that each time someone gave you their cash, you placed it at the bottom of your pile. My guess is that all the cash at the top of the pile were counterfeit bills. Therefore, no matter whether you won or lost, you always kept their cash."

The little bastard.

Zero gave a smirk. "That's an interesting theory, my friend."

"Please, call me Marc. So once again, I ask you, what was so special about that little girl that you actually paid her real cash as her winnings?"

Zero took another swig of his beer.

"*I just don't like ripping off innocent little kids.*" That was all this stranger needed to know.

The man who introduced himself as Marc, leaned back in the booth and gave him a partial smile.

Leaning forward, Zero crossed his arms along the table, being sure to flex his bulging biceps for added intimidation.

"*Now, how about you tell me what you really want?*"

4

DIESEL

*H*opping around his room, Diesel banged his head to music playing through his bedroom speakers. There was nothing better than the opening riff of "Enter Sandman" by Metallica. Stomping around his room, shirtless and wearing only a pair of loose-fitting shorts, Diesel used his fingers to pick at the strings of his imaginary guitar. Hundreds of screaming fans all around him cheered as they waited for him to take them out of their misery and down the rabbit hole with him.

Music and drugs were his escape. Oh, and alcohol. And sex. Fuck, there were a lot of things that he used for his escape. But fuck. His life was awesome. He lived in a castle, got paid to play with his dick, and whenever he got tired, he just took a trip into that magical land where anything was possible. Soaring high above everyone, feeling on top of the world...

Lifting the remote for his bedroom speakers, he turned

up the volume a few notches, knowing that Anders next door would probably be banging on his wall in... three... two... one.

Right on cue, there came a banging from the other side of the wall.

"Turn that shit down, asshole. Some of us are trying to watch porn in here."

Chuckling, Diesel turned down the music. He liked to remind the guys that he was here every so often.

Anders and Diesel had shared a bedroom wall ever since Isaac moved into *Cock Manor* a few years ago. At the time, Isaac had requested a room swap, claiming that the morning sun coming in from his window was murderous on his pale Irish skin.

Worst. Excuse. Ever.

In actuality, the little perve just liked listening to Jared beat off on the other side of the wall.

Diesel knew it. Isaac knew it. Jared was too into his muscles to notice.

Walking over to his bedroom mirror, Diesel ran his fingers through his hair and double-checked that nothing awkward was on his face. In their line of work, you never knew what might end up stuck to your face... or body. Always safer to do a quick status check.

Once, he walked out onto the patio for dinner with a used condom stuck to the back of his thigh. Granted, he was high at the time and half a bottle of whiskey in, but still, it was awkward when the rubber fell to the floor in front of Matteo and the guys. He could still hear the squishy, wet sound it made as the lubed condom hit the stone tile.

No one was impressed that day, and the guys didn't stop their relentless teasing until Isaac ended up getting a squeaky sex toy stuck up his butthole a few weeks later. Don't ask how it got stuck up there. Even the doctors were baffled by the positioning of the toy and the length of time it remained clenched between his butt cheeks.

Needless to say, everyone stopped talking about the *condom heard 'round the world.*

"Mornin', Bruno," Diesel said to the smiling demon face inked to his chest.

He flexed his pec muscles and watched as the creepy demon did a little dance for him, moving its face to the beat of the drums.

He loved his little Bruno. The crazy dude kept him company and kept his secrets. The two of them had been through some crazy shit together, and through it all, the little dude never judged.

In addition to the creepy-ass demon face, running along the right side of his torso were three rather large stab wounds inked just below his ribs. A reminder of the three people who had betrayed him: his mother, his stepfather, and his stepfather's son. If there was a cause for him turning out the way that he did, it was them. *Thank you, motherfuckers. Hope you die a painful death.*

Moving away from his emotional wounds, his eyes landed on the mantra that had become his words to live by, "Never Again." Those chilling words were scribbled just above his belly button. Those two words were a stark reminder of the weakness he fought so hard to forget.

Lost in his own mind, his thoughts drifted to the painful memories of his past.

It was autumn. The leaves were just beginning to change color, and the evening wind was starting to bring a chill that only a light jacket could satisfy.

They were at Great End Skate, a local roller rink that kids and families used to pass the time while waiting for their lives to pass them by.

Coming to Great End Skate was not something that Diesel and his younger stepbrother, Jordan, did, but his stepfather had promised to take them for Jordan's eighth birthday.

Diesel had been looking forward to it all week. He had never been roller-skating, and he hoped that his stepfather would teach him how to skate once they got inside. He knew that it was a long shot, but he hoped that perhaps Jordan's dad would teach them both like all the other dads did.

"Can we go inside?" Jordan whined, tugging on his step-mother's hand.

"No, your father will be back here any minute. He has the money for the tickets, and then we can go inside and skate for your birthday," his mother answered.

"But I want to go inside now!" his bratty little brother argued, yanking her arm and sticking out his lower lip in a pout. For eight years old, the kid was still a big baby.

"Joe, you do as your momma says, or else I'll slap you upside the head," Diesel's stepfather growled, opening the pack of cigarettes he had just purchased and striking a match as well.

"*Finally,*" *his little brother gasped, charging off toward the arena with his mother dragging her feet behind.*

Diesel stood up from where he was sitting on the hood of his father's car and took a step toward the arena as well.

"*Where do you think you're going?*" *his stepfather asked, pressing a hand against Diesel's chest and stopping him in his tracks.*

Diesel stood there for a moment, confused. Were they supposed to use another entrance instead?

"*Did you bring extra money for skating?*"

Money? His stepdad knew that he didn't have any money. Most kids got an allowance, but not them. His parents didn't believe in paying their kids to do chores.

"*That's what I thought. Lesson learned, kid. Always make sure you are able to pay your way in life; otherwise, you will miss out on everything.*"

Diesel stood there, seconds away from tears.

"*Here, I need you to wait in the car and watch this beer while we go and celebrate your brother's birthday. If you get hungry, there should be some crisps in the glove compartment.*"

His stepfather passed him his six-pack of beer and turned to walk away. "You're too old for skating anyway."

Smoke billowed from the side of the man's face as he walked off smoking his cigarette.

Jaw clenched, Diesel watched as the man who was supposed to provide for him, protect him, and guide him into the man he was to become walked off without a second thought for his well-being.

Never again would he rely on his stepfather to provide him with money for his ticket.

Next time, he would bring his own money and get to go skating with all the other boys and girls. Maybe then, one of the other dads would be able to teach him how to skate.

Fists still clenched, Diesel jumped when his cell phone alarm beeped, announcing to the world that it was just after nine a.m.

How long had he been standing there?

Moving toward the door, he grabbed his black sleeveless *Nine Inch Nails* T-shirt and threw it over his shoulder as he left the room.

Next stop, Jared's room.

Using best-friend etiquette, Diesel knocked once on Jared's bedroom door before turning the knob and letting himself in.

Diesel whistled.

Jared was bent over, ass hanging out, as he pulled his underwear up over his thick thighs.

"I see someone's been doing their squats," Diesel chirped, making his way across the room and over toward Jared's bed. He paused, taking a moment to inspect his buddy's sheets before deciding that it was safe to sit his ass down.

"What are you doing?"

"Checking to make sure I won't accidentally get pregnant if I sit on your bed. Don't need any baby Jareds running around."

Jared gave him the finger before reaching for his joggers.

"Want to go for a run?" Diesel asked, trying to remember the last time the two of them went jogging together.

The last few times Diesel had asked his best friend to go for a run, Jared had declined, choosing to spend time with his fiancé rather than get sweaty on a dirt path with him.

Seriously. Where were his priorities?

"Sorry, dude. Going to help Isaac with his boarding."

In case anyone cared, Isaac's favorite pastime—other than riding Jared's dick—was riding his skateboard in the home-made skate park Jared had built for him years ago.

Sweet, right?

Yuk! Make him gag.

Feeling the sting of rejection, Diesel tried to mask his feelings by giving his buddy his standard "I don't give a shit" shoulder shrug.

They had been best friends since they first met. Always together. Always there for one another.

Now?

Now he was lucky if he got to see Jared for more than thirty minutes before that skater-boy smurf hypnotized him with his magic-ass voodoo.

Seriously, how many times can two dudes fuck in a day before their cocks get all chafed and sore?

Frustrated, Diesel huffed as he got up off the bed.

"Whatever," he mumbled, walking out of the room before Jared could see the hurt in his eyes. Sometimes, he hated his best friend.

Making his way down the corridor, he skipped over

Isaac's room, knowing that the boy already had plans and continued on to Levi's.

He stopped in front of Levi's room and gave a hard knock on the door.

A second later, the door flew open.

"Jesus! You knock like a gorilla!" Levi hissed, sending daggers through his eyes.

Diesel smirked. Yes, he was an asshole.

"Whatcha doin'? Wanna play some *PlayStation*?"

Levi opened the door the rest of the way, revealing a half-naked Chase lying in bed, the sheets loosely clinging to his body.

"Sorry. We're having sexy times."

Of course they were. When weren't Levi and Chase fucking like bunnies? Ever since the two laid eyes on each other, their clothing of choice was lube.

"Hey, Diesel," Chase called from the bed, giving him a *what's up* head nod.

Okay, this was getting sad.

"Whatever," Diesel huffed out before turning and heading down the stairs, rejected once again.

Was everyone in this place fucking today?

Walking through the kitchen, he grabbed an apple from the fruit bowl and made his way outside. Perhaps Teo wanted to hang out and do something?

Biting into his apple, he stopped in his tracks when he saw Teo doing some weird-ass triangle pose on a yoga mat outside.

Fuck that nonsense, he thought to himself. He wasn't that bored.

Pivoting, he decided to check on Daddy M and see what the big guy was up to.

When he reached Matteo's office, the door was open, and two sets of voices were having a heated discussion. Not wanting to interrupt Daddy M and Daddy A, Diesel waited just outside the door and listened.

"Whoever told you that you were a master with a hammer was clearly lying to your face," Matteo hissed.

Point one for Daddy M.

"I'm surprised you even know what a hammer is, your Royal Highness," Ares responded.

Ouch! Daddy A with the return!

"I know a lot of things; I just dumb things down so you don't get lost when I speak."

Diesel let out a chuckle.

Both voices went silent.

"Show yourself," Matteo snarled in that pissed-off daddy voice of his.

Shit. He was busted.

Diesel took a breath, then entered the dragon's den.

"What?" Matteo asked, looking ten shades of pissed off.

Not wanting to seem like a clingy princess, Diesel shrugged his shoulders as if he didn't care.

"Just thought I'd check in and see if you needed a hand." Secretly, he hoped that Matteo would ask him to help put together what appeared to be a bookcase that the two of them were clearly struggling with.

Throwing a hand his way, Matteo signaled *no*. "No. I've got my hands full trying to deal with an overgrown man-child. Apparently, I need to show my love how to hammer in a nail so that it goes into the wood straight."

"But I thought you liked it when I go in at an angle," Ares commented, apparently deciding that his life was not worth living.

Matteo's eyes flared, giving the room a glimpse into the fires of hell.

"Go," Matteo growled at Diesel. "I can't today."

Fine. Fuck.

Now that everyone was coupled up and preoccupied with their "special human," it appeared that none of them had any more time for him.

Whatever. He turned and walked back to his room.

But what did he expect? It was only a matter of time, really.

Once inside his room, he began pacing the floor.

The story was always the same. Every time he got close to someone or felt like he belonged somewhere, it all came crashing down around him, usually in a glorious blaze of misery and fire.

First his family. Then his friends. Now these guys.

Did you really think it was going to last?

He'd secretly allowed himself to think that perhaps things would be different with Matteo and the guys, that somehow, he had found a home and a family to which he belonged.

How could he be so stupid? It was all just lies and fairy tales.

Now that they have their special someone, they don't need a low-life druggie like you.

You're nothing. You're pathetic. Who could ever love a loser like you?

Not even your family wanted anything to do with you.

They were right. All the voices of his past. He was alone. No one wanted him. No one needed him.

He had just been fooling himself.

Throwing on a pair of jeans and his hoodie, he grabbed his stash of cash from the back of his dresser drawer and stuffed his earphones into his ears.

Blasting Metallica, he closed his bedroom door and walked out of the château.

5

DIESEL

One week later

"Jesus," a voice gasped from somewhere off in the distance.

The world around him shifted as he suddenly felt light as a feather.

Ahh, he loved that feeling. Floating on a cloud. So peaceful. So light.

His body was jogged, and the joyous, floaty feeling suddenly didn't feel so light. Now he felt sick.

Fuck.

Diesel felt his body shift and bump and fall for just a moment before quickly coming to a level height once again.

Around him, someone gasped, then cursed, then said something that Diesel couldn't quite make out.

Where the fuck was he? What the heck was going on?

"Pass me that cloth," someone said. Matteo?

All around him, the sound was soft, then loud, then muffled once again.

How was it that sound could suddenly hurt your body? Was that even a thing?

Diesel felt something move across his face. The feeling was soft, gentle. Done with almost care and concern.

"Grab the door."

"Who the fuck stays in a place like this?"

"No judgment. You're here to help. This is our boy. Diesel is our family." That was Matteo's voice. Always the sweet, caring guy.

Where was he? And why couldn't he open his eyes?

He felt cool air against his body. Once again, he was feeling all floaty as someone—Matteo perhaps?—carried him off somewhere.

"Hospital or home?" someone asked.

"Home. I'll have the doctor come by the house."

"He looks like he needs a hospital."

"I'm not having him arrested. He needs a doctor, then his family. Now drive, dammit!" That was definitely Matteo. Only a man like him could command so much attention.

All around him, Diesel felt warmth. Loved. Safe...

That was when the sound and world around him went silent, and darkness took him once again.

Diesel wasn't quite sure how long he'd been out for. When he finally opened his eyes, the room was dark, and the light from the moon was streaming in.

Head throbbing, he looked around the room and cursed his life.

Fuck.

He had gone on another bender again. He barely remembered the events of the last few days. Glimpses, voices, and feelings all seemed to come rushing back as he struggled to remain conscious and not... pukey.

Diesel raised a hand to his head and noticed the tube stuck to his arm. He looked over at his nightstand and saw the IV bag set up next to his bed.

Damn. He must have been in rough shape. Matteo was going to kill him.

At least he wasn't in a rehab facility. That had to be a good sign. The last time he'd gone on one of these benders, he woke up in a private facility and held against his will. Apparently, Matteo had some powerful friends.

A noise at the door caught his attention.

Slowly, the door crept open, and voices were heard whispering.

"I'm just going to sit with him for tonight and make sure that everything's okay." Jared.

"The guy needs his rest. Leave him alone, and let him recover in peace," Isaac responded.

"I'm not going to bug him, just watch him sleep and make sure that the machines are working and stuff."

Diesel's heart was touched. It wasn't very often that people cared so much about him.

"Okay, Dr. Jare. Have a good night, and I'll see you in the morning." There was the sound of wet kissing.

Blah. Get a room, boys. Preferably not his.

Diesel watched as Jared slid his massive body through the tiny crevice between the door and the wall.

Why wasn't he opening it wider?

Because he's trying to keep out the light so it doesn't disturb you.

Oh, okay, that makes sense.

Tiptoeing like a creeper in the night, the muscled brunette grabbed the comfy armchair from the far side of the room and carried it over to the right side of Diesel's bed.

Was he...?

Yup. Diesel watched as Jared plopped his massive frame into the chair and checked the IV bag still hanging from its spot by the bed.

He must not have noticed Diesel's eyes open. This was too much fun to ignore. He closed his eyes, leaving them open just enough to spy on Jared and his secret dealings.

His best friend leaned forward and adjusted the sheet that was wrapped around Diesel's torso, pulling it up higher to keep his friend warm.

That was... sweet.

"You know, watching me sleep is psychopathic behavior," Diesel whispered, scaring the daylights out of his best friend.

"You're awake!" Jared's face lit up as he leaned forward against the bed once again. "How are you feeling?"

"Like I'm made of sandpaper." The IV would help with his dehydration, but it would take some time.

"Here, have a sip." Jared picked up the glass of water on the nightstand and brought it close to Diesel's lips.

Diesel lifted his head and took a few short sips. He still wasn't feeling right. Knowing him, he had probably spent the last few days mixing party drugs and drinking God knows what.

Fuck. He hated himself sometimes. Why did he do such stupid shit?

Because you're trash, and that's how people like you behave.

He hated that voice deep inside him.

Jared placed the glass back down before leaning back in his chair. He was dressed in a tight white shirt that clung to his massive chest—no doubt for Isaac's benefit—and light-gray joggers that, no doubt, were probably also for Isaac's benefit.

"You gave us all a scare," Jared noted, his voice calm and non-judgmental.

Diesel lowered his gaze.

"Yeah, sorry about that. Where did you guys find me?"

Giving Diesel one of the coldest stares he had ever seen, Jared's jaw tightened.

"Some drug den in Paris." Diesel cringed. "Judging by

the state of some of the people lying passed out around you, I'm guessing they'd been there for a while."

"Was Matteo pissed?"

Jared just stared. "We wanted to take you to a hospital to get checked out, but M insisted on bringing you home. He was worried they would arrest you or throw you into another rehab clinic or something."

Shit. Now Diesel felt even more like a complete asshole. Why did the man insist on taking care of him? He would have dumped his own pathetic ass ages ago. But for some fucked-up reason, Matteo insisted on trying to take care of him.

Looking back over at his best friend, he realized what a selfish thing it was that he'd just done. The guys didn't deserve to be put through all this bullshit, especially because of him. They deserved to live their happy lives with their perfect partners and not give a second thought about the dark cloud that was Diesel.

"Look. If you're gonna creep me while I sleep, at least make yourself comfortable in this massive bed. Don't worry, we don't have to cuddle."

Eying the big open space next to Diesel, Jared smiled.

"You better not let any rip while you sleep," Jared said as he jogged around to the other side of the bed.

And that, right there, is why Diesel did not find Jared sexy in the least. Call him old-fashioned, but any sex partners he had did not make sounds with any part of their lower body.

Turning to face the window, Diesel felt the bed sink as Jared's massive body slid into the space next to him.

His eyes opened once again when he felt Jared's arms wrap themselves around him. Jared pulled him up against his body and snuggled his chin into the crook of his neck.

"Don't ever do that to us again," Jared whispered into his ear.

For the second time in his life, Diesel felt loved and cared for.

"I won't," Diesel promised, closing his eyes and falling asleep in his best friend's arms.

6

DIESEL

*T*he next morning, as expected, Diesel got the thrashing of a lifetime. Matteo paced the room, seething, asking a million questions that Diesel didn't want to answer or have a reasonable explanation for.

It was clear from Matteo's tone that he was frustrated and pissed. He was a powerful man, always in control, and with Diesel, he didn't have any of that. Diesel was unpredictable, out of control, and did whatever he wanted.

Yet, still, for some reason, Matteo insisted on holding on to him.

"I just don't get it. Do you know how dangerous going on a bender like that can be? What if you overdose? What if you catch some disease? You don't even know what's going on half the time around you; anyone can do anything to you, and you wouldn't even know!" Matteo's blue eyes blazed with the fury of a thousand suns.

Diesel knew better than to say anything. While he might like pushing Matteo's buttons or talking back to him when warranted, seeing how angry and upset Matteo was right now, Diesel had too much respect for the man to show him any sort of lip.

Taking a seat on the bed, Matteo rested his elbows on his lap and lowered his head.

"Diesel, you got to help me out here. I think of you as one of my sons, and it kills me every time I have to go searching for you whenever you go on one of these benders. I'm terrified that one day I will find you dead, lying between one of those strung-out bodies."

Seeing this strong and powerful man so disheveled and vulnerable broke Diesel's heart. He didn't deserve this sort of stress or heartache. The man deserved to live a happy and stress-free life with the man he loved—who was apparently a cranky gun smuggler.

Swallowing the lump in his throat, Diesel didn't know what to say.

"I-I'm sorry, M. I don't know what's wrong with me or why I do the things I do."

Straightening back up, Matteo turned to face him once again.

"There's nothing wrong with you." Matteo stared at him with soft, pleading eyes. "You just have a lot of issues that you keep buried and refuse to deal with. Please. I beg you. When you are fully recovered, will you please go speak with a specialist? I really think that you need to talk to someone and work out all those dark feelings that you keep so closely guarded."

Hearing the pain in Matteo's voice, Diesel felt like the biggest asshole in the world. The man had been nothing but kind and generous and so fucking loving, and all he had done was bring pain and misery to this amazing man's life.

That had to change.

"Sure. I'll go speak to someone when I'm better."

Silence fell between them as Matteo no doubt tried to determine whether he was serious or just trying to end the conversation.

"I promise." He hoped that his eyes were sincere enough to reassure Matteo that he wasn't lying.

Nodding, Matteo placed his hand on Diesel's shoulder and gave it a gentle squeeze.

"Thank you."

Two weeks went by with Matteo barely leaving Diesel's side. Every fucking place he went, the overbearing Italian magically appeared. For someone whose parents died well before their time, Matteo had somehow mastered that Nonna ability to be everywhere and nowhere both at the same time.

Take now as an example: Diesel had come into the gym to do a few weights and burn off some of that pent-up frustration, and low and behold, Matteo was sitting in the corner reading a goddamn magazine!

"Don't you have an old-man dick to take care of?" Diesel asked, racking up the weights on the bench press machine he was about to use.

"Watch your language," the man responded, eyes never leaving the magazine.

Diesel smirked. "No. Seriously. Where is Daddy A? I haven't seen Ares in a few days. You guys fighting?" Perhaps that was the reason for Matteo's clingy behavior. He doubted he was that lucky.

"He's doing some business in the States."

Lying down on the bench, Diesel took a breath before lifting the bar into the air. Whoever said that exercise was good for people with addictions was a lying piece of shit.

His body hurt, and he was sweating like a pig.

It's your body detoxing, fuckhead.

After the eighth rep, Diesel sat up and turned to face his secret stalker.

In addition to the twenty-four seven supervision and invisible shock collar Matteo had no doubt placed around his neck, Matteo wouldn't allow Diesel to work the floor while he was recovering.

Matteo claimed that no one fantasized about the guy from *Tales from the Crypt*. Okay, that was an overexaggeration. Besides some dehydration and dark circles under his eyes, he still looked hot as fuck. At least that's what he told himself in the mirror each morning. Even Bruno agreed. Mind you, it was in the smiling demon's nature to lie his ass off. But still, Matteo was being unreasonable. And to be honest, Diesel was becoming bored as shit.

"How long before I can hit the stage again?" Diesel asked, not quite sure if he was going to get a response. Matteo could be a stubborn ass when he wanted to.

"When you stop smelling like weed."

Like weed? That was probably the least harmful drug he had been ingesting since he was fourteen. Weed was like water; it barely had any effect on him.

"But smelling like weed is part of my charm. It adds to that bad-boy persona so many guys here want. Do you really want to deprive your guests of my studly man-scent?"

Matteo glanced at him from over the top of the magazine.

"You're not that manly."

Diesel slid back under the pole and began benching another few reps. Then he sat back up and flexed his arms.

"You really gonna deprive all those thirsty men of these sexy-ass arms?" He knew he was starting to win over his jailer's bad mood.

The left side of Matteo's lip turned upward in a barely there hint of amusement.

"When are you going to start therapy?"

Damn. He hoped that Matteo had perhaps forgotten about his little promise made, oh, so many eons ago. It was probably coming up to just over a week and a bit at this point now.

"When I'm ready mentally," Diesel answered, letting out what he hoped was a desperate sigh.

He was going to have to hold up his end of the bargain. Matteo deserved that. But right now, he was soooo fuckin' bored! Then a thought came to him.

"Hey! How about, while I'm recovering, I go help Chase on his next assignment. I heard him say he is leaving for London tomorrow. A change of scenery would be good for me."

Matteo placed the magazine down and crossed his leg over his knee. He looked like he was posing for the cover of some fancy-ass fashion cover. He swore Matteo had his own specialized lighting following him around. Perhaps he had made a deal with the devil to always look young and beautiful. *Whatever happened to Dorian Gray? Did he become a vampire in the end or something like that?*

It was in that moment that Matteo's face contorted into what could only be described as an "evil-villain smirk." Diesel swore that the lights dimmed, and the air around them suddenly became stale. Something was wrong.

He didn't like the sudden look of amusement that seemed to take over Daddy M's face. He was up to something.

"You know what? That's actually a really great idea. And while you're out enjoying that new change of scenery—all nice and relaxed—you can meet with Dr. Annetta Bloom and begin your one-on-one therapy sessions. I hear that she has a lovely office right in the heart of downtown London. I'm sure that you will love it down there. How does that sound?"

Annoyance pooled itself in the pit of Diesel's stomach.

He wondered just how much he could challenge Matteo before he decided Diesel wasn't leaving the château. It wasn't worth it. He needed a change. He needed fresh air!

Hating that Matteo had won once again, he decided to give in to the brilliant man's trickery.

"Fine." Diesel huffed, finally accepting his fate.

Meeting with the doc was going to be *such* a shit show.

7

ZERO

*M*ovement at the front door caught Zero's attention. He watched as his target locked his front door and then hopped into his car to head off to work. It was always the same. The doctor left his home around six thirty a.m., then worked in the lab until about six, except for Mondays and Tuesdays when the man seemed to stay late and work until seven thirty at night.

Zero wasn't exactly sure what the doctor did at the lab. It was a high-security facility, so it wasn't like he could just walk in and take a snoop around. The man did have an advanced degree in biology and chemistry, and according to the journal that his boss showed him, the man was some kind of chemist.

The doctor did also have a secondary office that he kept, outside his home and the lab. Zero was still trying to understand why the man had the other office, but that was a question for another day.

Today, his goal was to break into the doc's house and

have a look around. See if there were any clues there that might help him with his investigation. The boss would be looking for results sometime soon, and so far, he was coming up with zilch.

Dressed as a cable repairman, Zero carried his box of tools around to the back of the house. It was always easier breaking in through the backyard, away from prying eyes. Not that he was any kind of super criminal. His specialty was cons, duping people out of their money. Breaking and entering was just a skill that he had developed over the years, hanging out with different sorts of questionable characters.

Once he reached the back of the house, he located the back patio door, then fished his cell phone out of his pocket.

"I'm here," he said into his phone and waited.

"Give me one sec." There was a forty-five-second pause before the voice came back on the phone. "Security cameras are looped. You have two hours."

"Thanks, boss," Zero said into the phone before hanging up on the man who hired him to do this job.

The man's name was Marc, and he lived in the United States. Apparently, he was trying to confirm some information and needed him and his skills to assist him with this investigation.

Zero still wondered if Marc made a mistake and hired the wrong man. Other than being great at conning people, he was far from a professional investigator. Perhaps it was his confidence and ability to adapt to ever-changing situations. That was one of the skills you needed as a con artist—the ability to switch tactics midstream and think on your toes. If you weren't convincing and sure of yourself, your victims would be on to you in no time at all.

Zero's mind drifted back to when he was ten years old and pulling scams with his father.

"Here, hang this around your neck," his father said, handing him a lanyard with a plastic ID card attached.

Zero flipped it over and looked at the picture. It was him, taken from one of the photos his father carried around with him in his wallet. He knew because he had seen his dad show his friends from time to time.

Scribbled just underneath his photo were the words "Press Pass."

"Dad, what does 'Press Pass' mean?" Zero asked, throwing the lanyard around his neck and making sure that his photo was facing in the right direction.

"It means that you are here to take pictures and then share them on the internet and in magazines."

"But I don't have a camera, and how do I share the pictures on the internet and in magazines?"

His father held up a camera. "This is just pretend, remember. If anyone asks, Daddy works for a big magazine and is here to take pictures."

"And what about me?"

"You are my assistant. Now are we done with all the stupid questions?" his father growled.

Zero knew better than to continue asking his father questions. Instead, he nodded and reached for his father's hand.

Nodding, his father took his hand, then walked them into the fancy hotel where all the pretty men and women were chat-

ting inside, smiling and laughing as they stood together and took photos.

"I'm a photographer from Green Velvet Cinema Maga-zine, *here to photograph the event and actors," his father said, holding up his pass to the woman at the door. She nodded, then gestured for them to enter the large conference room.*

Inside, there were rows and rows of tables covered with black cloths and sparkly items.

"Here, give Daddy your press pass," he heard his father say.

Zero turned and looked up at his father.

"But I thought I was supposed to be your assistant?"

"That was just until we got inside the door. Now that we are inside, you are going to pretend to be a famous child actor. If anyone asks, you are in movies made in the United States. No one in England ever pays attention to kids in US movies."

"But, Daddy." He wasn't sure what he was supposed to do. He couldn't think of any American movies that he had watched on the tele anytime recently. What if someone asked him what movie he was in?

"Listen carefully, kid. When we get to those tables, you're going to ask those nice ladies and gentlemen if you can have one. Then take it. If they offer you two or more, you take those as well."

"What are they?" Zero asked, looking at all the items on display at each table.

There were watches and tablets and fancy running shoes. There was even a table with cool-looking cell phones and cameras. He always wanted a cell phone, but his dad said that they couldn't afford one.

"These are all gifts that companies give actors and actresses so that they can use them and hopefully post about them on social media or wear them at movie premiers. People then see celebrities using these items and go and buy them themselves."

"All of this is... free?" Zero couldn't believe that people just gave all of this stuff to famous people.

"Yup. Now go to those tables and start getting free stuff. Daddy is going to stay here and take pictures of people."

Zero nodded, then walked over to the first table, where a man and woman were smiling.

They said hello and waved toward the row of items all laid out before him. He pointed to the first item, a handheld gaming device, to which the woman picked up a box and placed it in a bag for him. She waved her hand over the other items, and he slowly pointed to a tablet, which she placed a second box into the bag as well.

He continued making his way around the room from table to table, pointing at items and watching as people placed his selections into a bag.

After an hour, he walked over to his father carrying two bags while a guest services worker carried another six.

"Thank you, sir," his father said, taking the bags from the young worker and watching as the man disappeared back into the crowd. "Wow, looks like you did well, my boy."

They made their way out of the hotel and walked toward his father's beat-up piece-of-shit car parked at the back of the hotel.

"Daddy, do I get to keep all this stuff?" he asked, excited to play with the handheld gaming system.

His father gave him a mocking face. "No chance! Daddy's going to sell all this crap and make a shit ton of money."

Disappointment set in. He never got anything cool. All of his friends had gaming systems and new toys, but here he was, having to steal toys from his friends or fish old gaming systems from the trash.

His mind finally returned to the present.

Opening his tiny kit, he pulled out two metal objects that looked like tiny nail files. He inserted both tools into the locking mechanism on the back door and began fumbling around until he finally heard a click.

Bingo.

Placing the tools and kit back in his bag, he pushed open the door and stepped inside.

It was time to see what the dirty little doctor was hiding in his home.

8

DIESEL

Tossing his duffle bag into the back of the SUV, Diesel took a deep breath of fresh Parisian air and let the smell of freedom set in.

Okay, perhaps he was exaggerating. He wasn't locked away in a tower somewhere, but he was under the watchful eye of a certain overbearing Italian. And if you have ever pissed off an Italian, you know how scary their oversight can be.

"Wait up!" someone shouted from behind Diesel.

He turned, half expecting one of the security staff to remind him of something he'd forgotten. Instead, Chase and Jared were both making their way over to him.

"What's with the body bag?" Diesel asked, referring to the camouflage duffle Jared had slung over his shoulder. *Damn, the boy's muscles were huge.*

"It's filled with snacks for our trip." Jared smirked, tossing his bag into the back of the SUV as well.

Like Diesel would believe that Jared would eat his body weight in candy for one second. The man calculated his calorie intake at every meal just so that he knew how long he would have to work out in order to burn off the food he just consumed.

Guess Jared was joining them on their trip.

"And the Mrs. is okay with letting you out of his sight for more than ten minutes?" Speaking of the devil.

He watched as a streak of blue came barreling out of the front doors.

"Need my goodbye kiss," Isaac claimed, jumping into Jared's arms and making out with him like the two were searching for buried treasure conveniently located in the back of Jared's throat.

"Sickening, isn't it?" Chase said, stopping right behind the two love birds.

"Does Matteo know what he's doing by taking away Isaac's favorite toy? I pity the rest of the poor souls staying behind," Diesel quipped.

Chase gave a chuckle.

"Matteo's allowed them two weekend visits a month until all this is done. Here, give me your arm." Chase pulled a black wristwatch out of his pocket and held it up in his hand. "A gift from Daddy M."

Diesel held out his arm as Chase fastened the plastic device to it with an unsettling click.

"Why do I get the feeling that this isn't a love gift?" Diesel asked skeptically.

"It is. It's because Daddy M loves you that he asked me to

place one of Marc's nifty little trackers on you—you know—in case you decide to pull a Houdini on us again and run off."

Shocked and a little offended, Diesel raised his wrist in disbelief. He turned his arm and examined the pesky device that Marc had created. Marc was Chase's boss, a security expert and all-around genius. The man had designed and created his own mini tracking device that could be inserted into any piece of clothing or jewelry. It allowed the operator to track the person's movements using a third-party device. The thing was designed to be untraceable if someone were to scan the individual searching for tracking devices.

"Don't bother trying to remove it. There's a special key that's needed, and guess who's holding it?" Chase gave him a smirk.

"Can't believe I'm now basically tagged cattle."

"Hey! Doesn't it record voices as well?" Isaac asked with an evil smirk and puffy red lips.

Diesel's head snapped toward Chase. Isaac was right! He never felt so betrayed.

"Calm your nuts. Matteo insisted that the voice recording function be turned off. I guess he didn't want to suffer through all the vile things he was likely to hear."

"I make no apologies for the life that I live," Diesel defended, not sorry in the least.

It appeared that Big Brother wasn't listening... he was just... following.

Deciding to give it a little test, Diesel raised his wrist to his lips and whispered, "Matteo likes to suck old-man balls before showering his face with day-old spunk."

They all held their breath, waiting to see if their boss and surrogate father would come bursting through the doors.

Nothing happened.

"Okay, now that we're done playing around, let's get our asses moving," Chase ordered, opening the passenger-side door and hopping in.

They took Matteo's private jet over to London, making it easier to transport all their equipment. Chase already had a skeleton crew over in London doing some investigative work for him.

From what Diesel had overheard, their investigation hadn't been going well, and this was Chase's last-ditch effort at finding any incriminating evidence of the suspect's alleged crimes.

Perhaps Edwin had created a fake entry into his journal with the hopes that if it was ever obtained by the authorities, they might have one hell of a time trying to determine which entries were real and which were fake.

They needed to be sure that the crimes listed in the journal were real. The last thing they wanted was to take out a man who was innocent of the crimes he was accused of.

So far, Chase and his boss Marc had investigated a handful of entries over the past two years, all of which turned out to be real. Each of the monsters located suffered a fate befitting the crimes they committed.

One such prisoner was currently locked up in Matteo's

dungeon—yes, Matteo had a fucking dungeon at the château!

Landing in London, they headed right to the terraced house in which they were staying. When they arrived, Diesel took in the common-style row of attached houses, all perfectly matched, all soulless and plain.

What did he expect? Chase and team were on a tight budget, and considering there were a few of them staying here, he was lucky they weren't all being crammed into a tiny apartment.

The outer brick of the home was a dull brown stone. Judging by the discoloration and dirt built up around the edges, Diesel guessed that the structure was at least sixty years old. The windows themselves were another matter entirely. Considering the amount of rain that London gets each year, one would not expect the level of grime and waste caked onto the surface of the glass. It was as if the surface repelled water and soap.

The only redeeming quality that Diesel could see was the large bay windows that protruded from the property. Perhaps with a bit of elbow grease, people could actually enjoy staring out of the living room window—not that there was much of a view to look out onto.

Collecting his courage, Diesel followed the guys into the house, wondering what new horror awaited them inside.

Inside, the conditions weren't quite so bad. Yes, the floors still creaked to kingdom come, and the drapes looked like they were from a 1940s home-styling catalog, but at least the walls had been covered with a fresh coat of paint sometime over the past few years.

Diesel walked into the living room and admired the large old-fashioned fireplace set into the wall. It might be kind of cool to have a few drinks while roasting his balls by the fire.

The thought made him smile.

Next to the living room was a tiny kitchen. The appliances weren't new, but at least they weren't bought at the same time the home was constructed. The open concept of the kitchen made the place look bigger than it really was. Less claustrophobic and more... cozy? As cozy as cozy could be when the structure around you was a mixture of 40s, 70s, 80s... and, well, let's not push past the 80s. Still, the walls seemed sturdy, and Diesel didn't think the roof was ready to cave in just yet.

"Jared, you and I will take the beds in the basement. Diesel, you'll get the room at the top of the stairs," Chase explained before turning to the driver and instructing him to place the equipment they had brought into the living room.

Tired of listening to Chase bark orders, Diesel picked up his bag and made his way up the questionable stairs.

Once he reached the top, there were two bedrooms across from each other and a small bathroom set in the middle.

So much for living in luxury. He was starting to wonder if coming to London was a mistake. Matteo's watchful eye wasn't so bad after all. At least there, he didn't have to worry about what surfaces he touched or where he stepped. First thing tomorrow, they were ordering a cleaning person... or four.

Now, which room was his? Well, one door was open, looking empty and bare. The other door was closed. He decided to check out the closed door just to see if the room was a better fit.

Locked.

Chase did mention that they were sharing the place with the current team in place, so the bedroom must belong to one of them.

Fine. Bedroom number one it is!

9

DIESEL

*I*t was just after midnight, and Diesel was no closer to falling asleep than he was when they first arrived. His skin felt antsy, and his mind was running a mile a minute. Not to mention his dick was dying for some attention.

Fuck it.

Diesel hopped off his bed and quickly changed into a fresh T-shirt. He had showered two hours ago, but for some reason, lying in this house made him feel... *dirty.*

God, Matteo has turned you into some kind of princess.

Fuck that nonsense.

Would you like some scented candles and perhaps some Michael Bublé music as well? Whatever happened to that tough-as-fuck prick who slept in his car and beat on three guys at once? When was the last time you even got in a fight? You're going soft.

Was he going soft? Was he getting too comfortable with

66

Matteo's life of luxury? He was leaving himself vulnerable again. What was going to happen when it all came crashing down, and Matteo eventually asked him to leave? He wasn't going to be a hot piece of ass forever.

Creeping across the ratty floorboards, Diesel listened against his bedroom door before opening it.

Silence.

Chase and Jared must be asleep in the basement already. Diesel smirked.

Mistake number one: don't place the troublemaker on a floor alone with easy access to the front door and no supervision. It was like Chase was begging for him to sneak out.

Was it really sneaking out when you were twenty-five?

But he still lived at home with a "dad" and basically roommates. Granted, the house was a fucking castle, but still, it wasn't his, and he couldn't claim to be an adult. He could barely manage his own finances.

Closing the front door behind him, he began jogging down the road, searching for the nearest pub or club—any place that served alcohol and contained horny men or women. Actually, preferably, horny men. Men were more likely than women to spend the night buying him drinks, and, let's face it, he wasn't rolling in funds. Hopefully, he could find a nice, generous man to buy him a few drinks, then swallow his cock in the men's room.

It didn't take him long to find a dingy English pub with low lighting and a crooked sign hanging out front.

It was the perfect dive bar.

Once inside, he glanced around, looking for a potential mark or at least someone cute enough to fuck.

It didn't take him long.

Sitting at the bar, playing with a pint, was an elderly gentleman wearing a charcoal tweed blazer and a light-gray flat cap. The man was who you might picture having a beer at a local pub after a long day at work.

Adjusting his black hoodie, Diesel walked over to the bar and slid onto the empty stool right next to the smiling Englishman.

"How's your night going?" Diesel asked, leaning in closer to him.

He watched as the man's eyes dilated, and it suddenly became hard for the man to swallow.

Wow, looks like my guess was right, Diesel thought to himself, recognizing a man in lust the moment their eyes connected.

"I've been working construction all day and thought I'd stop in for a quick beer before I head home for the night. Anything worth drinking?" Over the years, Diesel had mastered the art of smooth-talking and getting what he wanted from men. The key was to find a mark who was quiet and willing to offer you the moon in return for some affection. Tonight was this tweed man's lucky night!

Looking nervous as hell, the man nodded to the bartender and ordered Diesel a beer.

"So, what does a sexy stud like you do for a living?" Diesel asked, giving the man one of his dangerous smirks and sliding his hand discreetly up the man's inner thigh.

"Umm..." the flustered man uttered, trying not to draw attention to himself and the fifty shades of red he was turning.

This guy was going to be too easy.

An hour and a half later and four whiskeys and two beers in, Diesel was feeling buzzed. It felt good to be free of his chains and not have his parole officer monitoring his every move.

Judging by the few remaining patrons in the pub, it was probably getting close to last call. Time to get his balls drained.

Placing his hand on the gentleman's lap, he began rubbing circles on his inner thigh.

The man swallowed hard, looking scared and uneasy.

Was this the man's first time with a guy?

"So, how about we head into the loo and get better acquainted?" Diesel whispered into his ear, paying no attention to the bartender washing glasses at the far end of the bar.

"Umm. I... I think I better just head home." The man quickly stood and dropped a handful of cash on the bar.

There were fifties and twenties all rolled together. The man didn't even take the time to double-check that he was dropping the right amount of cash on the bar.

Before Diesel had a chance to speak, the man was scurrying out of the bar.

Well, that was new. Usually, guys couldn't get to the bathroom fast enough when he asked. *Was he losing his touch?*

The sound of someone stifling a chuckle echoed across the bar.

Diesel turned, ready to tell whoever it was off, but stopped when he caught sight of the offending young man.

"That was painful to watch," the mystery man noted. "Didn't take you for the type of guy who enjoyed draining old-man nutsacks."

Diesel's face heated. *Who the fuck was this dude, and why was he all up in his business?*

"I don't recall ever asking for your opinion." Shaking his head, Diesel downed the last of his whiskey and slid the empty glass toward the bartender.

"No. But it's still painful to watch a strapping young dude spend his evening pimping himself out just so he can get a guy to buy him some alcohol."

"Still don't recall giving a shit what you think."

Another smirk. The man was handsome in that rough trade-boy kind of way. He probably worked construction and plowed his girlfriend every other day.

"You want to know the most painful part?" he asked, leaning even closer to Diesel.

The man was sitting two chairs away, just far enough that Diesel couldn't run his hands across the dude's short black hair and far enough that the bartender couldn't overhear their conversation.

Run his hands across? What was he thinking? Perhaps he was hornier than he thought.

Although, the dude did have a nice buzz cut, freshly

buzzed, as opposed to his facial hair that looked like it hadn't been clipped in at least three days.

Strangely, he found himself wondering how the man's scruff would feel up against his hole as he ate his ass out for hours.

Yeah, the dude looked like he enjoyed eating ass. Probably enjoyed it when a woman sat on his face and demanded that he service her.

Fuck. He needed to get his balls drained. It had been almost two weeks since he busted a nut. Having Matteo around him constantly tended to be a boner killer. Don't get him wrong, Matteo was a good-looking man but not boner-making material in his books.

This dude sitting next to him? Yeah, he wouldn't mind shoving his face down in the dirt as he laid claim to his tight firm ass. The dude would probably squeal like a pig.

He wondered how much whiskey it would take to make the guy... question...

"So? Do you want to know?" the man asked again, reminding Diesel that his lips were moving and that air was coming out of his mouth.

"Sure, entertain me."

"The most painful part had to be watching you get shot down by a horny old geezer." The man chuckled. He actually fucking chuckled.

Fuck this dude.

Diesel leaned back in his chair and grabbed a handful of his already hard cock.

"The poor guy probably realized that he didn't have the

gag reflexes to take all this meat," Diesel said, giving the man the cockiest grin he could muster. *Nobody talks down to him. Not ever.*

"Yeah, deepthroating takes years to master and talent to achieve. Nine's my best record," the man said, tossing a twenty on the bar and standing up from his stool. "Enjoy your evening."

What? Nine? Inches? Was the man saying...?

Confusion and uncertainty flooded Diesel's mind. What was the dude getting at?

He felt a hand tap him on the back as the mystery man walked past him and out the back door of the bar.

What the...? Was he hitting on him?

Diesel sat there watching the back door to the pub close as he tried to figure out what the fuck just happened.

Was the dude gay? Bi? Teasing him? Or was he being set up to get gay-bashed?

Fuck it. What was the likelihood of him getting attacked when he walked outside?

He hopped off the stool, hoping that his dick wasn't leading him to trouble and headed toward the back door.

Outside, the parking lot was dark, save for two overhead lamps that helped patrons find their cars if they chose to drive.

Diesel looked around the lot, wondering where the tattooed, confusing straight dude disappeared to. Then he saw the red glow of a cigarette being inhaled.

Throwing his hoodie over his head, he moseyed over to

where the guy was leaning against a dumpster. He was in no rush. The dude could wait for him.

"Usually, my tricks have a smoke after they've sucked my dick," Diesel explained with all the confidence in the world.

Eyes trailing down to Diesel's package, the man gave a smirk. "Is that so?"

Yeah, this was happening. The dude was sizing him up, probably wondering how much of his raw meat he could actually fit down that pesky throat of his.

It was time to see if the man was all talk.

Stepping forward, Diesel popped open his jeans and slid down his zipper until the thickness of his package was exposed to the night air.

"Hmm, looks like it might be worth my time," the cocky bastard supposed, tossing his smoke over his shoulder and dropping to his knees.

Grabbing onto the back of the man's head, Diesel guided him toward his throbbing hard cock. This wasn't going to take long. He was so fucking horny already. It had been too long since he blew his load.

Cool air touched his thighs as the scruffy, straight dude in front of him pulled his underwear down around his thighs. He let out a moan when Diesel's cock flopped out and smacked him in the face.

Take that, you cocky bastard.

As if accepting Diesel's challenge, the rough tradie grabbed hold of Diesel's stiff shaft and then swallowed his cock down to its base.

Holy. Fuck.

Only one other person has ever been able to take all of his cock, and that dude was a fucking porn star. Literally. For some world-famous porn studio that specialized in gay kink films and, apparently, world-class dick swallowing.

Placing his hand on the back of the dude's buzzed head, Diesel closed his eyes and let the cock-sucking demon have his way with his rock-hard cock.

Sucking. Slurping. Gagging.

The guy knew how to suck dick!

Unable to hold back any longer, Diesel unloaded his seed in the cock-hungry tradie's mouth.

It wasn't until Diesel stopped convulsing from his orgasm that the scruffy-looking *straight-my-ass* dude released his cock from his mouth and got up from his knees.

Smirking, the cocky bastard popped open his jeans and began unzipping his fly.

Judging by the bulge in his pants, he appeared to have his own lethal weapon tucked behind the overstretched material.

Too bad it was getting late.

Zipping up his jeans, Diesel gave the man a grin of his own.

"Thanks for the ball drain. Gotta jet before the crew notices I'm missing."

Loving the confused look on the dude's face, Diesel turned and headed back toward the house.

He kind of felt like a dick for leaving the guy with blue balls, but if Chase woke and happened to realize that he left the house, he was going to be crucified. Matteo would lock him in a tower and never let him out again.

He got what he came for. Free booze and ball drainage.

Hey, he never said he wasn't an asshole.

10

___

DIESEL

"*M*orning, sleepy head," Chase greeted as Diesel walked down the stairs and into the living room. He was hooking up some monitors to laptops and appeared to be loving every moment of it.

"Hey," Diesel responded, trying to walk off his massive headache. He was going to have to find where he packed his damn painkillers after breakfast.

Shouldn't they be in your toiletry bag? that annoying voice inside his head asked.

Yeah, you'd think, but when he checked this morning, they weren't.

Inside the kitchen, Jared was flipping pancakes without a shirt.

Back at home, Daddy M had a strict "must wear shirts at the breakfast table" rule that everyone followed—except Diesel because, hey, Bruno needed to breathe. But whenever Daddy M wasn't around for breakfast, Jared never seemed to be able to locate a shirt.

Diesel was pretty sure that, if given the chance, Jared would live his whole life never wearing a shirt. He was too proud of his body to ever want to cover it up. And, of course, if given the choice, Isaac would probably never wear pants.

The two of them were made for each other.

"Pancakes are almost done," Jared called over his shoulder. "Want to grab some mugs for coffee?"

Nodding, he began opening cupboards at random, searching for the highly coveted coffee mugs. Thanks to his lack of sleep and massive hangover, today was going to be a high caffeine intake day.

The sound of Jared humming caught Diesel's attention. He was shaking his butt while flipping pancakes in the pan. *How could one man be so chipper and energetic first thing in the morning?* He swore if Jared asked him to go for a run with him, he was going to have to punch the guy in the throat. Friendship be damned.

Grabbing three mugs from the cupboard, he finally had to ask, "What's with the endorphin overload this morning?"

Jared picked up the pan and flipped a pancake onto a plate like he was some sort of master chef or something.

"FaceTimed with Isaac this morning. Did you know the boy can do the pretzel?" Jared's eyes lit up as he talked about his fiancé and their stupid early morning sex games.

"Hope you washed your hands before making my pancakes."

"Don't worry, I whipped you up a special batch of

whipped cream. I know how much you love having cream on your cakes."

Diesel couldn't help but chuckle. The dude had a sick sense of humor which was probably why he and Isaac got along so well—well, once they stopped prank-flirting with each other and finally admitted that they wanted to bone... and cuddle... and all that other lovey shit that couples do when they decide to bind their lives together for some untold, freakish reason.

"Jare still shaking his booty?" Chase asked, walking into the kitchen and washing his hands in the sink.

"Yeah, it's sickening that one man should be so chipper first thing in the morning," Diesel responded, still eyeing his best friend.

"You didn't see what my boy did with his leg behind his head." Jared's smile was practically swallowing his face.

"Judging by the chub in your joggers, I'm guessing it was something dirty and demeaning," Diesel added, pouring himself a cup of coffee. He had taken a seat at the table facing the stove and Jared's shaking ass.

Jared and Chase finally joined him, each reaching for a cup as well.

"Why's there an extra plate?" Diesel asked, noting the extra place setting laid out across from him.

"It's for Zero. In case he joins us for breakfast," Chase answered, reaching for the pancakes and dropping two on his plate.

"Zero?" Diesel asked.

"Yeah, the guy staying across the hall from you. He's the

one who's been working this case these past few weeks." Jared picked up the maple syrup and began drowning his pancake.

Seriously, how sweet does this guy like his cakes?

"Speaking of the devil," Chase said, rising from his chair to shake hands with the man who had just entered the room. "Perfect timing."

"Yeah, I could smell breakfast from upstairs and had to come check it out."

From his periphery, Diesel watched as a body moved from behind him and circled the table, taking the spot directly across from him.

What the fuck?!

Color drained from both their faces as Diesel and their new breakfast guest locked eyes with one another.

Freezing mid-sit was the demon cocksucker himself—shirtless and looking sexy as fuck.

Eyes locked together, neither said a word.

"Zero, this is Diesel and Jared," Chase introduced, oblivious to the sudden awkwardness in the room.

Jared wasn't.

Time once again began moving forward, and the demon cocksucker, a.k.a Zero and, apparently, his new co-worker, finally sat his firm ass down at the table.

"I'm Jared," a voice said from across the table.

Diesel finally exhaled, remembering that breathing consisted of two ways—in and out. Kind of like how his cock was sliding in and out of Zero's mouth last night.

Fuck, this was going to be awkward.

"Nice to meet you, Jared," Zero finally said, extending his

hand across the table and releasing Diesel from his death-like stare.

Was this what mice felt like when caught in the gaze of a pissed-off snake?

Diesel felt a kick from under the table and glanced over to see Jared giving him a *what the fuck's up* look.

"And this awkward piece of shit is Diesel," Jared finally said, reminding Diesel that he still hadn't spoken.

"Does it talk?" the cocky cocksucker across the table asked Jared, giving a smirk as he reached for the plate of breakfast sausages.

"Most days, but it appears that today we got grumpy D instead."

Jared was going to die if he didn't fuck right off.

"Oh, sorry. Was just thinking about this disappointing hookup I had last night at a bar. Had to come home and rub one out to get that unsatisfied feeling out of my balls," Diesel said with a sly grin of his own.

"No worries, man. I know the feeling. I gave a mercy blow job to some dude who had been rejected at a bar last night too. Poor guy had the smallest cock dangling between his legs. Had to make him feel special somehow."

Jared and Chase both laughed. Diesel was seething.

Small dick, his ass.

"Good for you. Even the small-dick boys need a good BJ every once in a while," Chase added through a mouth full of sticky syrup.

Zero gave a nod as he raised his mug to take a sip.

Asshole.

"Wait," Jared said, head snapping around at Diesel. "You left the house last night?"

Dammit. Talk about ratting your own self out. Thanks a lot, fuck-face.

"Yeah, I was bored, so thought I would grab a drink at a bar."

"Why? Is Mr. Talkative not allowed out after dark?" Zero asked, seeming amused as he took a bite of his breakfast.

"No. Diesel is kind of grounded at the moment," Chase answered, giving Diesel a disapproving glare.

"Yeah, Daddy M even gave him a nifty little tracking bracelet," Jared added, pointing at Diesel's wrist with his fork.

"Wow, sounds like someone's been a naughty boy. Care to share?" Zero asked, appearing to love every minute.

Digging into his breakfast, Diesel refused to look over at the annoying man. *Who comes to breakfast shirtless, wearing only a pair of loose-fitting board shorts?* Then his eyes slipped to Jared. *Fucker.*

"Looks like his batteries might have run out again," fuck-face added.

"Ignore D. Sometimes he can get a little moody, especially before eleven a.m.," Jared offered.

Why was Jared being so chatty with the new guy?

"So, when do we get to meet the rest of the crew?" Jared asked, going in for a second helping of pancakes.

From the corner of his eye, Diesel watched as Zero's lips wrapped around his fork, gently pulling the meaty sausage from its tongs. The thought of those lips wrapped around his cock last night made blood flow right to his dick. He had to admit, he hadn't had a blow job that good in ages.

Still, the look of his smug face, scruffy facial hair and chestnut eyes... everything just made him want to bury his knuckles into his stupid lips.

And then force-feed him your cock?

Fuck that voice.

"Actually, I am the crew."

Sound returned to the room as Diesel caught the words falling out of Zero's mouth.

"What do you mean that you're the crew?" Diesel snapped, annoyed if it was just him.

"Zero's been here doing surveillance. Trying to see if there is any truth to the things written in Edwin's journal about the doctor. So far, he hasn't been able to corroborate the man's story." Chase was the one speaking. He looked annoyed and, quite frankly, pissed that they hadn't been able to uncover anything so far.

Reaching across the table, Diesel placed two pancakes onto his plate before reaching for the bowl of whipped cream. Yes, Jared wasn't kidding when he said he liked cream on his cakes. Whipped cream and strawberries were his favorite, but since there were no strawberries on the table, whipped cream alone would have to suffice.

"What have you found so far?" Diesel asked, still not sure how he was going to work with his annoying hookup. The whole point of having a hookup was so you didn't have to see their stupid face ever again.

Putting his fork down on his plate, Zero placed his elbows on the table and crossed his fingers under his chin.

Diesel couldn't help but notice the way the man's muscles seemed to bulge as he leaned forward on the table in contemplation. His arm sleeve tattoos seemed to come to life as he moved his body against the table. There was something about guys and tattoos that always made Diesel's dick hard.

Cocky bastard. Trying to show off his muscles like he was some kind of king shit or something.

"Not a whole lot." Zero's voice broke through the internal debate that Diesel was having. "I've been able to document his weekly routine. Mostly work, coffee, gym, and biweekly dinners at a friend's place. The guy is pretty average and seems to stick to his routines," Zero explained, seeming a bit flustered himself.

"Well, hopefully, we can change that," Chase added. "With more of us on the case, hopefully, we can find the chink in his armor."

Diesel wasn't sure how much he would be able to contribute to this case, but it was definitely going to be an interesting assignment. Still beats sitting at home, benched, until Master M deemed him fit for performing.

His eyes drifted up to Zero, who was already watching him as he placed another forkful of pancakes into his mouth. The man began chewing like he was making love to the freakin' batter.

Of all the people he could have picked up at the bar, it had to be the one guy who was sleeping across the hall from him.

Zero gave him a wink.

Diesel's eyes narrowed, hoping Zero could read the *fuck you* behind his glare.

Under the table, Diesel felt another kick. He glanced over at Jared who was giving him a questioning look.

Diesel just shook his head. He didn't need the guys explaining what he already knew—never shit where you eat. Jesus, could he fuck up any more?

Had he known, he would have told his dick to fuck right off and gone home to take a cold shower.

11

DIESEL

Standing outside the brown-and-black attached home, Diesel glanced at his phone to double-check that he got the right address.

65 Blossom St.

Yup, he was at the right place. Then he spotted it. The little brown plaque with gold lettering announcing that this was the office of Dr. Annetta Bloom, Psychiatrist.

Psychiatrist. Like he was crazy or something. The only people who went to places like these were schizos and psychopaths. Neither of which was he.

But he had to. He made a promise to Matteo, and this was part of Matteo's sentence. If he was a good boy, perhaps one day, Daddy M would take off his protective jewelry and let him run free once again. Until that day, he needed to earn back Matteo's trust.

Taking a deep breath, he slid his phone back into his jeans and made his way up the concrete steps.

"Mr. Pratt, welcome. Please come in," the friendly young woman answered on his third knock.

The house was much nicer than the dump that they were currently staying in. The walls were covered in a soft blue wallpaper with silver-and-black trimming, no doubt meant to provide a calm and soothing environment.

Diesel already hated the place.

He followed the woman into the living room where there was a large comfy-looking chaise lounge—don't ask him how he knew what the damn psycho sofa was called. He must have seen it in a magazine or heard Levi talking about getting one for his bedroom or something. The boy was so precious when it came to luxury items sometimes.

Next to the lounge was a plush-looking armchair—no doubt the queen's chair. Her Majesty's throne to sit upon while she writes down all the things that are wrong with him and his entire damn life.

Why was he here again?

"Please, have a seat." The woman gestured toward the dissection couch and waited for him to take his rightful place... under the microscope and awaiting judgment.

"Diesel. You can call me Diesel."

"Of course. Would you like some tea? Coffee? Water?"

"How about a whiskey?" Hey, it was worth a shot.

The woman stared at him for a moment before realizing that he was kidding.

"No, I'm fine. Thanks."

Diesel had purposely booked these sessions in the morning so that he could get the damn thing over with, then proceed to enjoy the rest of his day. Session one was off to a good start—that was sarcasm if anyone missed it.

Once they were both comfy in their respective spots—Diesel refusing to lie down like a helpless damsel in distress, instead choosing to sit with his leg over his lap and his arm resting on the back of the lounge—they began their session.

"Before we start, I wanted to make it very clear that whatever is said during these sessions stays between you and me. Nothing you say will ever be shared with anyone else, including your boss, Mr. Sabarino."

The doctor had been working with Matteo and the guys for several years now, so she was well aware of the château and what they all did there. Mostly, she met with newbies who were having trouble coping with the heavy amount of trauma that they all brought with them. Levi was one of those guys who met with the doc once a month, just for "fine-tuning," as he liked to say.

Diesel, on the other hand, didn't see any reason to come and let some strange woman judge him. If it weren't for the promise he made to his jailer, he wouldn't be here.

"Sure thing, boss." Fifty-nine more minutes. This was going to be painful.

Giving Diesel a gentle, reassuring smile, she opened her notebook. "Now, how about we start with a little bit about you? Feel free to tell me as much or a little as makes you comfortable."

Argh. This was so stupid.

"Well, as I'm sure you've probably read in my file, I'm twenty-five, six feet, bi, and like long walks alone through dark parks and meeting random strangers in dark alleys. Oh, and I have a tattoo named Bruno."

Listening attentively, the woman made a few notes in her notebook, then tapped her pen against her lips. "And Bruno, how long have you had him living on your body?"

Okay, Diesel could see why so many of the guys at the mansion loved her. Still, these sessions were bullshit and a complete waste of his time.

Diesel spent the next fifty-five minutes talking about all his favorite bands and T-shirts. He even went over all his tattoos and why each one hurt differently. Overall, he thought the session went well.

"Well, that's all the time we have set for today. I'll see you again tomorrow at the same time."

"I look forward to it," Diesel said with a fake-ass grin.

Leaving the doctor's office, he decided to walk the forty minutes back to the house. It would give him time to clear his head and figure out what he was going to do with his cock-sucking demon problem.

When he arrived home, the place appeared to be empty. Diesel went into the kitchen to grab himself a drink.

"I didn't think anyone was home."

Diesel spun around, startled, nearly dropping his bottle of water.

Standing in the entrance to the kitchen, towel wrapped snugly around his waist, was Zero.

Water slid down the man's bare chest, catching briefly on the ridges that made up his six-pack.

Jesus, did this dude live at the gym?

Realizing that he was staring at the man's obliques, Diesel cleared his throat and then turned back to close the fridge door.

"Umm, no. I just got back from my... thing." He hesitated before deciding that Zero didn't need to know all of his secrets. He already knew the taste of his cum; that was probably enough. "Where are the other guys?"

Not seeming to care that he was in a towel, Zero crossed the kitchen to where Diesel was standing, firmly planted against the kitchen counter.

"They went out to grab some groceries and pick up some surveillance equipment. I think Chase wants to try some new techniques."

Stopping in front of Diesel, the man placed his hands on both sides of the counter, effectively trapping Diesel in place. The asshole smirked, leaning in closer so that he was just inches from his face.

"You left me with blue balls last night."

The smell of fresh soap and toothpaste filled the empty space between them. Diesel was finding it hard to focus, especially when the muscles in Zero's arms kept flexing around him.

Normally, he wasn't this flustered. Guys were his plaything. He used them to get what he wanted, then moved on with his life. So why was he finding it so hard to focus when he was around Zero?

"That wasn't a kind thing to do."

He wasn't a kind boy.

Focus finally returned to its master.

"That sounds like a *you* problem, doesn't it? My balls were happy and empty," Diesel responded, using his hand to push away his captor and walk around him. "You should probably be more selective about which random dude you decide to suck off in the back of a dingy bar. Some of us are only interested in taking care of number one."

Behind him, he heard Zero chuckle.

"You owe me a blow job," he called as Diesel left the kitchen and headed up to his room.

Perhaps, one day. If he was feeling generous and in the mood for swallowing *questioning, straight-dude* dick.

But today was not that day.

12

ZERO

*R*eaching for another potato chip, Zero held the binoculars steady against his face. From where he sat, he had a perfect view of their subject as he browsed some fruit laid out by a local vendor.

Chase, in his infinite wisdom, had decided that tonight, he and his train wreck of a new partner should be placed together to keep an eye on the man that they were investigating—Dr. Nicolaus Baasch. He wondered if perhaps Chase had detected a bit of awkwardness between him and the cocky little bastard at the breakfast table the other day, and this was his way of forcing the two of them to sniff each other's butts and become best friends.

That only happens in the animal world, dipshit.

Too bad. He wouldn't mind getting up close and personal with a certain tantalizing behind. Perhaps knock some sense into that selfish little stoner.

He was familiar with guys like Diesel. He'd been dealing

with them his whole life. They were lazy, selfish, and couldn't be relied upon. Take what happened between them the other night. The second the guy shoots his load, he fucks right off, only caring about himself and his own selfish needs.

Focus. You're here to watch Dr. Creeps-a-lot, *not devise plans to teach bad boys a lesson.*

The sound of the potato chip crushing between his teeth filled the silent void around him.

"Could you chew any louder?" Diesel's annoyed voice came through the tiny earpiece he had shoved inside his ear. The irritation in Diesel's voice was loud and clear.

Zero added three more chips to his mouth and began chewing even louder.

"Great, they assigned me with an immature man-child."

"Immature man-child with a six-pack," Zero added for good measure.

"Not sure how, when all you've done since we started this stakeout is pig out on junk food."

"It's called working out. I hit the gym five days a week and watch what I eat... most days."

Zero turned his binoculars toward the park where a hooded Diesel was sitting on a bench, arm thrown over the back, pretending to be playing on his cell phone.

"So tell me. What's your workout regime?" Zero asked, curious about this walking gray cloud of sunshine.

"Whiskey."

A startled chuckle slipped from his lips before he had a chance to get himself under control. He wasn't going to give the guy the satisfaction of knowing that he found him amusing.

"There's got to be more than that. You work as a stripper, right? That means you've got to have a half-decent body buried under all those layers of clothing."

"Whiskey and sex. Lots of sex. So much so that people are amazed I even get dressed at all."

This guy was kind of funny. In a mean-girl kind of way.

"Well, I haven't seen the body, but you definitely got the porn star dick thing going for you." He decided to play nice and throw the man a metaphorical bone. A compliment here and there never hurt anyone.

"Thanks. It keeps me employed."

Now Zero couldn't help but chuckle.

Damn it.

"Remind me again why I'm stuck outside, alone in a dark park, and you're just chilling inside a warm car with music and snacks?" Diesel asked, turning his head toward the direction of the car.

"Because you're more believable as a sketchy bum just chillin' in a park looking to score some coke."

Diesel pulled down his hoodie and glared at the car.

"Hey, you're not allowed to break character. Get back into your stank-ass, druggy persona and appear like you're looking to score some dope." He was having way too much fun with this.

"You're such a dick." Diesel huffed back into the earpiece.

"You still owe me a blow job."

"Hate to tell you, but I'm straight," Diesel responded, turning his focus back to the man they were supposed to be surveilling.

"Keep telling yourself that, princess, and maybe one day your fairy godmother will bring you a pony as well."

Twenty minutes went by with nothing but silence between the two. Zero was now working on a bag of jelly beans which was basically all sugar and gelatin—and oh, so fucking delicious. Only downside? They were chewy as hell! He grabbed the cap off a pen and began trying to pick the gummy from the bottom of his teeth.

Fuck, he wished he had his toothbrush with him.

"So, what kind of a name is Zero, anyway?" Diesel's voice was low and sounded almost bored.

"It's a nickname."

"Meaning?"

Zero exhaled, thinking about the origin of his nickname. He wasn't exactly proud of his past, but what could he do? In the end, it all came down to whether or not you learned from your past mistakes and how you grew from those experiences. He wasn't a saint by any means, but he also wasn't the monster.

"Zero, as in 'zero patience.' Let's just say that when I was younger, I had a bit of an anger-management problem and went from zero to sixty in zero point zero seconds. People started calling me Zero, and the name kind of stuck." He tossed the bag of jelly beans onto the passenger seat of his car and picked up the binoculars once again.

Their favorite person was inside the gym, presumably working off whatever calories he had consumed that day.

"What about Diesel? Was your dad a car buff or something?"

"Couldn't tell you. Haven't seen the guy since I was four, and my mom and I weren't exactly the sit-and-chat kind of people." There was a certain darkness in the words that Diesel spoke. Zero wanted to ask more, but he wasn't sure how the man would react.

"So, if Zero is your nickname, what's your real handle?"

Lowering the binoculars, he gave the back of Diesel's head a smirk.

"Wouldn't you like to know."

13

ZERO

Two days had passed without making much progress on the Dr. Baasch front. Chase and Zero alternated surveillance methods, and thanks to Chase's fancy new toys, Zero didn't have to spend all his time sitting in his car watching the man outside his home.

It was just after eleven p.m., and Zero was busy scanning through surveillance video on his laptop—thanks to Chase's new remote wireless setup—while Diesel and the guys were in the kitchen, setting up for a game of poker.

Zero had placed a hidden camera across the street from Dr. Baasch's house so that he could monitor his activities from the comfort of the living room couch. Right now, there wasn't much going on. The light to his bedroom was on, and he appeared to be getting ready for bed. Hopefully, that meant that Zero would be off duty soon.

In the kitchen, Jared laughed at something Diesel had

said while Chase opened a bag of chips and poured them into a bowl.

He wondered how often they did this. Hang out together, shooting the shit. They seemed to be a close-knit group of friends.

Watching Diesel at the table, he seemed a lot more relaxed. His hoodie was down, and he barely seemed to check his phone.

Zero had started to notice that whenever Diesel was uncomfortable or didn't like the situation, he raised his hoodie over his head and seemed to retreat into himself.

His hoodie seemed to be his safe place.

"Okay, I'll deal," Diesel announced, picking up the deck of cards and beginning to shuffle.

Someone's phone rang.

"Oh, that's Levi. I gotta take this," Chase announced, grabbing his phone and jumping up from his seat. They all watched as Chase scurried off to the basement, presumably to have a private conversation with his fiancé.

"Guess it's just you and me," Diesel said with a nod to Jared.

"Guess so. Deal 'em."

Zero watched as the two began playing, each doing their best to fuck over the other. It was nice seeing Diesel smiling so much. From what Zero had gathered, the two were best friends, having worked at their magic *sex wonderland* longer than most of the guys there.

When he wasn't shooting daggers his way, Diesel didn't

seem like such a terrible guy. Perhaps they just got off on the wrong foot... or the wrong knee, in his case.

Diesel and Jared were just about to finish their first game when Jared's phone dinged. The guy's face lit up like it was Christmas morning.

"Isaac says he's got a boner. Time for some sexy times!" Jared announced, all excited and jumping up from the table.

He started moving toward the basement door, then stopped. He must have just realized that sexy times in his bedroom would involve Chase sitting right next to him, Face-Timing with his own boyfriend.

Head swiveling back and forth, Jared looked like he was trying to complete complex math in his head.

"Umm, hope nobody needs to use the bathroom for the next... umm... forty-five minutes. Later, dudes," Jared stammered, bounding up the stairs like a sex-starved inmate who just got out of prison.

"But... it's your..." Diesel began, pointing toward the deck of cards, before watching his friend disappear up the stairs.

Zero couldn't help but notice the wave of disappointment that spread across Diesel's face. He stared at the remaining cards he held before placing them down on the table and raising his hoodie back over his head.

Silence fell across the kitchen.

Perhaps one of the guys would end their call early and rejoin their buddy at the table for some cards.

As the minutes ticked by, it became clear that no one was returning to their card game anytime soon.

Lifting his laptop, Zero headed into the kitchen to join Diesel and his abandoned card game.

"Mind if I join?"

Diesel lifted his head and groaned when he realized who the speaker was.

"Honestly, it's getting kind of late. I'm just gonna head to bed. Help yourself to the snacks." He picked up his beer, then headed up the stairs.

Even though the man could be a selfish prick, Zero still didn't like seeing him so dejected. Something was going on.

On his laptop, nothing was happening. It looked like it was going to be another quiet night for the doc.

Somewhere above him, the haunting lyrics of "Bullets with Butterfly Wings" by the Smashing Pumpkins began to play.

Grabbing the bowl of chips and the remaining four-pack of beer from the fridge, Zero headed up the stairs to join his new housemate.

Knocking once, he turned the knob on the door and let himself into Diesel's bedroom.

"Dude!" a pissed-off Diesel barked as Zero walked in uninvited.

"Calm your knickers. I just need some help with something." He was lying through his teeth, but the angry wasp on the bed didn't have to know that.

Diesel's room was just as he would have imagined. Dirty clothes were thrown over every possible surface, with empty glasses and half-eaten bags of chips left on the floor next to the bed.

Ignore the mess. Ignore the mess.

"Still, you could have waited until I asked you to come in."

"And would you have asked?"

"Probably not."

"Okay, now that that's cleared up, shove a butt." Zero huffed, tapping a less pissed-off version of the angry wasp on the shoulder. Diesel slid over on his bed—but just barely enough to fit a bite-sized twink and perhaps his touch-up bag.

There was something fun and exciting about Diesel's need to challenge everything. He never just did what he was told and always did things the hardest way possible. It was as if he needed to remind people that he had an opinion as well and that his views mattered.

Fine. Have it your way.

Deciding to teach the boy a lesson, Zero flopped down on the bed next to Diesel, his ass half sitting on the side of Diesel's thigh while his shoulder pressed firmly against his chest.

"Well, this is cozy." Zero leaned in toward Diesel and inhaled his scent. "Mmm, you smell good too. Like angry douche meets horse-hung stoner."

He let out a chuckle when Diesel shoved him in his arm with the hand that wasn't trapped under his body.

"Okay, okay. Geeze. You can't even compliment a guy anymore these days." The stubborn hornet shifted under his body. "Here, hold this." Zero passed Diesel the bowl of chips and chilled cans of beer.

"You really came prepared," Diesel noted in that sarcastic tone of his.

"Yeah, well, I figured this might take a while." Shifting, he pressed his body further into Diesel's, not totally disliking the feel of their bodies pressed up against each other's.

Diesel's body was lean—not gym muscle lean, but rather, keeping active lean. Without Diesel's sweater on, it was much easier to feel the contours of his body pressed up against him. He could definitely understand why people would like to see him dancing onstage.

Settling down but still refusing to move over on the bed, Diesel looked over Zero's shoulder at the laptop he was holding.

"Let's get this over with, washed-up CK model," Diesel huffed out.

"CK model? It's because of my cut obliques, right? They would look killer in a *Calvin Klein* underwear ad." Was it odd that he kind of liked the half-ass compliment he got from the guy?

Zero was poked in his side by the annoyed young wasp.

"Hey, I work hard for these cum gutters. You should see me when I'm in my bulking stage at the gym. I'm a total beast."

Zero was proud of his body and all the hard work he put into it. He hated to admit it, but it was easier to pull scams when you were good-looking and in shape. People liked that you were giving them attention and just wanted to do whatever it was that you asked of them.

That was a sad truth about our society as a whole. If you

were good-looking, the world was your oyster. Take a look at salespeople and bartenders. The good-looking ones always made much higher sales and received better tips.

Feeling Diesel's breath on the back of his neck, his body began to tingle.

This was nice. This closeness and somewhat intimate connection. Plus, it wasn't so bad verbally sparing with the angry little ray of sunshine currently squirming under his weight. Diesel adjusted himself, sinking his back into the man's side and positioning the laptop so that they could both view the screen properly.

Zero could only imagine what they looked like. Two grown-ass men, both over six feet, pressed up against each other, balancing a laptop, beers and chips on a bed made for a daddy and two twinks at best.

"So, what do we got?" Diesel asked, appearing to have accepted his fate as Zero's captive body pillow for the night.

Opening a folder, he pulled up some old video footage from last week and began going through some of Dr. Baasch's daily activities. There wasn't much there, and Zero had already analyzed the footage, but hey, there was nothing wrong with a second pair of eyes taking a look. Plus, that wasn't the purpose of this little impromptu "hang out and chill" session.

Sliding his finger across the laptop, Zero tried to ignore the warm breath gently blowing against his neck.

God, how long had it been since he cuddled up with some-one? Probably ten years?

Not since he caught his ex-girlfriend shacking up with

the neighbor down the hall. That had been one fucked-up encounter. He nearly tossed the asshole over the balcony but thought better of it at the last minute. His ass was too sexy to go to prison.

Ever since that bitch cut out his heart, he'd been anti-love and feelings ever since.

Still, it was nice to feel another warm body pressed up against his own. Even if it did belong to a selfish prick who only ever thought about himself.

As they worked through the footage, Diesel asked questions and provided some thoughts that were actually worth taking a look into. It was interesting to see how the man looked at things from a totally different perspective. He seemed to always want to know why things were occurring.

"Everyone does things for a reason. If you can understand the purpose behind someone's actions, that might give you a clue as to their larger agenda. Take me as an example. When I was younger, I liked to take walks at night. It wasn't because I loved the fresh air; it was because I needed to escape my stepfather's home for a few hours. I hated being there, and going for a walk late at night also helped to avoid any arguments or judgments passed by the parental units."

"Hmm, that's an interesting point."

"You said that the doc likes to go for a walk through Grand Park every night after dinner?" Diesel asked, his cheek just inches from Zero's.

"Yeah, usually around nine before heading to bed at eleven."

"He goes to Grand Park every night except for Thursdays, when he takes a walk through Allistair Park instead." Zero nodded. "Why the change?"

Zero had always assumed it was because Allistair Park had street performers performing every Thursday night, but now Diesel had him wondering if his assumptions might be off. It might be worth taking another look into.

"Pass the chips," Diesel asked, reaching across his body toward the bowl that was just out of his reach. Zero lifted the bowl and passed it to him.

"Night, D." Jared's voice boomed through the other side of the bedroom door, causing them both to jump.

They glanced at the time on the laptop. They had been at this for almost an hour. Where had the time gone?

"Night, Jare," Diesel called back before settling back into his position as Zero's human man-pillow.

Leaning into each other wasn't feeling as awkward as it was when he first barged into Diesel's room.

"You guys have been best buds for a while, huh?" Zero asked, not sure if he would receive an actual response.

"Yeah, he and I were some of the first guys to join Matteo's *cock palace*." Zero couldn't help but chuckle-snort. "We've both been through some heavy shit, and it's nice to have someone around who understands the crap going on inside your head. With Jare, there's no judgment. He's always there when I need him, and he reminds me when I'm being an ass."

"So, he's your Jiminy Cricket."

"My what?" Diesel asked with a chuckle of his own.

"Your grasshopper. Your conscience. That little voice

inside your head that tells you what you're doing is asshole adjacent."

"No, that little voice inside my head is usually telling me how worthless I am and that people are better off without me."

Well, that wasn't what he was expecting.

There was something cold and unsettling about the words that Diesel used. Did he really feel so worthless and think so little of himself?

It was in that moment that Zero realized he really didn't know much about Diesel at all. Only what he did for a living and that he had a really nice dick. Perhaps there was more to the man trapped beneath him than a hot body and prickly attitude.

His eyes fell on the black watch that was strapped to Diesel's wrist. The same watch that he never took off and was apparently his parting gift when he left for this trip. Now was probably not the right time to ask him about it. He needed to earn the man's trust if he expected him to share his darkest secrets and perhaps open up about the demons of his past.

It was time for some lighter conversation. He opened a web browser and began searching for useless trending videos.

"You got to see this video. Pass the chips."

They watched pointless, trash videos and demolished the last of their snacks over the next two hours. It was sometime after two a.m. when Zero finally slipped back into his own bedroom, leaving a drooling, tattooed stoner boy asleep in his bed.

Overall, the evening hadn't been that painful to endure.

14

DIESEL

Seventeen Years Ago

*D*iesel's eyes shot open suddenly, remembering the excitement of the day!

Today was his birthday! He was finally eight!

Two more years, and he would be in the double digits!! That was practically a teenager!

Diesel threw the thin Spiderman bedsheet off his body and jumped out of bed with all the excitement of being the birthday boy.

Today was his day! Today, his momma was going to surprise him with something nice!

She hadn't mentioned anything about his birthday during these past few weeks, but that was because she was keeping it all a secret from him. She was going to surprise him with a big party, a big cake with lots of icing and candles, and maybe even some of those bottle rockets that he loved to swipe from the corner shop down the road. They fizzled and popped and made your tongue feel funny.

He ran into the tiny bathroom and took a pee while he thought about all the presents his mom was going to surprise him with. Jimmy, from school, got eight presents from his parents, and Alice from the trailer next door got three. He wondered how many his momma had decided to buy him? It didn't matter how many. He knew he was going to love them all.

Today was his day!

He washed his hands quickly, then ran out into the living room where his momma was sitting on the small sofa having her morning cigarette.

"Morning, Momma!" Diesel screeched, hopping on the sofa cushion right next to her.

"Oh, good. You're awake. Hurry up and go get dressed. We're going to be late."

To his surprise? *Shit! He better hurry and go get ready.*

Diesel charged into his bedroom and threw on the same jeans and T-shirt he had worn the day before. He was allowed to wear shirts for three days in a row before they had to be thrown into the bin to be washed by Mrs. Harris.

Not wanting to waste any time, he decided to bypass brushing his teeth and ran back out into the living room, too excited to wait any longer.

"Good. You're ready." His mom picked up her keys and threw her pack of smokes into her purse with the broken handle.

"Where're we goin'?" Diesel asked, jumping down the three steps that led up to their trailer in a single bound. Dirt puffed up around him as his feet landed in the grassless yard around him.

"To see a friend of mommy's," his mother answered, lighting another one of her cigarettes as they both got into the car.

They must be on their way to his big birthday party!

Today was his day! His momma must be planning something big. She had been having a lot of meetings with her friend, especially late at night. Sometimes, she wouldn't get home until it was time for him to go to school.

He couldn't wait to get to his party!

Fifteen minutes later, they pulled up to a tiny house with a metal fence around the yard and two bikes thrown across the lawn.

His mother drove up onto the driveway and turned off the ignition. She turned to him, holding an almost finished cigarette in her hand.

"I want you to behave yourself. Don't be giving me any lip and play nice with the other little boy."

Oh! His momma must have invited other kids to come to his party! He wondered if it was anyone from his class. His momma didn't send out any birthday invitations to his classmates, so perhaps she told their mums and dads.

Excited that they were finally here, Diesel tore off his seat belt and jumped from the car.

The backyard gate opened, and a man with a dirty ball cap stepped out from behind the fence and motioned for them both to come round back.

He must be the one running his birthday party!

Diesel ran past the man and into the backyard excited to see all his balloons and presents and friends.

Confused, Diesel stopped on the grass. The backyard was empty except for a broken shed and a picnic table with a small boy sitting at it. The boy looked at Diesel with the same confused look on his face.

"Momma? Where are all the—" Hiss voice caught in his throat when he turned to see his momma kissing the man with the dirty hat. "Momma?" Diesel asked once again.

Why was his momma kissing this man, and where were all his balloons? Did they still have to set up for his party? And why was his momma still kissing that man?

"Daddy?" the small boy at the table called, putting down the popsicle he was eating and watching his father with questioning eyes.

The sun above them beamed down, warming up the air all around them. Off in the distance, a bird chirped, and a car was heard revving its engine.

"Boy, come over and meet your new daddy. Bo and I are getting married next week, and you and I will be moving in here at the end of this week." His mother always called him boy, unless he was in trouble. Then she always called him by his full name—Diesel Alexander Pratt.

"Jordan, come over and meet your new momma and brother," the man with the dirty ball cap... Bo... daddy?... called to the boy sitting at the table.

Both of them walked over to where their parents were standing and locked eyes with one another.

Bo stuck out his hand. "Nice to meet you, boy. Heard you

have trouble takin' orders. I'm here to change all that. In this house, you do as you're told."

Scared, Diesel took the angry-looking man's hand and winced as the beast crushed his fingers.

What was happening?

Diesel looked up at his mother, who was busy smiling at the scary-looking man.

"Here, I have a present for you," his mother said, reaching into her purse and pulling out a baseball glove.

Yes! He always wanted a baseball glove! Perhaps now his momma would teach him how to catch so that he could play baseball with the other kids down at the trailer park.

Diesel froze as he watched his mother bend down and pass the baseball glove to the other little boy standing next to him— his new little brother—Jordan.

The boy's face lit up as he took the glove from his new mother and flipped it around in his hand.

"What do you say, son?" Diesel's new dad asked, startling him where he stood.

"Umm, thanks... Mom?" the boy said, appearing unsure of how he was to address the new woman standing in front of him.

But he was the one who had asked for a baseball glove for his birthday. He was the one who was supposed to be getting gifts today. It was his birthday, not Jordan's.

What was happening?

"Come, let's go inside. The game is about to begin, and the chili is almost ready," Bo ordered, placing his arm around Diesel's mum and leading her into the house.

Jordan followed after them like a happy little puppy.

Perhaps his party would begin once the chili was ready?

Diesel followed them into the house, his feet dragging a little slower than before.

He didn't really understand what was going on. Why was his momma marrying this guy who she just met today? Did she know him from before? Was he a friend of his real dad?

Still confused, Diesel walked into the living room, where his momma was sitting on the couch with Bo's arm wrapped around her shoulder, a freshly lit cigarette dangling from her fingers. On the floor by their feet, Jordan sat playing with his new glove.

Looking around the room, he didn't see any balloons or party favors. No snacks or wrapped presents waiting for him to open.

Perhaps there was a cake hidden in the fridge?

Sadly, Diesel knew better.

There was no cake. No presents. No... nothing.

This was not his day.

Casting aside that last glimmer of hope of having a birthday party this year, Diesel walked around the sofa and took a seat on the cold wooden floor. Away from his momma, away from his new family.

Little did he know that this was going to be his future.

Alone and barely an afterthought.

15

DIESEL

Give it your best shot, Doc. You'll never get a word out of me.

The ticking of the clock was the only sound that filled the space that used to contain a two-sided conversation. That all ended when the nosy bitch decided to ask him that stupid question.

"Mr. Pratt? Did you hear my question?"

Of course he heard her stupid question. It didn't mean that he had to provide her with an answer. She was the *quack doc*—she could figure out the answer on her own. Didn't she go to school to learn all about this stuff? Why did he have to do all the hard work for her?

"Why do you think it is that you go on these multi-day benders?"

Leaning back on the sofa, he pulled his hoodie down even further and began playing with the string around the end.

Time was ticking. Twenty more minutes until this stupid therapy session ended. Why did he ever agree to see this nut job? She had already spent the last two sessions trying to get him to speak about his childhood. If that didn't work, what made her think talking about his present was going to be any different?

Matteo said he needed to see a shrink; he didn't say that he needed to speak.

"Mr. Pratt. I know that digging into your past and getting to the root of your own personal trauma can be daunting and uncomfortable, but unless you are willing to face your demons, you're never going to be able to grow and heal."

She was persistent. He had to give her that.

"Let me start off with something a bit easier. How do you feel about Matteo?"

Her question caught him off guard, and he wasn't sure why she was asking.

Diesel shrugged. "He's a good guy. Generous, loving. What does it matter?"

Dr. Bloom pulled her silver-rimmed glasses from her face and placed them down on the table next to her chair.

"And why is he generous and loving?"

Diesel shrugged his shoulders again. "He likes to help people and never asks for anything in return."

"And has he helped you?" Diesel nodded. "How so?"

He stared at the inquisitive doctor and wondered how pissed off Matteo would be if he continued to ignore all of her questions going forward.

Matteo's trying to help you, that voice deep inside him said.

This voice was different than the other voice. The other voice liked to remind him how worthless and trashy he really was.

Straight from the trailer park. Now you're nothing more than a glorified stripper.

There he was. He wondered when that voice might appear during one of his sessions.

"Mr. Pratt?"

Jesus. Why did she insist on calling him by an old-man name? He was fucking twenty-five, not forty-five.

Deciding that it was easier to just end this nightmare of idiotic questions, he finally answered.

"M found me unconscious in a park in South London. I had mixed a bunch of party drugs and didn't remember even walking to the park. Three days later, I woke up in the hospital with all my medical bills paid and no idea what my next move was going to be. I had been living on the streets for the past six months and was turning tricks to make money for food and drugs. Matteo offered me a safe place to stay while I recovered and got myself back on my feet."

The doc nodded in agreement as if she understood everything that he had just said, but she didn't.

No one did.

Unless you lived in that world, you didn't understand the pain and the suffering. The feeling of powerlessness and anger. Anger that no matter how hard you tried, you just couldn't seem to get it right.

Matteo had seen all that. He somehow understood all the pain and suffering and anger that he felt. He didn't push, he didn't force, he just made an offer, then stood there for support. It was thanks to Matteo that Diesel was finally able to get off the streets. It was because of him, he was able to get a best friend. It was because of him that he was able to get brothers and a father, and a fucked-up and badass crazy family that he wouldn't change for the world.

All because Matteo gave him a chance.

And how are you repaying Matteo's kindness? that pesky voice inside him asked.

He was right. Matteo was once again trying to help him, and here he was, actively trying to sabotage his own future.

Feeling all that pain and suffering and anger building up inside him, he lifted his head and locked eyes with Dr. Bloom.

"I go on my binges to lose myself and numb the pain."

Speaking those words out loud, he felt like he was releasing an atomic bomb into the atmosphere. What would the fallout be? Would he survive? Would Matteo lock him up in a treatment facility indefinitely?

By the time he got home from his therapy session, Diesel was wiped and beat.

"Hey, buddy, welcome back," he heard Zero say from someplace in the living room. He didn't have the energy to spar with him. Not today. Right now, he wanted to lie down in bed and let the blankets swallow him whole.

Ignoring Zero's greeting, he walked up the stairs and into his bedroom.

He had just toed off his shoes and flopped down on the bed when his bedroom door opened.

"Everything alright, man?"

It was Zero.

Lying on his stomach, Diesel didn't have the strength to flip over and give him the finger.

"Yeah, man. Just wiped. Please leave."

There was a moment of silence where Diesel wondered if Zero had actually left the room. Then he heard an exhale.

"Right, dude. I'll be downstairs if you need anything."

The door closed, and Diesel was finally left alone. Alone to process his thoughts and wonder how the fuck he was ever going to fix himself.

A small rap at the door had Diesel opening his eyes and raising his head. The room was dark, and he had no idea what the fuck time it was.

Groggy and disoriented, he sat up on his bed.

Light creaked in through the bedroom door as it slowly opened.

"Whatever you do, don't scream. It's only me. Bloke from across the hall."

Further light filled the room as Zero pushed open the door the remainder of the way and took a step inside.

"You alive?" Zero asked, standing in the doorway like a six-foot-two menacing nightmare.

"It depends. Have you come here to murder me?" Diesel responded, sliding up so his back was pressed against the headboard.

"Not today, but if you keep stealing all the hot water, I can't be held responsible for my actions."

Diesel flicked on the lamp next to the bed.

Standing in the doorway, holding a tray, was the hookup who never left.

"I come bearing food."

"What time is it?" Diesel asked, reaching for his phone and tapping the screen.

It was just after eight p.m.

"What? Are you fucking serious? I slept all day?"

"You must have needed it," Zero said, placing the tray down on the nightstand next to the bed.

The food smelled amazing.

Diesel's stomach growled in response.

Chuckling, Zero passed Diesel the tray.

"Had to hide it from Jared. The boy eats everything in sight."

Not waiting for Diesel to offer, Zero plopped himself down on the bed.

"Yeah. He calls it fueling. Apparently, each of his muscles needs its own meal," Diesel added.

"Please. These muscles put his to shame, and I don't eat half the shit that he does." Zero flexed his bicep, not noticing the sudden shift in Diesel's jeans.

"Thanks for this. I'm fucking starving. What is it?"

"It's white-wine mushroom risotto with oven-roasted chicken breast. And for dessert…" Zero reached into his back pocket and tossed Diesel a pack of sour candies.

Wow. This whole thing was kind of… sweet. Why was the man being so nice?

Taking a forkful of risotto into his mouth, Diesel let the flavors slowly roll over his tongue. *Fuck.* He had never tasted anything quite so good.

"Damn, where did you guys order this from?" Diesel asked, moving over to the chicken once he swallowed his rice.

"We didn't. I made it."

Surprised, Diesel lifted his gaze and stared at the man. "Who knew that a washed-up underwear model could cook?"

Zero punched him gently on the leg. "A man has to have some secrets."

Yes, he does.

Staring into his chestnut eyes, Diesel wondered what other hidden talents the man was hiding behind that tradie rough exterior. Part of him was curious to find out, while another part didn't want to show that he was interested.

Pushing those thoughts aside, Diesel returned to his meal.

"So, where are the guys?"

Zero grabbed a piece of chicken that Diesel had just finished cutting with the side of his fork and popped it into his mouth.

Umm, rude much?

He appeared to ignore the slight growl that emerged from Diesel's throat and proceeded to answer his question.

"They're both out following the doc while he goes on his nightly walk."

That made sense.

Silence fell over them both.

"So, do you want to tell me what this morning was all about?" Zero asked in a gentle voice that Diesel had never heard before. The man seemed genuinely interested to hear what he had to say.

Not quite sure how much he wanted to disclose to the guy who sucked him off next to a dumpster, Diesel took another bite of his chicken to buy himself more time.

"It was nothing, really."

Bullshit. It was a lot.

Zero shifted on the bed, watching him, not saying a word. There was no judgment in his eyes, just pure curiosity.

"Look, I know we haven't known each other long, and for some reason, you refuse to see how irresistibly amazing I am." Zero gave his shoulders a slight shrug. "But I know what it's like to suffer in silence. Trust me, having someone to vent to or share things with can make things much easier to bear. And sometimes, it's easier to talk to someone who you don't really like."

Diesel struggled not to smile. The guy was an idiot.

"What I'm saying is that I got your back if you ever want to chat."

Who was this guy? He didn't know how to deal with this nice version of Zero. Perhaps he should just punch him in the throat and get the old Zero back.

Stop being a dick. He's just trying to be nice.

Fuck that annoying voice. Where was the other one that always told him what fun, wicked things to do? *He* would know how to handle this nice Zero pod sitting in front of him, offering him food and comfort.

Fine. He was going to throw the man a bone.

Placing his fork down on his plate, he shoved the food aside and took a deep breath.

"Not sure if the guys told you, but I'm seeing a shrink." Zero shook his head and remained silent. "Well, today, she asked me something that really made me think. So when I got home, I was all up in my head and couldn't deal with people, so I did what I always do and retreated into myself."

Nodding his head slightly, Zero played with the edges of the blanket on his bed.

"I know how exhausting and painful therapy can be. I've had a few friends attend court-ordered sessions and seen them come out looking wrecked and shattered. But in most of those cases, the guys told me that in the end, the sessions really helped." Zero placed his hand on Diesel's leg again. "It sounds like you had a great session today. You should be proud of yourself."

Standing, he began to walk to the door.

"Z?" Diesel called out, not really sure why or what he was going to say.

Zero stopped at the door and turned.

"Thanks for dinner... and for listening."

"Anytime. You're still a douche though," he said with a smirk before walking out the door.

Diesel couldn't help but smile.

16

DIESEL

The one problem with sleeping all day is that you end up staying awake all friggin' night! Diesel tried everything. He played games on his cell phone, cleaned up all the empty glasses, and threw out all the half-eaten stale chips. He tried watching television, but what's on at three a.m. other than infomercials and squiggly porn. He even tried reading a book he found that was currently being used to prop up a nightstand. That only lasted all of two minutes before he became bored and decided that reading still wasn't for him.

He rummaged through the fridge, searching for something that might satisfy his itch, but nothing there seemed worthy of eating.

"Fuck this." Ready to lose his mind, he decided to head back upstairs.

This is what happens when you go to therapy. You end

up walking around the house alone in the middle of the night.

Now who needs a shrink?

The house was quiet, except for the gentle breathing coming from Zero's room. Since they were staying in a pauper's starter home, the place didn't have any air-conditioning.

It didn't take long for the place to heat up, given that there were four beefy men occupying the space as well as several computers and monitors all going at the same time.

A gentle breeze wafted into the hallway, causing Diesel to pause. Zero's bedroom door was open slightly, probably to allow the air from the open window and bedroom fan to circulate and help keep the bedroom cool.

Curious, he took a few steps closer and carefully peeked through the tiny space between the door and the frame.

Inside, Zero was passed out, lying naked on his belly, two perfect globes pointed upward.

Diesel licked his lips.

Zero's ass was a thing of beauty. Muscular, firm, smooth to the touch. Not to mention the man has this sexy-as-fuck tattoo that runs up his left thigh and up his left butt cheek.

Fuck, could he be any sexier?

When it came to sex, Diesel was an equal-opportunity man. He liked it all. Top, bottom, side, you name it. He ended up either just doing oral or bottoming most of the time because guys seemed to have difficulty taking his dick. When he did find a guy who was brave enough to take his cock, he liked to fuck them doggy style so he could watch their ass jiggle as it slammed up against his pelvis.

Fuck. Diesel looked down at his joggers which were now sporting an awkward tent.

Good thing Chase and Jared were still out watching the doc.

A groan escaped Zero's lips, and his body slowly turned onto its back.

Holy. Shit.

The man was sporting some major wood. Like a mighty oak, the man's thick mushroom head pointed directly at the retired underwear model's face.

Do rough-looking construction-type men have underwear brands that they model? If so, Zero would be the perfect model for the job. His tattoos, firm jaw, rough tanned skin, and perfectly manicured facial hair all added to that rough tradie man fantasy that so many people craved.

Another groan. This one followed by a sultry breath of air.

Boner pressing tight against his sweats, Diesel gripped the head of his cock and gave it a little squeeze.

Fuck, he was horny.

He should go back to his room and give it a wank. Might help him fall asleep after all.

The bed shifted, catching Diesel's attention once again.

This time, Zero's right hand gripped his cock by the base, giving it a firm squeeze.

A breath escaped Zero's lips. Those perfect, supple lips. Diesel wondered what they tasted like.

Probably like whiskey and bad choices.

His favorite taste.

Slowly, Zero's legs shifted, giving him better access to his throbbing hard cock.

Diesel watched as the tattooed slab of beef began working his length, up and down. Nice and slow.

Another moan escaped Zero's lips, eyes remaining closed as his body fucked up into his tight grip.

"Yeah, take that cock, you mouthy little shit," Zero whispered.

Diesel's boner reacted as if the man had been speaking directly to him. Against his sweats, his cock bounced and throbbed, begging to be released and join in the fun happening in the next room.

All around Diesel, shadows whispered their judgment. Yes, he was being a perv and violating the man's privacy. But how much privacy could the horny dude want when he was yanking his dick with his bedroom door half open.

Barely open.

Slightly open.

Who cares. It was open enough for Diesel to enjoy the show.

Reaching into his joggers, Diesel pulled out his dick and began rubbing his length in time with Zero's. Fuck, the man was hot.

Reaching across his chest, Zero began pinching his nipple with his free hand.

Diesel let out a moan. Fuck, he wanted to lick that man's nutsack, then tease those nipples with both his hands.

As if wanting to put on a show, Zero used his legs to lift his hips off the bed and begin fucking up into his fist.

Fuck, the man was gorgeous.

Faster and faster, Diesel watched as his housemate jerked his fat cock, using his precum as lube to slide against his shaft.

With his eyes focused on Zero's hips and dick, Diesel lost himself in the show. His grip tightened around his cock, and he began jerking it with purpose.

"Oh yeah. Take that fucking cock like you were born to do."

Listening to Zero talk dirty while pleasuring himself was one of the hottest things he had ever seen.

"You ready to come? I'm almost there." Zero's voice was louder as he continued to fuck up into his fist.

His muscular legs flexed, and his biceps bulged with each tug.

"Oh yeah. Here I come, baby!"

Diesel jerked his cock fiercely while watching thick streams of jizz burst from his buddy's cock. There was no holding back now. With a muffled cry, Diesel shot his load all over the side of Zero's bedroom door.

He shook and convulsed and wondered what his own fucking name was.

Squeezing off the tip, Diesel gave his dick a shake, not seeing where the last of his load landed. By the time morning came, his cum would be dry and blended in with the history of the house.

Diesel smirked. He found that amusing.

"Maybe now you'll be able to sleep."

Heat flushed Diesel's cheeks when he looked up and locked eyes with Zero, staring back at him.

Fuck.

"You might want to get this wall looked at. There's some sticky white substance all over the place. It might be a health code violation," Diesel said, pretending to check out the wood on the door.

"Oh, it's definitely a violation."

Feeling cum drunk and chill, Diesel tucked his cock back into his sweats and turned to head back to his room.

Yeah, he was definitely ready to get some shut-eye.

17

ZERO

Raising his glass, Zero took a swig of his beer before placing it down on the coaster sitting just before him. He watched Diesel as he took his own drink and continued to act like he wasn't sitting right in front of him.

The man was being an idiot.

"So, how long are you going to continue to pretend that you're sitting here alone?" Zero asked, leaning back and placing his arm across the back of the booth they were sitting in.

Eyes never leaving their subject, Diesel continued to stare away from him. "I'm here to keep an eye on the good doctor, which is what I'm trying to do. Not sure why you keep trying to distract me like a needy little princess."

Zero gave a snort.

Needy? Him? Please.

If anything, Diesel was the one who was all needy and attention-seeking. Watching him sleep last night like an attention-starved little puppy. He could almost hear the man whimpering at the door as he tried to sleep. But that fucking heat. Heat always made him horny for some reason.

Lying on his stomach, he couldn't help but feel his boner pressing into the mattress. Wishing that he was pushing his cock deep inside two luscious mounds... *mmm*, he could feel his dick starting to thicken at the thought.

It was only after a few seconds of rubbing his cock into the mattress that he heard steady breathing coming from his door. It was then that he realized he had an audience to his very stiff situation. And what better way to get off than putting on a show for the horny perv staying across the hall. *His* horny little perv.

His perv? When did they become such a thing?

He's more like you than you think, that annoying voice deep inside him said.

Zero hated to admit it, but he could see a lot of similarities between them both. They both used sarcasm and insults to keep people from getting too close. They both struggled with addictions. Zero's had been painkillers, which, thankfully, only lasted for two years. He'd fallen off his motorcycle one day, breaking his arm and having to suffer through eight months of recovery, during which he became way too fond of the disassociated feeling that painkillers offered.

It was only after he woke up covered in blood—to this day, he still did not know whose blood it was or what had happened to the person—that he decided he needed help.

Part of him worried that he killed someone; another part of him was convinced that it was simply a bar fight. He didn't think he had it in him to take a man's life, but when you are out of it, do you really know what you are doing?

Across the bar, Dr. Baasch was having a drink with a young man probably half his age. They were both sitting on the same side of the booth, leaning into one another as they discreetly played with each other's... parts.

Zero had to give it to the doc—hehe was able to get some pretty hot tail. If he had to judge the doctor in the looks department, he would give the man a solid seven out of ten. He wasn't ugly or anything, just very plain and ordinary-looking. Perhaps that was why no one else in the bar seemed to notice that the two were quickly rounding second base.

"Geez, at this rate, the dude will be pregnant by morning," Zero whispered to no one in particular.

"My guess is they fuck in the bathroom."

"My money is on them boning in the alley."

"I'll take that bet," Diesel said, finally turning and acknowledging that he was not sitting at the table alone.

"And what do I get when I win?" Zero asked, raising his glass to his lips, wondering how far he could take this. He was getting horny watching the two playing "pet the weasel."

"I'll let you eat my ass."

Zero stared at him from behind his glass trying to assess whether the man was joking or being serious. With Diesel, you never could tell.

Placing his glass back down on the table, he asked, "How is eating your ass a reward for me?"

"Have you seen my ass?" Diesel asked with a cocky smirk.

"Given the wicked reputation of my tongue, it still seems like a prize tailored in your favor."

Diesel took a swig of his beer before locking eyes with Zero. "Fine, what is it you want?"

"You to eat *my* ass."

A mischievous smile spread across Diesel's face.

Was this what the devil looked like when he was making a deal for an evil man's soul?

"Fine. You got a deal."

They both reached across the table and shook each other's hand.

"Here, you might want to put this on." Diesel reached into his jeans, then pulled out a tube of lip balm. "I like my men nice and smooth."

Zero rolled his eyes.

"Sounds like all you've been with have been boys. Real men are rough and hairy."

Eyes locked on his, Diesel took a drink without saying a word.

Movement caught Zero's eyes. The good doc and his meal for the night were on the move. Which way would they go?

They watched with fascination as both men walked toward the bathroom.

"See?" Diesel said in that confident tone of his.

Just as the boy was about to push the bathroom door open, the doc grabbed him by the hand and pulled him past the bathroom and down the hallway leading to the back alley.

"You may want to lube up your lips," Zero said, standing up from the booth and making his way toward the back door.

Diesel sucked back the last of his beer and then followed.

Once they reached the back, Zero opened the door carefully and glanced around to make sure that the coast was clear.

"Stay close," he whispered over his shoulder.

Zero slipped out of the bar with Diesel close behind. He glanced around the alley, wondering where their target had disappeared to.

Just when he was about to call Chase and let him know that they lost the doctor, he heard whispered moans.

Pressed up against the wall, hidden behind some discarded empty boxes and crates, were the doc and his horny male companion.

Zero pulled Diesel down a stairwell leading down to the back entrance for the restaurant next door. From there, they could keep an eye on them and make sure that nothing bad happened.

"Seems a little pervy sitting here in the dark watching them fuck," Diesel noted, flipping over a crate and taking a seat next to the door.

Zero sat down on one of the steps and turned to face his mouthy partner. From here, he could at least hear the doc and his companion's evening activities. He didn't need to view them to know what was happening. It was easy to tell when a man was being murdered versus sucking a dick.

He hoped the man wasn't going to be murdered. He

wasn't in the mood for dealing with blood and screams and death.

"So, what do we do now?" Diesel asked, picking some dirt off his shirt and flicking it away.

"Well, you do have an ass to eat."

Diesel's eyes shot up.

"What? Seriously? Now?"

Zero chuckled. "What? Stairwell sex is beneath you?"

Shrugging his shoulders, Diesel didn't look insulted.

"Tell you what. I'll give you a pass on the eating my ass portion of the deal if you answer me one question."

"What's that?" Diesel asked, looking mildly interested.

"What made you decide to go and work at the strip club?"

"It's not a strip club."

"Fine, the whorehouse."

"It's not a whorehouse," Diesel responded, looking rather annoyed.

"Fine. The mansion."

"You're an idiot."

"So, which is it? Hot-ass meal? Or honest conversation?"

The minutes ticked by as the stoner stripper boy weighed his options. If he was being honest with himself, this would be a difficult decision for him as well. He did have a fucking delicious ass, after all.

Seeming to finally come to a decision, Diesel let out a breath, then leaned his head back against the wall of the restaurant.

"Fine. But if you begin to judge me or say anything

stupid, I'll stop sharing and punch you in the fuckin' throat," Diesel threatened half-heartedly.

"I'd never make fun of someone's difficult past."

Diesel stared at him once again as if trying to convince himself that sharing this information with him was going to be okay.

"A few years ago, Matteo found me passed out in a park, barely breathing. I had mixed a few too many party drugs and basically was on my way to death. M took me to the hospital, which pretty much saved my life. After I recovered, he offered me a room to stay in at the château until I was able to get my life back in order. He didn't ask me for anything, and there were no strings attached, just concern that if I went back onto the streets without a plan, I would end up back in the hospital in no time." Diesel looked down at his fingers as he took a moment to breathe.

Diesel's hoodie was still down, so that was a good sign that, emotionally, he was still okay to talk. The last thing Zero wanted was to push Diesel to talk about something that he wasn't ready to talk about.

"After a couple of weeks, I started helping out around the mansion to try and contribute where I could. Guests kept tipping me as I walked past them without even having to dance or anything. They kept saying how hot I was and that they would love to buy me a drink sometime. Within a week, I had made close to eight hundred euros, and nobody even sucked my dick. That was when I realized just how much money Matteo's boys were making. So I asked M if I could try dancing one night—"

"And let me guess, you were a hit?" Zero jumped in.

Diesel shrugged his shoulders and gave a little smirk. "Have you seen my dick?"

Zero began to chuckle before slapping his hand across his mouth. *Shit.* He had to remember that the doc was only a few feet away, giving some dude a physical exam.

"Needless to say, I was very popular with the crowd that night. So I decided to ask Matteo for a job. Hey, it's easy money, and there's nothing wrong with using your body to make a living."

"But isn't it dangerous? Can't guys hurt you or force you to do things that you don't want to do?" Zero asked, suddenly concerned for Diesel's safety. The man wasn't a small guy, but still, all it took was one pill or one surprise attack for things to go very wrong.

Diesel shrugged his shoulders.

"No matter what job you do, there will always be risks. But Matteo really does love all of us, and he takes a lot of measures to help ensure our safety. He does background checks on all members and has security and cameras all over the place. Plus, I think all of the members are actually afraid of the guy. There have been... *incidents* in the past which have led to some guests turning up for work with black eyes and broken limbs... and even a few who were never heard from again." Diesel looked conflicted before adding, "We are all operating under the assumption that these men just simply moved away."

Zero wasn't so sure how he felt about that one. All the guys he had met who worked at *La Maison* seemed like pretty decent men so far. He didn't think that they were the type of guys to work for someone who murdered his clientele. *No judgment, remember?*

"It sounds like you really enjoy it," Zero added once Diesel had finished explaining.

"I do. But now, we are more than just co-workers and employees. We are family. Those guys are my brothers, and Matteo and now Ares are both our fathers. We trust them and would do anything to protect them."

"Which explains why Jared followed you on this trip."

"Yeah. He's my best mate."

Further down the alley, someone gave a grunt and then cursed.

"Sounds like the good doctor is finally done taking the young man's temperature up his butt," Zero joked.

Diesel shook his head. "You're such an idiot."

For some reason, that warmed Zero's belly and made him smile.

18

DIESEL

Sitting on the roof of the house, Diesel took a swig of whiskey from the half-empty bottle clutched in his hand. He drew his arm across his nose and wiped the moisture that had been collecting there.

He hated nights like tonight. These were the nights that often led to his all-night benders or, worse yet, all-week melt-downs. If he weren't trying his best to keep his promise to Matteo, he would have hit the closest drug den he could find and welcomed the instant release that accompanied copious amounts of cocaine and whatever else they had on hand. He stayed away from heroin. That was a line he wasn't willing to cross. Anything else was fair game.

It had all started innocently enough. A simple comment followed by an innocent question. Something that any normal, well-adjusted bloke could have simply answered and moved on with his life. But not him. No. He was ten shades of fucked up and fifty ways of screwed in the head.

So here he was. Sitting alone on the roof of their rental, downing a bottle of whiskey at three a.m. Perhaps he would fall off the roof in a drunken stupor and break his neck. Hey, at least with all the alcohol he had consumed, he probably wouldn't feel a thing.

Death by broken neck, what a way to end a worthless life.

Got any brothers or sisters?

Simple enough, right?

Nope. Not for him.

They had been enjoying a nice dinner, Jared, Zero, and Diesel—Chase was busy rummaging through the good doc's trash can searching for clues—when Zero asked about Jared's family. They were getting to know one another when Zero turned his attention to Diesel and asked the same question.

"So, what about you, D? Got any brothers or sisters?"

That was the last thing he remembered hearing before ending up on this roof nearly six hours later. He couldn't remember what he started off with. Was it the beer or the shots? Whatever it was, it wasn't strong enough. He walked down to the local shop and picked up two bottles of whiskey. One was currently keeping his bed warm downstairs, while the other was dangling between his fingers, grasping at its last few sips of life.

Siblings. What an innocent yet horrible thing.

Diesel downed another mouthful of the bitter liquid and felt his mind pull away from him.

The sound of people laughing blared through the television as the main character of the show did something stupid, which was apparently funny to all those watching. If they were even there. He thought he'd read somewhere that television studios used prerecorded sound bites while filming sitcoms. A fake studio audience. It made sense when you stopped to think about it. This way, the show was guaranteed laughs even if their writers didn't have a funny bone in their body. Diesel didn't get it. It sounded dumb and stupid and fake.

Kind of like this fake-ass family thing they had going on.

Sitting on the couch, his so-called mother was leaning into her pig of a husband. He didn't understand what his mother saw in him. Was it the security of having someone take care of her? It wasn't because he was a nice man. If anything, he treated her like dirt, and Diesel was pretty sure he was sleeping around with other women. But he couldn't tell his mother that. She was too far gone in love with the man—seeing nothing but love and devotion for a man who didn't deserve it.

It made him sick.

"I'm going to my room," Diesel mumbled, getting up from his spot on the floor by the wall. His *spot*. Ever since the day he met his new "family," the spot on the floor by the wall had become his. Most people had a favorite chair or side of the couch. No, not him. He had a... spot. That was it. A place far enough from the lumps of shit he called "family" but close enough that they wouldn't complain that he was being antisocial or rude.

"Move your ass from the TV," Bo, his stepfather, grumbled as he walked past and headed toward the bedroom that he shared with his younger brother.

Well, stepbrother. There was no relation or shared bond between them. The only thing they shared was a space to sleep.

"*What are you doin' in here?*" *a pissed-off pimple-faced ass greeted as Diesel walked into his room.*

Diesel shut the door behind him and flopped down on his bed.

"*Kiss my ass, douchebag,*" *Diesel responded, pulling his pillow in close to his chest.*

He hated this fucking place. Only two more years until he turned eighteen, then he could get the fuck out of this godforsaken hellhole.

Closing his eyes, Diesel thought about where he would like to move to. Perhaps Scotland or Dublin. He heard that those places were a lot of fun, and he didn't have to worry about learning another language. Or perhaps Belgium. Did they speak English in Belgium? He would have to check.

Two years ago, he started saving whatever cash he could find or earn, doing odd jobs like cutting Mrs. Jenkin's lawn in the summer and shoveling Mr. Roger's driveway in the winter. Whatever cash he could get his hands on, he tucked away into the loose floorboard next to his bed. Last he checked, he had about two thousand pounds saved up.

He knew that wouldn't be enough to live off of, but it was enough to buy him a train ticket and a roof over his head for a few months—hopefully.

Banging on the front door made Diesel and his shit brother jump in their beds. They sat up and looked at each other, startled.

"*What the fuck do you want?*" *Diesel heard his mother shout. Classy as always.*

Diesel watched as his stepbrother jumped off his bed and

headed toward their bedroom door. Diesel couldn't give a shit about whatever drama was unfolding in their living room. Probably some pissed-off neighbor complaining about the volume of their TV or something.

"We've come to search the house," they heard a male voice say coming from someplace in the living room.

"You're not searching, shit!" his stepfather growled in that half-drunk tone they were all used to when it came to the evenings.

"Dad!" his stepbrother shouted before jerking their bedroom door open and jumping back, startled.

Standing in their doorway was a huge, uniformed police officer.

Diesel jumped out of bed, suddenly interested in what was going on.

"Is it just you two in here?" the man asked. He looked well over six foot three and appeared like a giant standing in their doorway.

Diesel nodded his head. He wasn't sure what was going on, but he had seen enough television shows to know that when police officers came bursting into your home late at night, it was never a good thing.

"You two, stand over there against the wall and don't move."

Diesel nodded, not sure what to do. He stepped next to his brother—stepbrother—and waited as the officer placed handcuffs on both of them.

Once on, he turned to face the officer. What was going on? The cold metal of the cuffs felt foreign on his skin.

"Don't move while I check your room," the officer ordered.

A moment later, his mother came flying into their bedroom and wrapped her arms protectively around his step-brother. He wasn't surprised. Why would his mother give a shit about protecting him? He was just an accessory, after all.

"Ma'am, you're not supposed to be in here!" the large man growled, closing the small dresser drawer he had just finished searching through.

"They're my sons, and I'll watch over them as I please."

It was strange hearing those words fall out of his mother's mouth. He could almost hear the fake studio audience laughing.

The officer reached into the closet, and a few minutes later, he pulled out a red-and-black knapsack. He pulled back the zipper and reached inside.

"Care to tell me where this came from?" The officer stood, holding a handful of gold necklaces dangling from his fingers.

Diesel's mouth dropped open. Where the heck did all that jewelry come from? He glanced over at Jordan, who was staring at his feet, looking guilty as fuck.

That little shit!

"Officer Platell! I found the goods here in the bedroom." The officer stood waiting for his partner to join him. "So which one of you broke into Saxman's Jewelry and stole all this shit?" The officer was still grasping the chains when his partner entered the room, holding his handcuffed stepfather by the wrists.

Both his mother and father looked at Diesel and his younger brother, shocked by what they were seeing.

"*Well? Which one of you was it? If you don't confess, I'm arresting you both,*" *the giant officer said, glaring at Diesel.*

"*It wasn't—*" *Diesel began before being cut off by his stepfather.*

"*It was the older one. The damn shit's been stealing shit left, right, and center. I tried beatin' his ass, but the stubborn shit keeps doing it.*"

Diesel's head snapped toward his stepfather. What the fuck?! He'd never stolen a thing in his life!

"*No, I didn—*" *His voice was cut off again, but this time by his mother.*

"*Yes, officers, it was my son, Diesel. The boy has a problem. I never thought it would escalate to this, but clearly, he's out of control.*"

"*What?! Mom. Why are you—*" *Now it was his turn to be cut off by his little brother.*

"*It was him. He told me last night that he broke into the store and took the chains after the place closed up.*"

"*See? The boy is a menace!*" *his stepfather growled, sealing Diesel's fate.*

"*I've heard enough,*" *the one officer said, grabbing Diesel by the arm and pulling him toward his bedroom door.*

"*But... Mom! Help me! You know I didn't do it!*" *Diesel cried out.*

He had never relied on his mother for anything before in his life, but he couldn't understand why his mother was choosing to believe this man over her own flesh and blood. He was her son, for fuck's sake!

"*Please!*" *Diesel shouted one last time.*

His mother just stared back at him with those dead eyes of hers, clutching his stepbrother in her arms.

"I'm sorry, son, but you need to take responsibility for your actions. You're out of control."

That lying bitch!

How could his mother betray him like this?

Staring into his mother's eyes, he realized that he never really had his mother's love. Even when he was younger, she never gave a shit about him or his well-being. So why should this be any different?

It was in that moment that Diesel finally realized one hard truth: he was all alone.

He had no one.

Then his sadness turned to anger.

Never again.

Never again would he be weak.

Never again would he be vulnerable and powerless.

Never again would he give power over himself to anyone else.

Never again would he trust anyone.

It was with that final thought his mind drifted back to the present. The promise he had made to himself all those years ago. The promise that kept him safe. Kept him protected. Kept him...

The cool night air brushed his face, reminding him of the promise he'd made to another man. A promise that he would try and pull himself together. A promise that, if he intended to keep, should not involve getting shit-faced alone on a rooftop.

While he might be breaking one of his own promises to himself—*never again would he give power over himself to anyone else*—Matteo was someone worth breaking his own promises for.

Placing the cap back on the bottle of whiskey, Diesel stood up and stretched out his back.

Fuck, he was getting old. Five more years, and he'd be thirty.

How many more years did he have before his balls began to sag and his boners became less... *stiff*?

With that sad question in mind, he climbed down the side of the house and stepped back through his bedroom window.

19

DIESEL

The world around him was dark and black. Well, not black per se, more like a very dark tint of see-through black... Dark, but not so dark that he couldn't see the world around him.

Tilting his head upward, he stared at the stucco ceiling and wondered if the doctor had it placed on the ceiling herself or if the ceiling came with the bubbly design when she purchased the place. Did she buy the place? Or was she renting?

What are you going on about, you whack job? Perhaps Matteo was right, and you really did need to come see this head doctor, that pain-in-the-ass voice said to him.

He hated that voice. That voice was no fun and always tried to think with his conscience.

"Jiminy. He's your Jiminy Cricket," Zero had called it once. His conscience.

Whatever. His conscience was dumb.

"Diesel? Did you hear the question?" a voice asked, interrupting the insightful argument he was having with the voice inside his head.

Turning his head, Diesel let out a sigh, then removed the sunglasses from his face.

Color and light returned to the room around him, and so did a searing headache thanks to last night's stargazing whiskey fest. Jared didn't have a clue about his early morning activities, but he got the feeling that perhaps Zero had caught him. If he had, he didn't say a word.

"What was the question, Doc?" That should buy him a bit of time to formulate a lie.

How are you going to get better if you don't answer the doc honestly? that pesky voice inside his head interjected.

Like seriously, perhaps he and the doc should have a talk about the inner voices he kept hearing. That had to be some sort of problem. A tumor? Multiple personalities? An unborn twin?

Perhaps she would give him some nice uppers. Something to calm his nerves and make his head all floaty.

Yeah, you're making really great progress...

Fuck. You. He told the asshole inside his head.

"I asked you what happened after your trial?"

Oh yeah, his big court case, thanks to his mom and stepdad. Thanks to them, he was arrested, charged, and convicted for a crime he didn't commit.

Deciding that the only way he would be able to keep his promise to Matteo and get better was by telling the doc the truth.

He let out a sigh.

"The judge found me guilty and sentenced me to two years in a young offenders' institution."

"That must have been hard on you," Dr. Bloom noted, seeming sympathetic to what she had just been told. "And what about your parents? How did they react to your conviction?"

Diesel turned his stare back up at the ceiling. *His parents. What a joke.*

"Don't know. They never came to court to watch my case. Once the judge made her decision, I was carted off to juvie prison and locked away with all the other outcasts and undesirables." He felt his jaw clench. Thanks to those assholes, he lost two years of his life.

"What about when they came to visit? Did they ever show remorse or guilt for what they had done?"

"My mom only came once, and I think it was just because she wanted to know what date I was being released. She never apologized or tried to explain why she'd done what she did."

Diesel felt his throat tighten up. *What mother throws her kid to the wolves and then lets them rot in jail?*

"That bitch stopped being my mother the day my pops walked out on us."

"You seem to have a lot of pent-up anger toward your mother."

"Uh, yeah, ya think? It's because of that cunt that I'm as fucked up as I am." Diesel could feel the anger building inside. It wouldn't take long before it spilled out in some form of destructive event.

"What do you mean?" Dr. Bloom asked, pen tapping her bottom lip.

"It was during my time in jail that I first tried cocaine."

He glanced over at the doc as he watched her begin to make all the connections.

"It was about three months in when I tried my first bump with my cellmate. There wasn't much to do in jail besides sit, eat, work out, and jerk off. Getting high at least took your mind off things and was a great way to numb the growing pain you felt inside."

Silence fell across the room as Diesel let himself process the words he'd just spoken. It was because of his family's betrayal that he began to distrust all those around him. Family was supposed to be the people who you relied on, who kept you safe in times of need. But not his. His didn't give a shit about no one.

The pain of betrayal and abandonment had been too much for him to bear, so he tried his best to numb it with drugs and alcohol.

"I think it's probably best if we end this session here. Give you a chance to refocus and digest what we've just discussed here today. It was a great session, Mr. Pratt."

Diesel sat up in the lounge chair, his *psycho chaise*, as he liked to call it.

"Any chance at getting *Daddy Dearest* to remove my kiddie tracker?" Diesel asked, raising his wrist to show off his watch.

Dr. Bloom simply shook her head.

Hey, it was worth a try.

On the way home, he stopped by his favorite deli and bought himself a sandwich. He wasn't really sure how he was feeling about today's session. Reliving his past always took a lot out of him. All he ever wanted was to forget that those years ever happened and keep his eyes focused on the future.

When he finally arrived home, it was shortly after one p.m. The house was quiet, and everyone appeared out. He walked up to his room and stopped when he heard strange noises coming from inside Zero's room.

Was Zero... fucking?

They weren't grunting sounds or the sound of a head-board banging up against the wall. It was more of a heavy breathing and deep panting.

Perhaps he was having a wank.

A mischievous grin spread across Diesel's face.

Gripping the knob of Zero's bedroom door, he gave it a twist before pushing it open with his shoulder.

"If you're not careful, you'll go bl—" Then his voice caught in his throat.

All he saw was bare man-ass and balls dangling in front of him.

Was that how he looked while onstage at La Maison?

Was this really what people paid to see whenever they cheered him on onstage?

Once time began to move forward again, the rest of Zero's body came into focus.

Bent over a yoga mat, Zero appeared to be in some sort of

intense yoga position. One that provided the world with full-view access to the man's partially spread butt cheeks and front-row view of his neatly trimmed balls.

A pair of dull brown eyes popped out from between the man's thighs, appearing curious about who the sudden intruder was interrupting his private naked stretching time.

"Oh, hey there, sunshine! How's the weather looking?"

"Umm, what?" Diesel asked, eyes still locked on Zero's butthole. He swore the thing was winking at him.

"I asked how the weather is?" Zero asked, lifting his head out from between his thighs before turning and bending over backward in some sort of freak-of-nature body-bending bridge formation. The human body was not supposed to bend to that sort of angle.

"Umm, weather? *What*?" Flustered, he shook his head. "What the fuck are you doing, man?"

Diesel had seen Teo doing yoga. Hell, he even joined him occasionally. But in all those sessions, they never once involved licking your own nutsack or airing out your asshole.

"I'm doing naked yoga! You've never done it before? It's so relaxing and freeing," the man said, arching his back even higher, causing his cock to rise up toward the ceiling.

What pervy hell was this bullshit?

Diesel watched the muscles in Zero's arm, thighs, and stomach all flex and contort. It was a display of pure power and strength.

Damn. The man was fit as sin.

Zero lowered himself down on his mat, still making no attempt to cover himself. And why should he? With a body like that, it should be on display twenty-four seven. Covering it up with anything was just a crime against humanity and decency.

"No, I prefer to keep my junk covered when doing downward-facing doggy."

A smile crept across Zero's face. "Well, with a cock like yours, that's probably safest. Wouldn't want you accidentally poking out an eye."

"Still obsessed with my dick, I see."

"Just making conversation. Plus, you still owe me a blow job." Zero gave a wink, then stood.

Stalking toward Diesel, Zero made no attempt to cover his junk as it flopped around with each step he took.

Before Diesel knew it, Zero had crossed the room and was standing just inches from his chest.

"Is that why you came into my room? To see if I was ready for that BJ?"

"I came in because it sounded like a pig was squealing, and I wanted to make sure that no farm animals were being harmed."

"I like to save my squealing for when I'm being pounded hard from behind."

The wicked smirk on the man's face left no doubt in Diesel's mind that Zero loved to take it rough from behind.

Behind his zipper, Diesel felt his cock begin to stir.

"Hmm, looks like someone likes the sound of that," Zero said, lowering his gaze to where Diesel's cock was silently betraying him.

His jeans were jutting out, barely able to contain the

boner that was raging behind the material. One of the downsides to having a big dick—when you got hard, everyone noticed.

"I don't do repeat hookups. You had your taste of the Diesel dick. Now it's time for you to move on."

Smirking, Zero took a step back before reaching for a pair of shorts. "Yeah, but you haven't tasted the *Z dick* yet. That's one piece of meat that'll keep you coming back for more."

"Sure, buddy," Diesel said with a chuckle. He turned and left the room, this time not stopping until he was safely inside his bedroom.

20

ZERO

"Watch where you step," Zero whispered over his shoulder.

"What? Ouch!" a painful voice behind him hissed.

It was just after one a.m. The office was dark, and the street was empty except for the late-night streetwalker or junkie looking to score. Most manner of civilization had retired for the evening, as was the acceptable mode of behavior for a Wednesday night.

"Exactly."

"You're a dick," Jared called from behind.

"So I've been told," Zero said with a slight chuckle.

Reaching into the bag slung across his chest, Zero pulled out another flashlight and passed it over to his companion.

"Here, use this," he noted, taking stock of the fact that Jared was standing straight and walking normal. Other than his pride, nothing else seemed to be bruised or injured.

"What are we looking for again?"

"Anything that might explain what the doc is doing to his victims. We need dates, times, locations. Any information that might explain what he is doing and how he's been getting away with it," Zero explained.

They still had nothing on this case, and it was getting to the point where even he was wondering if the man was innocent. They couldn't keep wasting time and resources on someone who was innocent.

"Wow, sounds like a lot." Jared pulled open a set of filing cabinets and began rummaging through some files. "Wow, who uses a filing cabinet anymore? How old is this guy? Seventy-five?"

Zero could sense the sarcasm dripping from Jared's words.

Ignoring the man's comment, he began looking behind pictures, feeling under surfaces, even tapping on walls, hoping to find a hidden door or entrance to an evil secret lair. Something. Anything.

Behind him, Zero could hear Jared rummaging through files and pulling folders from the cabinets. Hopefully, he finds something useful.

"I don't get it. I'm assuming that the doctor has an office at his lab and at his home, so why would he need an office here?" Jared asked, still rummaging through some documents.

That was the exact same question Zero had when he discovered that this secondary office existed last week.

"That's exactly what I'm hoping to find out. Seems a little odd to me," Zero answered, moving on to the next picture on the wall.

"All I'm seeing here are copies of receipts for purchases of electronic surveillance equipment, shipping manifests, and resumes for security guards."

"Does it say where the shipping was sent?" Zero asked, glancing over his shoulder at the man currently studying a file.

"No, that line had been redacted."

"Hmm, that's odd. Snap a picture of that file and anything else you think sounds odd for a man who spends all day testing and making drugs."

What was the connection? The doctor spent his days as a chemist in a lab, testing and formulating drugs. There are multiple victims who all wake up in various locations with no memory of how they got there or what happened to them during their blackout periods. They all have physical signs of distress, wounds, bruises, and even dirt under their fingernails, but no signs of sexual assault. That last one was a good thing. And now, this office? Why would a chemist need to keep a secret office separate from his work and home? And what was with all the surveillance equipment?

It all made no sense. Sometimes, he wondered why Marc and Chase had decided to hire him. He wasn't a trained investigator and knew fuck all about forensic evidence. Marc claimed he was hired because he was good at thinking on his feet and adapting to situations. That was a skill that all con men knew well. But still, sometimes, he felt like a fraud, playing detective and trying to impress Chase with the lack of evidence he was able to find.

Shaking those fears of self-doubt from his mind, he decided to focus on more important things.

"So, how long have you and Diesel been friends?" Zero asked, stealing a glance over at the six-foot-tall wall of muscle.

Jared stopped flipping through a file he was holding, appearing to take a moment to think about his answer.

"Ever since he came to *La Maison*."

"And has he always been so... cheery?"

Zero's lips turned upward when he heard the man begin to chuckle.

"Yeah, D's always been a bit... guarded."

"That's one way of putting it." Zero continued tapping along the wall as he made his way toward the doctor's desk. He had searched the doc's office a month ago but didn't find anything interesting. He hoped that this time might be different.

"Diesel's like an abused dog," Jared explained, lifting up junk from the doctor's shelves and putting them back in their places. "He's suspicious of anyone who he doesn't know and always makes sure that he's never ever cornered. It may take a while, but once you've earned that trust from him, he's the most loyal guy you'll know. There isn't anything that he wouldn't do for my brothers and me. Even if he won't admit it."

"Yeah, Diesel mentioned that you were all like family."

"We are. Think of *La Maison* as a sort of orphanage for unwanted, emotionally damaged men. Matteo is our daddy who watches over us and makes sure that we are fed and have a roof over our heads. He basically ensures that we don't die." Zero let out a chuckle. "We all came to *La Maison* for different reasons. Some, like Diesel and me, were saved by Matteo and decided to stay because we wanted to. Over time, we all kind of became one big fucked-up family."

"Saved?" Zero asked, already knowing some of the story but wondering about Jared's.

"It's complicated. For me? Matteo brought me back from a very dark place. For D? Well, that's his story to tell if he deems you worthy."

That was the big question, wasn't it? Would Diesel ever truly feel comfortable enough to fully let him in?

"I don't think he likes me much," Zero admitted, rummaging through some of the papers left on the doctor's desk.

"Like I said, defense mechanism. He's sniffing you out, trying to determine whether you are friend or foe."

"Yeah, I guess." The sting of disappointment suddenly made Zero realize just how much he wanted Diesel to like him. Not in that "let's get married and have a million babies while braiding each other's hair" kind of way. But it would be nice to hang out from time to time, perhaps exchange blow jobs and even cuddle occasionally. There was something about cuddling that *cloudy ray of sunshine* that made him smile. Diesel would hate cuddling... it would drive him nuts. But it would be so much fun to feel him squirm in his arms in protest.

Zero smiled.

"Shit."

Zero's head snapped up, wondering what Jared had just found.

Strained chestnut eyes stared at him, making him feel like he was suddenly being analyzed.

"You two didn't fuck did you?" Jared asked, giving him a "please say no" look in return.

Zero's breath caught in his chest. He and Diesel hadn't exactly discussed whether or not to tell the guys that they had hooked up, and judging by how Diesel reacted the morning they met, he didn't seem too eager to share the news.

"Shit. I can see it in your eyes."

"My eyes?" Zero asked, wondering what sign he was possibly giving away.

"It's that look guys get when they hook up with someone that they shouldn't have, then wonder how much trouble they're going to be in if they get caught."

"What?" Zero said a little too high-pitched for a guy with balls that had descended. "I don't know what you're talking about." Yup, Jared knew. Even he could tell that he was lying through his teeth. Hopefully, Diesel wouldn't get too pissed off that his best friend knew they exchanged cum. Well, he received Diesel's cum, and Diesel just pulled up his drawers and walked away.

Come to think about it, it was time to pay back that asshole for the blue balls he left him with that night. It was time to teach the fucker a lesson.

"Look, I've seen what D is packing downstairs, and I know it might be hard to pull away once you get stuck in that thing's gravity pull, but if you have any decency in you, don't fuck around with Diesel's feelings. He might be all hard shell and crusty attitude, but just beneath that cheap plaster is a gooey inner core that just wants to be loved."

Zero locked eyes with Jared, not really sure what to say. Yes, sex with Diesel would be fun—hell, even hanging out with the guy might be interesting—but he wasn't looking for a relationship. No feelings exchanges for him.

"That, and if you hurt my brother, I'll have to beat your ass down," Jared added, giving Zero a wink.

Given that Zero was a head taller than the buff stripper-man, he found it amusing that the guy would be so confident in himself. Mind you, the man would be defending his family's honor, so he would probably fight like a rabid pit bull. There was something to say about fighting for a cause.

"Don't worry, he can trust me," Zero found himself saying. He hoped that he was being honest.

Gazing back down at the stack of papers on the good doctor's desk, his eyes caught on something.

He reached down and pulled a black-and-red card out from under a pile of drug order forms.

A silver-lettered invitation to attend a party at the Black Door Lounge in two weeks was stenciled against an all-black backdrop. The invitation did not disclose who was hosting the party, just a date, time, and password.

Staring at the invitation, Zero wondered if the passwords were unique to each invitation or generic for all attendees. That was something he would have to look into. Over the past two months, the doctor had never been invited to such a party before. He wondered what kind of party it was. Perhaps this was the clue they were looking for.

"What's that?" Jared asked, walking over and peering over his shoulder.

"An invitation."

"To what?"

"That's what we have two weeks to find out."

Jared quickly entered the lounge's name into his phone and opened its website. The website said the space was used for private parties and to call if interested in booking rates. However, the page did not list an events calendar, so he couldn't get any information on the event that way.

He wondered how else he could get more information on the event. Perhaps Chase would have some ideas.

Zero took a photo of the card, both front and back, then slid it back into its original place tucked between the doctor's business papers. They didn't want to leave behind any evidence of their presence.

"It's time for us to leave," Zero ordered, checking his watch to confirm the time.

Jared nodded and followed him out.

21

ZERO

"**C**an you at least throw on a pair of underwear? I swear, I can practically see your butthole when you bend over like that," Diesel complained from somewhere behind him.

Zero stood up and closed the fridge door before turning to face his annoying housemate. Co-worker? Mistaken one-night stand?

Argh. Whatever you call a pervy bastard who jerks off while watching you sleep.

A chuckle tried to escape him. The thought of making the stubborn man all hot and horny made Zero all warm and fuzzy inside. This little cat-and-mouse game they were playing was also adding to the excitement he felt building up inside. Was it possible to be annoyed by someone yet also want them around, both at the same time?

"He's just saying 'hello.' Don't be rude. Give the guy a little kiss and see if he needs anything," Zero finally responded to Diesel's crack about his... crack? Hole? Butthole? Whatever.

"The only thing that hole needs is a shot of penicillin and a warning label for those who try to gain entry," Diesel quipped back without missing a beat.

The corners of Zero's lips turned upward slightly. No, he was not going to laugh and prove to the prick that he found his comebacks funny. Speaking of cum, he wondered where Diesel liked to take it? On his back? In his mouth? Painting his insides?

The thought of Diesel being covered in cum had Zero's cock quickly thickening.

Fuck.

He needed to go back upstairs and throw on a pair of underwear. Otherwise, the guys were about to get an eyeful. Or a mouthful. Depending on whether Zero could convince Diesel to open wide.

Shit. Boner. Time to run!

Biting into his apple, Zero gave Diesel a smirk as he walked on past him. Water from the shower he had just taken slid down his bare chest, making him look like the biggest thirst trap or douchebag—whichever you preferred.

He walked past Jared, giving him a head nod, as he combed through some old surveillance videos, looking for clues.

Movement at the front door caught Zero's eye as he was just about to jog up the stairs.

The doorbell rang.

Turning the lock and pulling open the door, he was

greeted by two men: one with spiky blue hair and the other with jet-black hair.

"Can I help you?" Zero asked, forgetting that his boner was set to partial-chub and practically reaching out to greet his new visitors.

"Hi! Wow, holy shi—" the blue-haired one began, his eyes quickly falling on the thick piece of meat reaching toward him from under the towel.

The blue-haired dude's cheeks flushed red as he stood there speechless.

"Isaac?" Jared's confused voice called from where he sat in the living room.

Smurf-boy's eyes darted to the living room seconds before his smile swallowed his face.

"Jared!" the boy shouted, charging past Zero and leaping into the man's lap.

It took all of two seconds before the blue-haired freak was assaulting Jared's mouth and face with kisses. It was like watching an excited puppy seeing his master for the first time in over a year. There was no stopping that pup from spraying all over the couch.

"Eww, you guys are gross. I liked it better when you hated each other," Diesel grumbled as he entered the living room. "Hey, Levi."

The second man at the door gave Zero a nervous smile before slipping past him with a simple, "Hey."

Considering that the one hyperactive little gremlin was busy sucking face with Jared, Zero assumed that they were all friends and decided that *stranger danger* didn't apply to this situation, so he closed the front door.

"I'm Zero," he introduced, extending his hand toward the purple-eyed twink.

"I'm Levi, Chase's—" Then his eyes lit up.

Zero had never seen a small body move so fast. It was like watching a beam of light shoot across the room.

Chase gave an *oof* when the speedy little twink, also known as Levi, collided with his beastly body.

Could a man that size even hurt a tank like Chase?

A squeal escaped Levi's mouth as he leapt into Chase's arms and began making out with the man porno-style.

Was this how everyone got greeted back at *La Maison de M*?

"Yeah, it's about to get very uncomfortable down here," Diesel said, walking past Zero and heading up the stairs. "Let me know when you freaks are done dry humping," Diesel hollered over his shoulder at the slobbering hot mess of bodies moaning in the living room.

That was Zero's cue to head upstairs and get changed.

Thirty minutes later, Diesel announced that the coast was clear, and he could rejoin the living on the main floor.

"Sorry about that," the man known as Levi apologized, reaching out to Zero and shaking his hand once again. "It's been two whole weeks since Isaac and I have seen our guys, and let's just say, our cocks short-circuited our brains."

Zero chuckled.

"That's understandable. I hope to be greeted by someone in the same way one day. I'm Zero, by the way."

"So you're not seeing anyone?" Isaac asked, sitting on the counter, sipping a whiskey.

Someone should tell the boy it's only two p.m.

Zero shook his head.

"Neither is Diesel," Levi added as if Diesel was part of the conversation.

"Don't understand why not. With a dazzling personality like his, guys must be lining up out the door," Zero added, giving them both a sarcastic smile.

"Oh, they're lining up alright. They just have dirtier, more demeaning things that they want to do with me." Diesel took a seat at the kitchen table and leaned back in his chair. "So, what are you fuckwads doing here?"

"Isaac's dick went on strike and refused to make an appearance until he got a chance to play with his best friend," Levi explained, giving the whiskey-sipping hormone a smirk from across the room.

"Fuck you. It was taking a nap and resting, knowing all the sex it was going to have when someone came to visit."

"Yeah. I think Matteo's words were, '*Your limp dick is no use to me onstage. Go see your man, and don't come back until your member has been resurrected.*'"

Levi ducked as an avocado flew at his head.

These must be the brothers Jared was talking about.

They seemed fun, in that fucked-up and emotionally stunted kind of way.

"I've missed you too," Jared added, wrapping his arms around his man and pulling him into his lap.

God, all this lovey-dovey bullshit was going to give him a cavity.

"So, fill me in. What did I miss? Has the new guy tried to murder Diesel yet?" Levi asked, eyes twinkling like that was the greatest thought he had ever had.

Zero chuckled. Okay, these guys were cool.

"No, not yet. But his choice of fashion has me wondering," Zero answered.

Diesel raised his middle finger.

"Love you too," Zero responded, puckering his lips and gesturing toward the man.

They spent the next few hours drinking, chatting about the guys back at *La Maison* and what new death threat their surrogate father, Matteo, had made to his partner, Ares. Apparently, Matteo was now the proud owner of a crossbow, and Ares was on his best behavior.

Zero couldn't help but steal glances at the moody piece of joy, also known as Diesel, who appeared to be lost in the laughter that surrounded the table. It appeared that Diesel's standoffish personality only surfaced when he was around people he wasn't familiar with. Shocking as it was, Diesel managed to keep a smile plastered to his face for the past two hours.

Now, if Zero could only do something about those beady little eyes that kept staring at him from across the table.

To be honest, they were kind of starting to freak him out.

Diesel was wearing a fitted white tank top—yes, the kind often associated with alcohol and domestic violence. It wasn't the tank top that was making him feel uncomfortable, but rather, the beady little eyes of something staring at him from just above Diesel's shirt collar.

"Freaky, isn't it?"

Zero turned to face Isaac sitting to his right.

"It's like the damn thing is waiting until I close my eyes before it sneaks up behind me and sodomizes me," Zero whispered under his breath.

Isaac, Jared, and Levi all laughed.

Apparently, Zero wasn't quiet enough.

"I know! I never turn off the lights when Bruno is in the room. I don't trust that creepy little perv," Levi added.

"Bruno?" Zero asked, wondering who else he had yet to meet.

The three men turned to face Diesel.

"You haven't introduced him to Bruno?" Levi and Isaac both shouted in unison.

Diesel shrugged his shoulders. "Bruno's still trying to decide whether to murder the man in his sleep."

Shocked, the blue-haired skater boy turned his attention back to Zero.

"Bruno is Diesel's comfort tattoo. It keeps an eye out for danger while he sleeps and keeps him company when he's alone and lonely."

Diesel raised his middle finger again.

"What? It's true. That's why you insisted on bringing

him to life by giving him a name." Isaac turned back to face Zero. "It's kind of like that killer toy doll that only seems to come to life when no one is watching."

Zero glared at the suspicious-looking eyes on Diesel's chest that now appeared to be following his every move.

Fuck. They were kind of freaky.

Finally having enough of this eeriness, Zero shook his head in frustration. "Okay, take it off. Let's meet Bruno, the murderous tattoo." Zero motioned for Diesel to take off his shirt.

"No. You're not getting me out of my clothes that easily." Diesel huffed, taking another sip of his whiskey.

"Would you prefer if I put on some music and gave you a twenty?" Zero asked, reaching into his pocket, pretending to fish out some bills.

He wasn't opposed to slipping Diesel a few bills, especially if it meant seeing the tattooed grump without his shirt on. But Diesel and the group didn't need to know that.

All the guys joined in cheering and taunting. Finally, Diesel let out an exhausted breath before pulling off his shirt in one fell swoop.

There, sitting over his left pec muscle, was a grinning demon's face. Yup, the thing was definitely giving off an "I'll wait till you fall asleep, then murder you in your bed" kind of vibe.

Eyes drifting across his body, Zero took in the number of tattoos inked on Diesel's skin. His body was a canvas of art and meaning.

Running along the right side of his rib cage were realistic-looking stab wounds rendered with intricate details, making it appear as though they were part of his skin. The design only added to the menacing physique that was Diesel. The man really did play into that "bad boy, I don't give a shit, fuck everyone and everything" attitude.

Finally, Zero's eyes landed on the cryptic message scrawled in bold, almost frantic script just above his belly button—"Never Again." He wondered about the significance of the words. Did they serve as a warning or a reminder?

He had noticed something scrawled on Diesel's belly while he was down on his knees sucking his dick, but it was too dark to read the writing.

Who are you kidding? You were too distracted with that big hog of a cock to care what the fuck was written on the man's bloody stomach.

That was true. Big dick? Or belly tattoo. He would choose big dick every fucking time.

"Meet Bruno," Diesel announced, flexing his chest muscles and bringing the evil creature to life.

Zero watched as the damn thing smiled, then winked, then possibly cast a curse upon him and his family. His family? It was just him and his dad—well, a dad he hadn't spoken to in over five years. Not since his father was arrested and thrown in jail for scamming people out of their life savings. It was thanks to his father that he spent his childhood pulling cons instead of going to school and learning skills that might actually get him a high-paying job. Instead, he learned how to lie, cheat, and scam people out of their money. *Always play on their emotions*, his father used to say.

Quite frankly, he didn't care whether Bruno placed a curse on his father or not. Have at it!

But him? He didn't deserve or have time to be cursed.

Where on earth was he ever going to find a man to give him "true love's" kiss?

The curse would never be broken, and he would be stuck in hell, being punished, all because he asked to see Diesel's gremlin tattoo.

"It's nice to meet your little goblin monster," Zero noted with a touch of sarcasm dripping from his voice.

He lifted his glass of whiskey and downed the rest in a single gulp. Staring at Diesel without a shirt on and knowing what the man was packing below his joggers was starting to get to his head.

Under his jeans, Zero's dick began to stir.

22
ZERO

The night was getting late, and the fire was beginning to burn out. Zero had lost count of how many beers he had but was feeling pretty fucking awesome when he thought about it.

"I'll throw some more wood on the fire," Zero said, forcing himself out of the lawn chair and grabbing a few logs from the pile of wood they had set out earlier. He tossed three on and watched as the fire shot back to life.

"Woah!" everyone gasped, startled by the sudden explosive heat given off by the fire.

"I think it's time we went back to my hotel," Isaac said to Jared, nestling his nose up under his chin.

Jared smiled, no doubt imagining the dirty things they were about to get up to. "Yeah, it's way past your bedtime."

The guys laughed.

"I'm amazed you guys were able to hold off fucking as

long as you did." Levi chuckled, leaning back into Chase's bare chest.

Zero had no idea how the chair was able to support both their weights. It wasn't so much Levi's weight. The damn guy weighed less than a sack of potatoes soaking wet—okay, fine. That was an exaggeration. But still, the slender twink weighed just about nothing. It was more Chase's solid frame plus the weight of the small sack of potatoes sitting in a lawn chair that should have been retired a decade ago. Still, the stubborn chair held its shape.

"I'm good at playing hide the sausage while in public," Isaac bragged as he pulled up his shorts which were riding low around his butt. Then the group watched as Jared adjusted the opening of his shorts.

The stealthy little bastard!

"Damn, you guys are masters!" Chase uttered, thoroughly impressed that his buddies were able to fuck without anybody being the wiser.

"I knew they were fucking," Diesel said, raising his beer and giving the campfire a cocky grin.

"No, you didn't," Zero added, deciding to call Diesel out on his bullshit.

"Jared shot his load right when Levi was going on about how he ripped a hole in his favorite shirt. Jare's left leg spasmed, and his thighs began to flex."

All eyes turned to Jared, who was sitting there with the biggest smile plastered on his face.

"Yup. The guy knows his orgasms," Jared confirmed,

standing up next to Isaac and downing the last of his beer. "Shall we call a cab?"

Isaac nodded. He decided to book them into a hotel for the weekend when he heard that Jared and Chase were sharing a basement. He needed to get his brains fucked out, as Isaac so eloquently put it. None of the guys argued.

That left Levi and Chase the basement. Zero hoped that sound didn't travel quite as well through multiple layers of flooring.

"We're going to head in as well," Chase announced, lifting Levi up and throwing him over his shoulder. Levi squealed.

The two looked so happy and in love. Love really looked good on some people. Sadly, he was not one of them.

Zero watched as the backyard emptied, leaving just him, Diesel, and a raging fire.

"Guess it's just you and me now," Zero noted, glancing over at his flatmate.

"I'm grabbing another beer," Diesel grumbled, attempting to get up from his seat. It appeared that grumpy Diesel had returned to the party.

"Grab me one as well?" Zero asked, watching Diesel slowly get up. "You sure that's a good idea?" He knew that Diesel could drink his weight in booze, but he kind of liked it when Diesel was sober enough to have a decent chat with.

"I'm not even close to being drunk," Diesel exclaimed, twirling around in a dramatic display of sarcasm and *fuck you.*

The *gods of justice* thought differently.

Diesel stumbled and fell to his knees, dropping right between Zero's sprawled-out legs. His hands landed right on the chunk of Zero's thighs, just hard enough to cause him to lurch forward in his chair.

Zero tried not to laugh as he locked eyes with Diesel. "You were saying?"

Staring up at him, with flecks of orange ambers reflected in his eyes, the one-night stand that wouldn't end stared sinfully into Zero's questioning eyes.

There was something in those eyes gazing back at him.

Was it passion? Desire?

A need to devour his prey?

Locked in his gaze, Zero found himself being drawn more and more into them. It was like a peacefulness had fallen over him. He didn't feel nervous or afraid. Or have the desire to throat-punch the jerk for being an idiot. Just a calming desire to give in to him.

Time seemed to stand still as the air around them grew thick.

Eyes never leaving his, Diesel's left hand slid under Zero's shorts and made its way across his hairy thigh.

What was happening?

Still locked in a game of visual foreplay, Zero held his breath as Diesel's hand wrapped itself around his rapidly thickening dick.

Fuck, he was so damn horny.

"What... are..." That was all that Zero was able to get out

before Diesel pulled his cock out from the side of his shorts and leaned in toward his thigh.

Zero's eyes rolled back as warm wetness dragged itself against the underside of his balls.

Fuck. He loved having his balls licked.

So many people forget the importance of giving a guy's balls attention. But, fuck, Diesel wasn't forgetting a thing!

Using one hand to stroke Zero's cock, Diesel used the other to play with his balls as he licked them in circular motions.

"Fuck, that's good," Zero whispered, finally giving in to the pleasure shooting up through his balls.

Through hooded lids, Zero gazed down at the tattooed stoner. He couldn't believe how fucking hot Diesel looked while sucking on his balls.

"Right there. Jesus. Fuck, you're a good boy," Zero found himself gasping. Apparently, Diesel's mouth on his balls had him whimpering all sorts of affectionate compliments.

Appearing to take no notice of Zero's words, Diesel slid his tongue across his shaft until he reached the tip of his mushroom head. He lapped his tongue around the top twice before diving down and inhaling the whole eight inches in one fell swoop.

A desperate moan escaped his lips. Having a man swallow his cock like that was both alarming and impressive.

"Damn, boy," Zero whimpered. Before he could say anything else, Diesel began sucking his dick like it was going out of style.

Up and down, fast and slow. Diesel swallowed his cock like his life depended on it.

"Holy. Fuck." Zero groaned, lost in the pleasure that was Diesel's mouth. "Jesus. Christ," he gasped out, legs shaking as his cock and balls quivered under the hungry dancer's lips.

Zero gripped the arms of his chair and held on for dear life. He'd never had a guy suck his dick quite this good. At this rate, he was going to bust his load any second.

Throwing his head back, Zero let the pleasure in his balls take him. There was no stopping it now.

"I... I'm—" Then it happened. His balls tightened, his lower back tingled, and he shot the biggest load he'd ever had.

Refusing to let up, Diesel continued his assault on Zero's cock, swallowing every last drop of cum until Zero's balls were empty and his body stopped shaking.

Panting, Zero stared up at the evening stars and wondered what the fuck had just happened? He didn't just receive a blow job from some horny stoner dude, he experienced a ball drainage from the *god of blow jobs*!

Getting up from his knees and sporting the biggest woody Zero had ever seen, Diesel dropped down in the chair next to him.

"You're welcome," the cocky bastard said, leaning over and grabbing another beer. "It's not every day that I swallow."

"With skills like that, it's a crime against humanity if you don't." Zero panted, still trying to catch his breath and regain feeling in his dick.

Diesel chuckled.

"Don't get used to it. I don't do repeats."

Turning his head, he stared at Diesel. "We'll see about that."

23

DIESEL

A slight breeze passed, causing Diesel's body to shiver. He was both cold and hot. His nose and chest were cool, and so were his forearms, yet his back and ass were warm, and so were the back of his thighs.

What the?

Then he felt it. Thick and firm, pressed right up against his ass.

His eyes shot open when he realized what was happening.

Firm muscular arms tightened their grip around his waist.

"Where do you think you're going, sweet cheeks?" the last voice he ever expected to hear whispered into his ear.

Body stiff, he lay there for a moment, trying really hard to remember the last six to ten hours. Even four.

Did he? Did they? What was he...?

Shifting behind him, he felt the man's manhood press up against his butt, inching ever so closely to that well-protected hole of his.

Well protected? He could hear his inner voice laughing its ass off. *That thing has seen more dick than a two-dollar whore on New Year's Eve.*

Shut up. Was it his fault that guys liked a well-hung dude, covered in tattoos, with a bad-boy attitude?

Diesel turned his head slightly, looking over his shoulder at the man currently holding him at *dick point*.

"I was trying to get away from you and your heavenly morning breath." That was a lie, but Diesel didn't know what else to say. In actuality, Zero smelled pretty good for first thing in the morning.

He felt Zero's body shake as the man let out a chuckle.

"If anyone's got morning breath, it's probably you. I can basically smell the cock breath from all the way over here."

Now it was Diesel's turn to chuckle. Memories of last night came flooding back. Slobbering on Zero's dick, sucking it nice and deep until finally swallowing down his delicious, glorious load. *Fuck, the man tasted good.*

Glancing down toward his ass, he didn't feel hopeful when he noticed that his shorts were down around his thighs.

"We didn't... did we?" Diesel asked.

"No. No, we didn't. You wanted to cuddle before bed, and when I wrapped my arms around your body, you insisted that your shorts were too itchy and tugged them down around your thighs. Who was I to argue with a man who insisted on playing hide my salami with his butt cheeks?"

"So, you did fuck me last night?" Diesel asked, face still turned toward him.

"Trust me. If I had my dick in your ass last night, you would definitely be feeling it this morning."

"Cocky much?"

"When you're aggressive like me in bed, and you're working with the size I've got, you tend to leave a stinging impression."

Diesel's cock plumped up. The thought of Zero pinning him down as he went all caveman on his ass had his dick *very* interested.

Resting his head back against Zero's body, he lay there in the morning light, wondering what the fuck he was doing. His body was telling him that it was very much interested in the hunky man behind him, but his mind and heart were telling him that he was swimming in dangerous waters. That he should walk away before anyone got close, and he eventually got hurt. After all, they all leave in the end.

Tightening his grip around Diesel's body, Zero's breath tickled the back of his ear.

"I'm sorry that I teased you the night we first met." Diesel's body stiffened. "I thought you were just another douchebag trying to take advantage of vulnerable guys."

Well, he did use the older guy to buy him drinks all night, but he was going to repay him with a load down his throat.

Guilt tugged at Diesel's chest. "Yeah, I guess I should apologize for leaving you with blue balls that night as well."

"They're not blue anymore." Zero chuckled.

"No. Now they're just empty and sad," Diesel added.

"I know one way you could make them happy again."

Fighting against his grip, Diesel turned himself around until he was chest-to-chest with Zero.

"Really? And what way is that?" he asked, sliding his hand in between them and grabbing hold of Zero's hard cock.

Heat exploded in Zero's eyes. "Well, that's a pretty good start."

Eyes locked together, Diesel began jerking Zero's cock while the man held him close against his chest. The closeness, the intimacy, was like nothing Diesel had ever felt before.

Normally, when he fucked, he preferred not to make eye contact or hold each other so close. Eye contact meant intimacy, holding each other meant comfort. When he was banging a one-night stand, he wanted neither of the two. Yet somehow, lying outside the burnt-out campfire on what appeared to be a ratty old blanket—*seriously, where the fuck did this thing come from?*—being so close and intimate with Zero felt kind of... perfect. It felt right.

Picking up speed, he welcomed Zero's hand when it reached between them and began jerking his cock as well.

Fuck. Feeling the man's dick throb in his hand, with his warm breath gently brushing his lips, he wanted nothing more than to lean forward and close the gap.

Kissing? Kissing was something that he never did with anyone. Kissing was definitely a line he never wanted to cross. Even with clients at *La Maison*, he always explained that was one thing he would not do. It was just too... intimate. Too personal.

Yet for some reason... he...

Focusing on the warm chestnut eyes staring back at him, he felt his balls tighten and his cock stiffen.

"Fuck, I'm gonna come." Diesel gasped, jerking forward and nestling his head in the crook of Zero's neck as he shot his load all over their bellies.

"Shit, so am..." Zero gave a loud grunt seconds before wet warmness shot against Diesel's stomach and chest as well.

Zero spasmed, firing off shots like he was putting out a fire.

Talk about having your bodies painted!

"Shit," Zero muttered.

Diesel raised his head to see what the matter was.

"I shot jizz in Bruno's eye. The creepy dude's gonna hate me now."

Diesel looked down at the demon who'd been looking out for him since he was eighteen. The poor guy had creamy white cum splattered up against his left eye and sliding down into his mouth.

He wasn't sure how he felt, sharing his man's horny juice with the creature living on his chest. Was he really ready for a three-way?

Chuckling, he slid his finger across his chest and wiped up the remnants of Zero's warm man seed. Staring into Zero's questioning eyes, he lifted his finger to his lips and licked the cum right off his finger.

Yup, Zero's cum tasted like sweetness with a touch of horny man-beast.

"God, that's sexy," Zero breathed out, eyes dilating as he licked his lower lip.

Ya, the man was hooked.

24

DIESEL

The guys left after two days. It was great seeing Isaac and Levi, and he loved that they came for a surprise visit—even if they didn't come to see him specifically—but he couldn't help the feeling of disappointment every time the guys went off on their own for a little "alone time."

He couldn't blame them though. Being apart from the guys they loved had made them all extra horny. So rather than host an orgy at which no one shared, it was probably for the best that they went to their own private rooms to get naked and sweaty.

"What's got your panties in a bunch?" Zero asked, walking into the living room in only a pair of loose-fitting shorts. He did that a lot. Diesel was starting to wonder if the man was peacocking. Or just had an aversion to wearing a shirt and underwear. Not that he minded, but still.

"Huh? Oh, um, nothing. Just thinking of the guys."

"Isaac and Levi?" Diesel nodded. "Yeah, it was nice meeting them. They seem like really cool guys."

Zero flopped down on the couch next to him. His thigh pressed up against his. It was a three-seater couch, and both were over six feet. Well, Diesel was six feet, and the *retired wannabe straight-boy* next to him was a head taller than that.

"Oh, good. You're both in here," Chase muttered walking into the living room from the kitchen holding his tablet. "We got some intel."

Diesel sat up, noting that Zero didn't move or budge. His leg was still firmly pressed up against his.

"What did you find, boss?" Zero asked, folding his arms across his chest.

Was he flexing his biceps? Diesel tried not to pay attention to the soft, smooth skin that was not pressing up against his arm.

Unfortunately, Diesel's dick took notice.

Why didn't he bust a nut this morning?

Chase took a seat in the armchair across from the couch.

"Marc was able to hack into the doc's email and noticed a reservation for tomorrow night at a seedy motel two hours outside the city."

"Do we know what he's doing out there?" Zero asked, shifting his body forward and resting his arms on his knees.

"Anytime a man with money books a room at a shady motel in the middle of nowhere, you know he's up to no good," Diesel noted.

He'd met enough closeted rich dudes who took him back to their motels to party and fuck, before returning to their wives and families. Seedy motels were where secret deals were made and sinful pleasures were kept.

"Diesel's right. Nobody asks questions at motels. Most know to keep their eyes down and their noses where they belong. When I was on the police force, anytime we were searching for a criminal on the run, ninety percent of the time, we found them at a motel," Chase explained.

"Okay, so what do you need us to do?" Zero asked, eyes laser-focused on his boss.

"I'm sending you two to follow Dr. Baasch and see what he's up to. Perhaps this will be the clue that we need. Marc and I are still trying to gather further info on this party going on. I don't like going in blind, so hopefully, we can find out more."

"Sounds good, boss." Zero nodded.

"You're following too close," Diesel noted, taking a bite into the monster sandwich he had purchased when they stopped to fill up at a gas station.

Zero glared at him from the corner of his eye. If he could smother a man with just a gaze, Diesel would be on his way up to those pearly gates this very minute.

Oh, who are you kidding? With the life you've led, you'd be on your way down to meet the man in black and all the monsters and party goblins he's got waiting for you down there.

"I know how to follow a man."

"You sure? Cus to me, it looks like you know how to make a guy aware that you are stalking his ass."

Diesel was getting a kick out of busting Zero's balls. The man was so uptight and taking this undercover, secret spy bullshit way too seriously. Christ! He was even wearing sunglasses and a baseball cap on his head.

That's because it's summer, jackass. The shades keep the sun out of his eyes, and the ball cap keeps the man from getting sunstroke.

In a car?

Yes, in a car. Were you always this stupid? No wonder your family fucked you over so easily, that nasty voice inside his head said.

"Shut up and eat your nasty gas station sandwich. Who even buys food at a gas station?" Zero's eyes were hidden from Diesel's view, but the horrified lips on his face said all he needed to know.

"Hungry men do. You going to question what every burly truck driver eats? The men have balls the size of your head. I think they know what they're doing."

Diesel took another chomp at his sandwich as they continued their drive, following their target. Twenty minutes later, their target pulled into the motel parking lot.

Zero parked their car across the lot, backing into the space so they had a perfect line of sight of the doctor.

They watched as the man grabbed his black overnight bag and headed into the main office to check in.

Fifteen minutes later, they were watching the shady doc unlock his motel room door and head inside.

This was going to be fun.

Two hours later, they were still sitting outside the motel, watching a closed door, praying for some kind of movement.

Diesel's stomach began to gurgle.

He shifted in his seat, trying his best to act normal and not let on that he wasn't feeling the greatest. Perhaps that sandwich wasn't the best thing to consume, especially when on a stakeout.

Using the back of his hand, he swiped at the sweat that was beginning to form off his forehead.

"Dude, you feeling okay?" Zero asked, lowering his binoculars and twisting his face in concern. His soft brown eyes grazed over him, checking him out from head to toe.

"Yeah, I'm fine. Mind your business."

"Honestly, man, you don't look so hot."

"I'm—" He had no time to finish his sentence.

Diesel shoved open the passenger-side door and bent his body out as best he could. He had no time to move or position himself to minimize the damage. The next thing he knew, he was throwing up along the side of the car.

He had no control. Every time he thought he was done, another wave hit him. His stomach continued to curse him as his throat cried out in pain. His brain switched itself off and abandoned him, leaving him to deal with all of his shame and disgrace.

He was so fucking embarrassed.

"Here, use this," Zero whispered, crouching down next to him, his foot barely missing a puddle of his own disgrace.

The car door was open as Diesel braced himself between the door and the side of the car.

Blindly, Diesel reached for whatever it was that Zero was trying to pass him.

It was some tissues.

Grateful, he took the tissues and began wiping his mouth.

Fuck, he hated his life. Between being found passed out in a drug den by Matteo and now puking his brains out in front of Zero, he felt like the biggest piece of trash alive.

"Thanks," was all he could think of to say.

"Stay here. I'll be right back."

Diesel wasn't going anywhere. He still felt nauseous, and his mouth tasted like trash. *Oh, great. Now his stomach was starting to cramp. Could this night get any worse?*

After God knows how long, Zero finally returned to the scene of Diesel's self-imposed humiliation.

"Here, come with me." He reached into the car and wrapped his arms around Diesel's chest, helping to lift him from the front seat.

His body was warm and gentle, taking on most of Diesel's weight in order to support him on his feet.

Talk about a sad sight. Worthless stripper-druggy can't even stand on his own two feet. God, he was pathetic.

"What? Where are we going?"

"Inside. I got us a room," Zero explained, leading them toward a room on the far side of the motel.

The motel was L-shaped, so they could still monitor the doctor's room if they chose to. Well, Zero could, but Diesel wasn't so sure that he could remain standing for very much longer.

Once inside, Zero helped him to the bathroom and sat him down on the edge of the bathtub.

"I'll be back in just a sec."

Zero vanished into the bedroom, leaving him wondering if he had left him there to die. Diesel wouldn't blame him. Nobody wanted to watch a man throw up their guts and then have to carry their sorry ass around.

Go on, run. Leave me here to die alone. We all end up alone in the end anyway.

"Here," Zero said, entering the bathroom and startling the shit out of Diesel. The man was holding up a toothbrush in one hand and a travel-size bottle of mouthwash in the other. "Thought you might want to brush your teeth."

Confused, Diesel stared at him for a moment. That was... thoughtful. He was just going to rinse his mouth out with nasty motel tap water, but hey, brushing his teeth with actual toothpaste was even better.

Wait. Toothpaste. He didn't see any in his hand.

"Oh," Zero blurted before reaching into his back pocket and pulling out a travel-size tube of toothpaste.

Jesus. The man thought of it all.

"Umm, thanks," Diesel whispered, struggling to stand up from the tub. He was still embarrassed as fuck, but the feeling of death was helping to push that feeling of embarrassment back to the side.

Within seconds, Zero was by his side, helping him over to the sink and then holding him up as he slowly brushed his teeth.

As he moved the brush back and forth in his mouth, Diesel's eyes drifted to Zero, who was staring at his body with a look of concern.

Was he... worried about him?

But why? He had been nothing but an asshole to him since the day they met. Okay, fine, so he sucked his dick and cuddled with him the other night and maybe showed him a bit of kindness here and there. But seriously, most guys would have walked away and let him deal with his shit on his own.

Once Diesel was done, Zero helped him to the bed and stripped him down to his underwear.

"I take it you probably don't want to rest in soiled clothing," Zero explained.

Fuck. Just another thing to add to his humiliation. He couldn't even puke right without getting some shit on his shirt and jeans.

Zero tucked him in bed and placed a trash can next to the nightstand.

"Just in case you can't make it to the toilet."

Diesel tried to smile, but his face and body hurt too much. He was exhausted, and his stomach felt like it was having a boxing match with his organs.

"Fuck. I'm sorry, man," Diesel whispered, eyes glancing up at Zero.

He felt horrible. Not only was he embarrassed as shit, but he had also fucked up their stakeout. Who knows what they missed while he was busy throwing up his liver and kidneys?

"None of that," Zero said, tucking Diesel in like he was five years old.

"What about the doc?"

Zero looked over his shoulder and shrugged.

"The only thing that matters right now is you getting better. Food poisoning can be dangerous." He began walking toward the door. "I'm just going to grab some water and ginger ale. Can't have you getting dehydrated on me."

Diesel tried to laugh but was interrupted by another wave of nausea coupled with intense stomach pains. Fuck his life. He jumped out of bed and ran to the bathroom, slamming the door behind him as he entered.

This was not going to be pretty.

"I'll be back in a few," he heard Zero shout from the other side of the door.

His mind disconnected from his body as the demon from gas station hell ripped apart his body. He was never eating food from a gas station again.

He eventually emerged from the bathroom, drained and ready to die.

"Here, let me help you," Zero offered, wrapping his arm around his shoulders and guiding him back into bed.

Diesel was too exhausted to argue or be embarrassed. He closed his eyes and wished for death to take him.

Grown men don't do well with being sick.

"Get some rest. I'll be here if you need me," Diesel heard Zero say as he pulled the bed sheet up over his chest. His body was starting to sweat and shiver at the same time... because... of course.

25

DIESEL

"*T*hanks," Diesel heard Zero say just before hearing the sound of the motel room door close. *What the fuck?*

Slowly, Diesel opened his eyes and waited for his vision to focus. Hunched over the tiny table next to the window, Zero was opening a paper bag and pulling out multiple Styrofoam containers.

Zero appeared to be razor-focused on the contents, searching among things he couldn't seem to find. There was a sweetness about his look—eyebrows scrunched together as he dug through the bag and its contents.

"What's all that?" Diesel whispered, barely able to lift his head. *God, why did eating rotten food wreak havoc on your body?*

Turning, Zero's face lit up, giving him a warm smile like he was happy to see that he was still alive. He placed the item he had just lifted back down into its brown-paper prison.

Diesel had no idea what time it was or how long he'd been sleeping. All he knew was that the room was dark, and he had puked another two times before finally falling asleep, dead to the world.

"Dinner! Thought you might want to try eating some toast to help get some solids into you."

Diesel groaned. He had no desire to eat. Just the thought of food made him want to be sick.

"None of that," Zero responded as if anticipating Diesel's resistance. "You need to shut up and start letting people take care of you."

Diesel's heart stopped in his chest. *Take care of him?* No one had ever taken care of him before, other than Matteo and, occasionally, Jared when he was feeling extra generous.

There had been one time when he was twelve, that his mother and stepfather had decided to go to the monster truck show when he had been sick with a temperature of one hundred and two. At the time, Diesel didn't realize how strong a fever that actually was, but what twelve-year-old really knows what a high temperature is anyway?

As he grew older, he came to realize the reality of those actions; his parents were monsters and never really gave a crap about him.

Reluctantly, Diesel nodded.

Zero picked up a container, some toast, and a bottle of water before joining him on the bed. Reaching over, Zero placed the soup and the bottle of water on the nightstand.

Carefully, Diesel forced himself to sit up and waited patiently for Zero to pass him the food.

"Not today, my *little ball of sunshine*." Zero swatted his hand away and began feeding him toast like he was a little kid or something. "Save your strength."

"I can feed myself," Diesel grumbled, trying to regain some of his manhood and self-esteem. His body refused to obey his commands.

"I know you can, but I'd like to keep these sheets clean and dry," he cracked, lifting the lightly buttered toast toward his mouth.

Fine. Feed me like I'm two years old.

"Take a few bites, then we can see how the food settles. At least this will give you a base in your stomach."

Diesel wasn't quite sure how he should feel. He didn't like giving up control to someone else. It almost made him feel weak and out of sorts. But it was also nice knowing that he had someone else around to take care of him. That he could relax and not worry and just focus on getting better.

He didn't have to do everything for himself.

It felt... kind of nice.

Moving the bread closer to Diesel's mouth, Zero suddenly froze and stared.

"What? What's wrong?" Diesel asked, wondering if the man had changed his mind about taking care of him. He couldn't blame him. Having to feed him and watch him be sick was a lot for any person to take in.

"It's staring at me."

Okay. Now he was even more confused.

"What?" His voice pitched upward, having no clue as to what the man was referring to.

"Bruno. I swear his eyes moved when I started bringing the bread closer to your face." Zero's eyes flicked up toward Diesel's. "Does he bite?"

Diesel chuckled. The guy was pure idiocy.

"Only if he's hungry."

Turning his attention back to Diesel's chest, Zero's eyes narrowed as if challenging the protector inked there.

"Look, Bruno. Your master is not feeling well, and I need to get some bread and water and soup into his skinny little ass before he shrivels up and dies of *gas station sandwich syndrome*. I promise I won't hurt him, so please don't bite my hand off." Zero continued to approach Diesel's mouth with the piece of toast.

"Fuck, you're an idiot," Diesel couldn't help but acknowledge. He gave a slight chuckle before his stomach barked back at him.

"Hey, I'm not takin' any chances around that thing. I'm still trying to figure out a way to smother it while we sleep tonight."

"That's definitely one way to get your hands bit," Diesel warned, taking a small bite of the bread being shoved between his lips. He really didn't feel like eating, but it was nice having someone take care of him. So he would soldier on and pray that he kept the food down.

The smirk tugging at Zero's lips did all sorts of weird things to the butterflies that were beginning to take up residence inside his belly.

After two tiny bites, they tried some chicken soup. He

ate a few spoonfuls before Zero placed the soup down, suggesting that they wait a bit to see how the food settled.

The man was right. The cramping in his stomach had stopped, but he didn't want to take any chances. His throat was still sore from being sick, but the warm broth seemed to be helping.

"You should go check on the doc. There's no point in wasting this opportunity just cus I'm an idiot and decided it was a good idea to eat a gas station sandwich."

Zero straightened and shot him a glare. He bent over the bed and grabbed Diesel by the jaw.

"First off, don't ever call yourself an idiot again. I hate hearing people talking down about themselves. The world is full of enough hatred and meanness; we don't need to be doing that to ourselves as well." Diesel wasn't sure how to respond to that, so he remained silent. "Secondly, I set up a dashcam to record the doc's activities while you were sleeping earlier. I can review the footage tomorrow to see what we missed."

Relief settled in Diesel's stomach. At least tonight was not a complete loss.

"Okay, so what do we do now?" Diesel asked, watching Zero clean up the mess from his somewhat dinner.

"Now we watch squiggly TV." Zero grabbed the remote and squeezed in next to Diesel on the bed.

It was in that moment that Diesel realized there was only one bed in the entire room.

"Sit up a bit," Zero ordered.

Diesel did as he was told and froze when he saw the man slide his arm behind his body.

"Come. Lean here and relax."

Diesel allowed himself to be pulled down so that his head was resting against Zero's chest. Behind him, he felt Zero pull his body firmly against his.

"Comfy?" Zero asked as he flicked on the television.

Diesel nodded, unsure if he was or not. His head was screaming for him to pull away and insist that Zero sleep on the floor, but his heart was telling him to relax and let the man take care of him.

That feeling, that need to be taken care of, was so foreign to Diesel. He was so used to always having to rely solely on himself.

Then there was his dick. His dick apparently hadn't gotten the memo that his internal organs were splattered all across the motel parking lot and the motel bathroom. Instead, the fucker was preparing for war by flooding himself with blood and preparing itself to invade whatever hole was available.

Not now, Big D. Talk about inappropriate timing.

Sinking his body into Zero's warm embrace, Diesel finally decided to relax and let his guard down. This was nice. This was comfy. This was... *sweet.*

"Now. What shall we watch on TV?" Zero asked, beginning to flick through the channels.

Diesel didn't care. He was warm and comfy and loved the feel of Zero's warm body pressed up against his.

He wasn't sure how long they lay in silence watching old re-runs of *I Love Lucy*. Eventually, sleep came to claim him, and he willingly gave in to its welcoming embrace.

26

DIESEL

Shifting slowly, Diesel's body protested. His cheek was pressed up against something solid, and his back was slightly curved upward. The last time he felt like this, he'd spent the night sleeping in a bathtub, a reminder of days he would rather forget.

His eyes jolted open when the surface beneath his face lifted before descending once again.

What the?

He jerked upright, startled, forgetting where he was for a moment. Then he saw Zero's sleeping face.

The man looked so peaceful, lying there, mouth slightly open, chin pressed against his chest. The poor guy had fallen asleep propped up, no doubt not wanting to wake him as he slept.

He remembered them watching TV and Zero's chest jiggling every time someone did something funny on the show. At first, it had been annoying—his head constantly being jolted around every time the man laughed at something stupid—but eventually, he began enjoying his laugh, especially when he began rubbing circles on the top of his arm. The gentle caress was calming and made him feel safe and taken care of. Other than Jared cuddling him to sleep when he was recovering from his weeklong bender at that skeezy drug den, he couldn't remember the last time anyone ever held him in such a way.

Zero was a good man. He may be annoying as fuck and pissed him off at the best of times, but considering how quickly he jumped into caretaker mode, doing his best to take care of him and make him as comfortable as possible, Diesel couldn't help but admire the guy.

Damn it. He was starting to kind of, sort of, maybe like the guy?

He's not so bad.

Plus, he sucks dick like a champ, the devilish voice inside him added.

Yeah, but do you really want to let another guy in? The more you let in, the more it's going to hurt when they all leave you, that other voice inside him said.

He did spoon-feed you dinner.

Damn. The voice was right. Zero put aside everything last night to tend to him and his needs, not worrying about watching the doc or finishing the job he was being paid to do.

The man cared about him.

Slowly, Diesel lifted himself out of bed, not wanting to wake the sleeping giant next to him. Once he was safely on the carpet, he tiptoed across the room and headed into the bathroom to take a leak.

Once he was done relieving himself, he looked around for his clothes, then remembered. There was no way he was wearing last night's clothing.

"Mmrmm, there's a bag on the table," Zero mumbled, half asleep. He slid down the bed, making himself more comfortable, and rolled onto his side.

Diesel opened the plastic bag on the table and pulled out a pair of dark-green gym shorts and a T-shirt with a large bass on the front. He smiled. The jerk really did think of everything last night.

"Sorry, that's all they had. Come back to bed."

"Get some rest. I'll be back in a bit," Diesel whispered, throwing on his shoes and heading toward the door.

"Where are you..." Zero's voice trailed off. The poor man was exhausted.

Grabbing the room key from on top of the TV, he slipped out of the room without making a sound.

As he walked across the parking lot, he searched for the doc's car. It was gone. Damn. He must have gotten up early and left. Hopefully, he went back home and not off to do some bad thing that they probably could have stopped had he not been such a fuckhead and eaten the last gas station sandwich sitting in the display case. He figured that if it was the last one, they had to be good. Or perhaps it was the only one because no one ever bought them, so the clerk just never bothered making more. The latter seemed more likely now.

Twenty minutes later, he returned with coffee and some

donuts. He was feeling much better this morning, but he still wanted to tread carefully when it came to food.

The room was still dark and quiet when Diesel slid inside, hoping not to wake Zero. The poor man needed rest.

"You don't have to creep around in the dark like a horny little stalker."

Diesel grinned.

He pulled back the drapes slightly to let in just a bit of light.

"Where did you go?" Zero asked, lying on his stomach with his head resting on his folded arms.

He was now shirtless and looked fucking delicious spread out on the bed.

Diesel felt his cock stir.

"Went to grab us some coffees and grub." He placed the donuts down on the table and carried both coffees over to the bed.

Shifting his gorgeous body, Zero flipped over and sat up in the bed. The sheet slid down, revealing just a hint of his underwear band.

Guess he wasn't naked under there after all.

Diesel passed Zero a coffee and slid onto the bed next to him.

"Thanks," Zero whispered, lifting the lip of the lid and taking a sip. "Mmm, that's good."

A sliver of sun fell over Zero's bicep as he lifted his arm for another sip.

"I wanted to thank you for last night. It was really cool of you to take care of me, and I'm sorry I fucked up our stakeout."

Zero turned his head slightly.

"Wow. Something nice just fell out of your mouth," Zero joked.

Diesel nudged him gently with his shoulder.

"Don't tell anyone. I wouldn't want to ruin my street cred."

"Your secret is safe," Zero said, patting Diesel's thigh with his free hand.

Heart pounding, Diesel slid his hand over Zero's. He wasn't sure what he was doing, but in that moment, he really wanted to touch him.

Zero's hand froze. They sat there for a moment, Diesel's rough hand resting on top of his.

Just when Diesel was about to remove his hand, Zero turned his over and interlocked his fingers with Diesel's. The gesture caught him off guard, and his breath caught in his chest.

Had he lost his mind? He didn't hold hands with guys. He didn't hold hands with anyone. Holding hands was too... intimate. Like telling someone that you liked them and didn't want them to leave.

Without saying a word, Zero began rubbing the skin on the back of Diesel's hand with his thumb, just as he had last night while Diesel rested on his chest. The feeling was so amazing.

Zero took another sip of his coffee.

"Do you think anyone famous has ever stayed at this

motel?" Zero asked, staring at the television at the end of their bed.

Diesel took a sip of his coffee. The hot Colombian liquid swirled around in his mouth. He prayed that his stomach would take mercy on him today.

"Not unless they were cheating on their spouse or snorting coke off some hustler's dick."

Zero turned to face him. "You don't think they'd snort coke off a dude's dick in a five-star hotel?"

His face was so serious that Diesel couldn't help but burst out laughing.

"You're such an idiot." Diesel chuckled, placing his coffee on the nightstand and slinking down onto Zero's chest. He put his head down and let his body sink into Zero's. "Tell anyone about this, and I'll stab you in the eye."

Zero placed his hand on Diesel's upper back and began caressing his right shoulder blade.

"Wouldn't dream of it."

27

ZERO

The drive back home was spent talking about their lives. Diesel spoke mostly about his time at *La Maison*, changing the subject whenever Zero tried to ask him anything about his family. He wasn't ready to open up about that part of his life. He got it. For now, he would spend the time getting to know Diesel's present.

"Do you think you'll ever give up working at the club?" Zero asked, not quite sure if he was crossing a line.

"I'm sure at some point. Nobody wants to see saggy balls and a wrinkly ass dancing around onstage."

Zero was having trouble getting that mental image out of his head.

"No. I guess you're right."

"It's good money. Where else can you get paid to drink, party, and get your dick sucked?"

"Just about every strip club and whorehouse across Europe," Zero added teasingly.

208

"Yeah, I guess you're right. But where else can you live in a fucking castle with your best friends and brothers?"

"You got a point. What about your boss? That daddy guy who's got you grounded?"

Diesel lowered his eyes. "Matteo. He's the closest thing we all have to a father. Without him, I would have died a long time ago."

Zero glanced over at Diesel, not wanting to take his eyes off the road for too long. "What do you mean?"

"It was Matteo who found me when I was nineteen years old." He turned to look out the passenger window, appearing lost in a memory.

Perhaps the topic was too painful to discuss. Zero was just about to change the subject when Diesel began to talk.

"When I was eighteen, I was living on the streets, crashing at whatever place I could find or whichever sugar daddy or mama would take me in for the night. It wasn't a life that I enjoyed, but it was better than the alternative."

Zero watched as Diesel turned to look out his window once again.

"I started hanging out with this crew—other street kids who liked to party it up and did what they could to make some extra cash for drugs and booze. Some worked for local drug dealers, selling on corners and getting their fix on the side. Others, like me, took advantage of lonely men and women looking for a bit of attention and willing to pay for the pleasure of my company." Diesel turned to face Zero once again. "Hey, at least all the money I made went to me and not some drug lord who would beat my ass if I didn't make his quota." He turned back to face the window. "Anyway, me and my friends were stupid as fuck. Partying it up when we could, not giving a fuck who we hurt or fucked over in the process. I was convinced that they were my crew. My family. The people I could trust to have my back if something went wrong."

Diesel began playing with the fabric of his cheesy gym shorts. His body was tense, and he looked uncomfortable talking about his past.

Zero reached across the seat and placed his hand on his thigh. "You don't have to talk about it if you're not ready."

Turning, Diesel gave Zero a half smile.

It looked like he wanted to talk about it, but just needed a reassuring hand letting him know that it was okay to open up to him. Zero got the sense it wasn't often that Diesel let people in.

"No, it's fine. Just makes me hate myself sometimes when I think about the past."

Diesel lifted his hand and placed it over the top of Zero's. Their fingers intertwined, and Diesel resumed his story.

"Anyway, so one night, I was partying with this dude who paid me five hundred pounds to suck me off. Hey, it was easy cash, plus I needed the money. After I left his motel, I hit up a buddy for some coke and K. Back then, I liked to mix coke with ketamine; yes, I know mixing them was stupid and dangerous, but no one thinks about that when you're eighteen and living on the streets. Anyway, after that score, I was feeling good and decided to party it up with my friends down in the park. At some point, I must have gone into a K-hole and passed out without realizing it. When I woke up, my friends and cash were gone, and I was lying on the ground shaking. I don't even know when I passed out again or when Matteo found me, but I woke up the next morning in the hospital with an IV bag hooked up to my arm.

"Do you know that the damn guy stayed with me in the hospital for three days? He kept bringing me magazines and chocolate and asking if there was anyone who I wanted him to get in touch with. I think by the third day, he finally realized that I was all alone."

Hoping to provide him with comfort, Zero rubbed gentle circles with his thumb.

"Once I was finally feeling better, M asked if I wanted to come stay with him for a while, just until I was able to get back on my feet. Of course, I thought the guy was just perving on me and trying to get me to drop my pants, but what did I have to lose? When we arrived at the château, he escorted me to my room and made it very clear that he was not interested in anything sexual. He was just trying to help someone who looked like they could use a hand at the moment.

"Matteo really did save me that day in the park. The doctor said that my heart rate was dangerously high, given all the drugs that I had been mixing. And it was a good thing that Matteo found me when he did."

Diesel was back to looking out the window once again.

"So that's how he found me. Don't judge me. I was working through a lot of things in my head back then. I still am."

"Is that why you're seeing a shrink?"

Diesel's head snapped around.

"You know about that?"

"It's not that big of a secret around the house. I hear Jared and Chase talking about it all the time. He's worried about you, you know. He scared you're going to lose control and overdose sometime." There was no judgment in his voice, only worry and concern.

Diesel lowered his head. "Yeah, I know. I owe it to the guys to work out the shit that's rolling around inside my head."

Zero gave Diesel's hand a gentle squeeze. "I hope you know that I'm here for you whenever you need me. Just say the word, and I'll be there."

Diesel nodded. "Thanks, man. I appreciate that."

They arrived back at the house just after six in the evening. They made a few pit stops along the way, some to grab food, some to check out things Diesel kept spotting along the way.

Zero had decided to take the scenic route home. He wasn't in a rush to get back to the house, and to be honest, he was kind of liking the one-on-one alone time with his grumbly ray of sunshine.

Who would have guessed that Diesel was into stained glass? While driving through a small town, they came across a little farmhouse where the owner made stained glass pictures and other small trinkets. Of course they had to stop inside.

Lost in the sea of artwork, Diesel kept eyeing a particular stained glass picture of an old church sitting in front of one of the most beautiful sunsets Zero had ever seen. There was something about the colors—purples, oranges, reds, and greens. They were all mixed together as if supporting one another to create one of the most spectacular views imaginable.

When it was clear that Diesel had no intention of buying the picture for himself, Zero waited until he went to use the bathroom before discreetly purchasing the item and shoving it into the trunk of their rental. He would give it to Diesel once they got back home.

"Hold up a sec?" Zero asked, just as Diesel was about to walk up the pathway when they got back home. There were no driveways, so everyone had to use street parking.

Zero reached into the trunk, pulled out the tissue-wrapped picture, and handed it to the confused young man.

"What's this?" Diesel asked, taking the item and flipping it around in his hand.

"I saw you staring at it in the shop and couldn't figure out why you wouldn't buy it. So I did."

Pulling the paper away, piece by piece, Diesel unwrapped the item and gasped when he realized what it was.

"But... why?"

The question was innocent enough, but it still caught him off guard.

"Because... I wanted to." That was the truth. He saw something that appeared to make Diesel happy, and he wanted to always see that look on the growly young man's face.

People didn't realize how good-looking Diesel was when he wasn't scowling or busy insulting your ass.

"Zero... I—" He paused, staring down at the gift, seeming lost for words. "Thank you. This was really nice of you."

Now it was Zero's turn to be stunned when Diesel wrapped his arms around him and gave him a hug.

What. Was. Happening?

"Tell anyone that I'm hugging you, and I'll stab you in the neck," Diesel whispered into his ear.

Ahh, that was more like it. Diesel wasn't himself if he wasn't making smart-ass comments or threatening to stab your ass.

Zero hugged him back with one arm.

"You boys done boning? I want to hear about your trip," Jared shouted from the living room window.

Always the gentleman.

Groaning, Diesel pulled away and headed inside.

When they entered the house, Chase was huddled over his laptop at the kitchen table while Jared was flipping through the TV.

"Want a pop?" Jared asked, holding up a can of soda.

They both shook their heads. They had been snacking and drinking sodas the whole drive home. Zero wanted nothing more than to hit the gym and eat something healthy for a change.

"So, how did it go?" Chase asked, walking into the living room.

"I'm going to review the footage tonight, and I'll let you

know," Zero responded, hoping that was the end of the conversation. It wasn't.

"What do you mean, let me know? What did you guys see last night? Did the doc meet with anybody?"

"I'm not sure," Zero choked out, not really sure how to respond to his boss.

"It's a simple question. What did you guys see? Did he meet with anybody? Was he there fucking some chick? Some dude? What?"

Chase's cheeks were beginning to flush, the more annoyed he became. The one thing that Chase didn't have patience for was beating around the bush.

"I don't know. I didn't see," Zero responded a little more aggressively than he intended to. He wasn't about to throw Diesel under the bus. Chase could hold his horses and wait until he was done reviewing the footage to get his friggin' report.

"You guys fell asleep, didn't you?" Chase asked, placing his hands on his waist and planting his feet firmly on the floor. "Fuck. I knew I shouldn't have sent you guys."

"Hey!" Diesel shouted, startling all three of them. "It's not his fault."

"Diesel, don't," Zero began.

"No, Zero," Diesel said, eyes glaring at him. "It was my fault."

A huff escaped Chase's lips, sending murderous rage coursing through Zero's veins. Who the fuck was this guy to huff about Diesel?

"Of course it is. What fuckup did you do this time?"

Chase growled, turning his angry eyes toward his future brother-in-law.

"He didn't fuck up. He got sick," Zero interjected. There was no way he was letting Chase make the poor guy feel bad for getting food poisoning.

"You got sick?" Chase asked, his voice suddenly showing a hint of concern.

"Yeah, I got food poisoning from that damn gas station sandwich I ate."

Jesus Christ, D, keep your friggin' mouth shut. Zero ground his teeth. It's like he enjoyed throwing himself in front of flying bullets.

"You got sick from a gas station sandwich?"

Oh, here comes the lecture.

"Who the fuck eats deli meat from a gas station?" Chase shouted, raising his arms in disbelief.

Diesel just stood there, eyes fixed on the floor in front of him. He knew he fucked up. But either way, he didn't deserve to get reamed out for something he couldn't control.

"That's enough," Zero shouted, stepping in front of Diesel and throwing his own hands on his hips. Two could play at that game. "I set up a camera to surveil his room, so I am going to go watch the footage now. I'll let you know when I have something."

He turned and grabbed Diesel by the arm.

"Come, you're helping me go through the footage."

Zero stormed up the stairs, not bothering to look back over his shoulder. His boss could go suck a dick until he was done.

28

DIESEL

*A*fter placing his gift down on his bed, Diesel stared at the stained glass picture and wondered whether the artist created the scene on sight or created it from memory. To be able to witness such beauty must have been such an exhilarating experience.

Getting high was like that sometimes, as well. Depending on the drug one took, they could hallucinate—witnessing colors and images never before seen in real life or become witness to eye-bending sensory manipulation that allowed the mind to see whatever sort of phenomenon it wanted or craved.

He had watched a documentary on the Discovery Channel once that talked about how many famous artists took mind-altering drugs or alcohol to allow them to tap into that imaginative subconscious that others rarely got a chance to experience. It was through those hallucinations that artists were able to create some of the most mind-blowing works of art that the world has ever seen.

Staring at the way the colors of the sunset were placed strategically together behind the church made the painting appear to come to life. Kind of like how people swore they witnessed Bruno's eyes move as they stared at his tattoo. The mind is a powerful thing, able to convince us of just about anything. Our sight, our senses, our emotions, all that information being fed into our brains only to be spit out and interpreted by our minds. It was incredible if you really thought about it.

Turning his head, Diesel glanced at his open bedroom door. He wasn't sure how he felt about Zero buying him this gift. Yes, he loved the picture. Yes, he couldn't wait to hang it up and admire it each and every day. But he wasn't sure what this meant for their relationship.

Yes, Zero was a hot guy, and they had some hot-ass fucking times together, but did this mean that Zero wanted more than just orgasms?

He did take care of you while you were sick. He did cuddle you and make you feel safe and protected while you struggled to stay alive.

Okay, that last part was an exaggeration, but he did feel like he was dying and about to puke himself into oblivion.

Perhaps Zero really was a nice guy. Maybe it was time for him to stop being such a fucking asshole around him and give the guy a bit of leeway.

Fine. But first, shower.

Diesel grabbed a pair of joggers and a fresh T-shirt from his dresser and walked over to Zero's room.

Zero was sitting on his bed, fiddling around with some surveillance equipment.

"I'm just going to take a quick shower, then I'll come and help you go through the footage," Diesel announced from where he stood standing in the open doorway.

Glancing up at him, Zero's warm brown eyes seemed to pop against his soft, tanned skin and jet-black hair. Just like the painting, Zero was a vision to behold.

"That sounds good," he said, giving him a gentle smile. "I'll grab us some sodas, then meet you here in ten."

Twenty minutes later, they were both sitting on Zero's bed, staring at the laptop resting on Zero's lap. Zero had downloaded the footage from the dashcam and was currently scrolling through it.

"Can you slow down a bit? We're going to miss something important." Diesel huffed over Zero's shoulder.

They were pressed up against each other, with Zero's back and shoulder resting against Diesel's chest as he balanced the laptop.

It was a small bed.

Okay, it was a decent-sized bed, but it was a small laptop. And how else was he supposed to see the laptop if he didn't press himself into Zero's back?

Why does he smell so good? Diesel wondered to himself.

Smells good? Do you know who smells people? that annoying voice inside Diesel's head asked. *Serial killers. That's who.*

He wasn't a serial killer. A doped-out drug addict who sold his body for money and had major trust and abandonment issues... sure. But a serial killer? No. He didn't have the drive or dedication to be one. Or the stomach, for that matter.

"Relax. Stop backseat driving. Do you know how many hours of footage we have to get through? And I don't know about you, but I don't want to be here watching a closed door all night, waiting for *Dr. Pervs-a-lot* to make a move."

But you smell so nice. It was a genuine manly scent. Like sweat mixed with sandalwood, mixed with muscle. *Fuck*, he loved the smell of a man pressed up against him.

"D? Is that..." Zero's voice trailed off.

"Is that what?" Diesel asked, looking over Zero's shoulder and down at the image of the closed motel room door. Unless he missed it, the doc still hadn't left his room and still didn't have any visitors.

Diesel watched as Zero's finger moved over the laptop and stopped an inch away from his junk. Then it happened. Zero poked his boner with his finger.

Shit. He was so busy inhaling Zero's scent that he hadn't realized the smell had awakened the beast slumbering in his joggers. And, of course, he was freeballing it.

"Fuck." Diesel groaned. "Sorry, dude. Guess I'm feeling better."

Ask anyone, and guys will always say how much they wished they had a bigger dick and how lucky guys were who were hung. But nobody ever stops to think about the downside to having a big dick. You can't just use any condom; it has to be XL or magnum—have fun purchasing those at a pharmacy!

Whenever you pop a boner, *everyone* fucken knows! There is no being discreet or going unnoticed. It's just there —out there for everyone to bloody see.

When fucking? You need to use a shit ton of lube and take your time sliding it in. There is no jamming or shoving it right in. There are patience and waiting periods. It requires using your fingers or toys to help spread open the person you're about to fuck before you even dream of sliding your cock into home base. What's the saying? Big dicks are nice to look at but a real pain in the ass. Truer words were never spoken.

"Jesus, dude. You need to get that thing registered as a deadly weapon." Zero chuckled, poking it two more times before returning his hand to the keyboard. "We need to be good. We have video footage to review."

Yes, he needed to focus on the task at hand and not the image of his cock disappearing between Zero's luscious lips.

"Stop. I can see your dick twitching from the corner of my eye."

Diesel chuckled. "He's just saying hi."

Zero gave a quick wave before continuing to fast-forward through the footage.

"Wait," Diesel blurted, pointing toward a figure that just appeared in the frame. "Press play."

They both watched as a large man in a brown leather jacket approached the doc's motel room, holding a black briefcase. A second later, the door opened, and the doc signaled for the unknown guest to enter. Ten minutes later, the mystery man emerged from the room without the black briefcase and disappeared from the shot. They continued to scroll through the hours of footage until six a.m. when the doc left his room and checked out of the motel, holding the black case.

"What do you think was inside the briefcase?" Diesel asked.

Zero shook his head. "No idea. If he made the effort of collecting the item all the way in the middle of nowhere in the dead of night, I'm guessing he doesn't want people to know about it." Snapping shut his laptop, Zero glanced over at where Diesel's beast was currently sleeping. "Hmm, looks like the little guy decided to take a nap."

"Hey..." Diesel began as Zero hopped off the bed and headed toward the door. "Where are you going?"

"To go report our findings to that pissed-off man I call a boss."

Diesel slid his body along the bed until he was lying flat on his back. He placed his hands behind his head and stared up at the ceiling.

"Meh, he's not that bad. Hurry back. Someone wants you to kiss him goodnight."

Zero froze when he reached the door. He turned slowly.

"Umm, come again?" Zero asked, looking so confused.

Hands behind his head and still staring at the ceiling, Diesel flexed, causing his semi-erect cock to bounce up and down—a plus side of having a big dick. Having the ability to wave hello from across the room.

Zero's lips parted until they curved up into a horny smirk. "Fuck..." he groaned out. "You're such a tease. Don't start without me."

Diesel chuckled. He never saw a man dash out of a room so fast.

29

ZERO

*Z*ero's debrief with Chase left more questions than answers. The only new information they had discovered was that the doctor had been given a briefcase by an unknown man in a brown leather jacket. Jared was able to confirm that the doc did arrive home carrying that same suitcase, so at least they knew that the case hadn't been passed off. Whatever was inside it, the doctor needed.

When their discussion ended, Chase advised that he was going to call his boss, Marc, and run the situation by him. Perhaps he had some insight or suggestions that might help them with their case.

Other than the party this coming weekend, the team had no new evidence or information that might indicate whether the doc was an evil man or just an odd scientist.

Zero hated the fact that he had not been able to find any evidence to support their suspicions. Multiple victims all claimed the same type of scenario, but none of them were coherent enough to provide any concrete, solid information. There were too many similarities amongst their accounts for Chase and his boss to turn a blind eye.

All victims, both male and female, were junkies—high as fuck for anything that they said to be taken seriously by the authorities. They all claimed that they went to a party, all woke up with no memory, and all had signs indicating a struggle.

The police treated each case as a separate incident as there was no physical evidence connecting them—or, more likely, they just didn't care. But Marc and Chase had seen the connections; all victims were of a particular type—junkies. This helped to ensure no one would believe a word they said... possibly. While each victim was found in a different location, none of them had any memory of what happened or how they got there. Then there was the physical evidence; all victims were found covered in cuts and bruises, barefoot, muddy, and bleeding. It wasn't signs of an attempted murder, more so, evidence of a struggle, a fight, possibly an escape attempt from their captor. Who knew?

Marc and Chase also had something the police did not— Edwin's journal. To some, it was known as the *Book of Sin*. In it were the suspicions of a man they could not trust. Hidden within the journal were truths and lies, details of horrors and accusations that Zero and his team were desperately trying to decipher.

Was the doctor abducting random junkies? Were these victims all survivors of some deranged plot the doctor set in motion?

All of these questions frustrated Zero. He would never forgive himself if someone else got hurt because he was too stupid to connect the dots.

No. The authorities did not believe a word the victims said. They took their statements, got them medical treatment for their wounds, and then tossed them back onto the streets as an inconvenience to their evenings and a waste of time.

Once Zero was done discussing the next steps with Chase, Zero went back upstairs to his bedroom. When he pulled open the door, Diesel was passed out on his bed, arm thrown over his eyes, legs spread out like he owned the whole fucking thing.

Zero smiled. These were some of the rare moments when Diesel actually looked and acted like a decent human being. The rest of the time, he looked and acted like a fucking asshole.

Yeah, but that's all just a defense mechanism. You've seen how he behaves when he's around the people he cares about, like Jared and Isaac and all the other guys from the club. Even Chase, he assumed.

Not wanting to wake Diesel, Zero silently slipped across the room and grabbed a towel to take a quick shower before bed.

Twenty minutes later, dripping wet and in nothing but a towel, Zero slipped back into his bedroom. He contemplated taking Diesel's bed, considering his was currently occupied by a slumbering stoner and his creepy-ass demon tattoo. But hey, why should he have to sleep in sheets that were probably covered in potato chips and dried cum, when his sheets were perfectly clean and fresh smelling.

That, and he secretly hoped that Diesel Jr. might wake up demanding attention and wanting to paint his insides. It had been a couple of weeks since Zero had been fucked, and he was dying to get dicked down by that monster cock of Diesel's.

He could only imagine the depth and stretch that thing would inflict.

Standing next to the bed, he watched Diesel sleep. He was still wearing his joggers but had removed his shirt at some point during the past twenty minutes when he was in the shower.

Zero watched as the man's chest rose and fell, relaxed and deep in his dreams. Damn, the boy looked so cute, just lying there all vulnerable and peaceful. He really was sweet when his mouth wasn't open and offending the world.

As he stood there, being the creeper that he was, Zero got the unnerving sensation that he was being watched. His gaze flickered up to Diesel's face, whose eyes were still closed and unmoving. Then, against his better judgment, Zero's eyes moved lower. They slid down Diesel's neck and across his smooth, lean chest until they landed on Satan's little minion.

"Fuck you, Bruno," Zero whispered at the creepy little demon's face. "I hated you in that kids' movie, and I hate you now on Diesel's chest." Zero stood there for a moment, giving the judging demon the evil eye. He swore the damn thing smiled back at him.

Diesel let out a groan, then shifted in bed.

Zero watched as the material on Diesel's joggers began to rise. God bless morning wood and uncontrollable boners!

Doing a silent prayer to the gay sex gods, Zero dropped his towel onto the floor and slid naked onto his bed.

Diesel let out another moan as his legs slid open even further, and his dick rose another inch. Fuck, there was nothing more delicious than watching a sexy man pop a boner. Seeing that thick piece of meat expand and grow until it reaches its full potential. And then watching it bob up and down, demanding attention.

So. Fucking. Hot.

Propping himself up on his elbow next to his slumbering fuck buddy—is that what they were now?—he lowered his other hand onto Diesel's hard cock and gave it a nice firm squeeze over the material.

"Mmm." Diesel groaned, and his body shifted as he slowly left the dream world. "Mmm, that feels nice."

Zero glanced up at Diesel, whose eyes were still closed, but his lips were slightly parted. He released his dick, loving the heavy thump Diesel's cock made as it fell against his stomach. That thing really could be used as a weapon. Talk about being beaten to death by a thick piece of meat—fuck, talk about a sexy way to die.

Not wanting to waste any more time, Zero slid his hand under Diesel's waistband and took hold of his massive shaft.

Fuck, the man's dick was hot and solid. He was amazed that the guy hadn't passed out, considering how much blood must be sitting in the man's cock that very moment.

"Thought you'd be back sooner." Diesel moaned, his eyes still closed but clearly enjoying the late-night hand job.

Little did Diesel know, but in about two minutes, that glorious hard-on was going to be buried balls deep inside his fucking hole.

"Had to shower and get ready..." He let his words drift off.

Diesel's soft brown eyes slid open when Zero didn't finish his sentence.

Turning, Zero reached into his nightstand and pulled out a condom—a magnum, of course—and a bottle of lube.

"Hmm, looks like someone is horny," Diesel said, giving him a cocky smirk.

There was a hunger in his gaze.

He was suddenly glad that he'd stretched himself out in the shower. He didn't want to waste time prepping and stretching himself out, delaying the pleasure of that hungry look staring back at him. Nope. He was well stretched and ready to hop on the man's dick and take the ride of his life.

"Shut up and lie there," Zero ordered, pulling down the man's joggers so that they were coiled around his thighs.

Using his teeth, he ripped open the condom and spit the foil onto the bed. He didn't have time for pleasantries and proper etiquette. He needed that dick buried deep inside him, stretching his hole and pounding his prostate.

"Wow, someone's bossy." Diesel chuckled, not making any attempt to move.

Ignoring the sarcastic comment, Zero rolled the condom down the thick length of his shaft and wondered how he was ever going to fit all of that meat inside his tight little hole. He'd been fucked by large dicks before, but Diesel's was in a whole other category of his own.

Grabbing the lube, he applied a generous amount to Diesel's cock, before applying the same to his hole.

He was both excited and terrified.

Excited at getting his ass pounded and his prostate assaulted, but also terrified that the damn thing wouldn't fit and then he would have to listen to endless jokes about how Diesel was too much man for him, and how his cock was a god and only the lucky few were able to enjoy its presence.

Fuck that noise.

He was going to take every last inch of that monster and make Diesel beg to bust a nut in his magical, powerful hole.

Taking a deep breath, he threw his leg over Diesel's torso and lined Diesel's throbbing piece of meat up with his hole.

"Ah, you may want to—" Diesel began but threw his head back in pleasure when his cock began to slide into Zero's tight heat.

"I told you to shut up and lie there." Zero huffed. He grimaced as he concentrated on opening himself up and welcoming every inch of Diesel's legendary manhood.

Fuck, the stretch and resistance were like nothing he had ever felt before. This was another reason why it was important to stretch out beforehand because this sting was next-level bullshit.

Christ, he had never had a dick this big in his ass before.

It felt fucking amazing.

Hurt like a bitch but felt fucking amazing.

Then it happened. The head of Diesel's cock brushed up against his prostate.

Holy. Fucking. Hell!

He sat there for a moment, eyes closed, his ass resting on Diesel's thighs, and his hole stretched to its limits.

He needed a minute.

Was this what it felt like to fuck yourself to death? If so, he would die a very happy man.

Big, rough hands gripped both of Zero's ass cheeks, bringing him back to the present. Zero's eyes slid open and landed on the heated eyes lying beneath him.

Slowly, Zero began moving his hips, loving the feel of Diesel's giant cock sliding in and out of his once-tight hole. Fuck, he felt so full and stretched out.

"God, your ass feels so tight." Diesel moaned, staring up at him like he was a juicy steak waiting to be devoured.

That heated look went straight to his dick.

"Shh. Daddy's going to show you how to ride dick." And with those heated words, Zero began the ride of his life.

Hands pressed against Diesel's chest, Zero thrust his ass down on his cock, loving the way Diesel's mouth gaped open at the tightness around his cock. Eyes locked together, he began building up speed.

Panting. Groaning. Zero worked his hips, loving the deliciously sinful sounds escaping Diesel's lips.

Beneath him, Diesel gritted his teeth, digging his fingers into the soft flesh of Zero's ass cheeks.

Why was great sex always so violent and carnal?

"Fuck. I love that dick." Zero gasped, throwing his head

back as flashes of light danced across his eyes with each powerful stroke against his prostate.

Jesus Christ, the man's cock was amazing.

"Holy. Fuck." Diesel panted, spreading his ass cheeks apart as far as they would go. "I... gonna..."

The man looked like he was in pain, trying to hold back his orgasm. Zero was glad Diesel was about to come. He wasn't sure just how much more his poor ass could take.

"Do it. Come for me," Zero ordered, picking up speed, then wishing he hadn't the moment Diesel's cock thrust up against his prostate. "Fuck!" he screamed, unable to stop the load shooting out of his cock. It was the first time he had ever come without touching his cock.

Beneath him, Diesel let out a feral growl as he snapped his hips upward, unloading his seed into the condom.

Gasping for air, Zero flopped down against Diesel's chest. Panting and exhausted, he tried to get his breathing back under control.

"Holy. Hell. That was one fucking magical ass, dude." Diesel huffed into Zero's ear.

Zero couldn't help but chuckle.

He lifted his head slightly. "Yeah, well, that's what happens when it's filled with porn star dick."

Now it was Diesel's turn to chuckle. It was such a beautiful sound.

Shifting his body, Zero stared down into the hooded eyes of the man who had just fucked his brains out. He looked so gorgeous smiling.

Eyes on each other, he leaned forward, locking their lips

in a heated, passionate kiss. He wasn't sure what came over him, but in that moment, he needed to be close to Diesel. He needed to feel his rough lips, taste his magic tongue, and feel his lean body pressed against him.

To Zero's surprise, Diesel wrapped his arms around his back and pulled him closer into his body.

A desperate moan escaped Zero's lips.

God, this felt perfect.

They continued to make out for the next forty-five minutes, clawing at each other's bodies, lips never leaving one another's, until Diesel finally rolled them over and began sucking Zero's dick.

It didn't take Zero long before he was spilling his seed down Diesel's throat as well.

Fuck, the man had mad bedroom skills.

30

DIESEL

*L*ight drifting in from the partially opened curtain landed on Diesel's back, warming his skin and reminding him that the secrets of the dark were no longer protected by the shadows of the night. This was why booty calls left before sunrise. Because once that sun came up, everyone was faced with the harsh realities of life.

Lying there, he gently caressed the arm that was draped over his body. His back was to the man he had just spent the last three hours sharing pleasures and orgasms with.

Now, in the harsh light of reality, he was faced with two choices: pretend like this was just another one-night stand— be cocky and rude and hope that the man didn't see through all of his bullshit—or be honest. Tell the man who has spent the last few days... hell, even few weeks being nothing but nice to him that he, in fact, might, possibly, maybe, for sure have feelings for the sexy retired Abercrombie model.

He wasn't sure what to do. His mind was telling him to

play it off as no big deal. It was just another night of shared orgasms and no different than any other one-night stand that he'd had in the past. Get up and leave before anyone gets the wrong impression.

His heart, on the other hand, was telling him a different story. This, right here, was not like all the other one-night stands. This man, the one with his arm around you, holding you and comforting you, has the potential of becoming something great. He took care of you when you were sick. He asks you for help and listens when you talk. He even asks you questions and takes an interest in your life and the things that you do. Hell, how many guys have looked at you with such passionate desire while riding your dick?

There was a moment last night, while their eyes were locked together, that Diesel swore he felt his soul being pulled into Zero's eyes. The way he was looking at him made him want to crawl inside his body and live there forever.

The only problem was that if he listened to his heart and discovered that he was wrong, he would be left with nothing but shattered pieces of a heart he didn't know still existed.

Apparently, Bruno was guarding a lot more than just his person. The fucker was also hiding his heart.

Brushing down Zero's arm hair, Diesel tried to ignore the fluttering feeling deep in his chest. He loved touching the grown man's skin.

Behind him, Zero's body jerked as if startled in a dream. He wrapped his arm tighter around Diesel and pulled his body closer to his.

Diesel couldn't help but smile. He liked being someone's comfort human.

"Jesus. I think you broke my ass," Zero grumbled against Diesel's ear.

Diesel chuckled softly in his captor's arms.

"Hey, I was told to just shut up and lie there. If anything, I think it was your ass that broke my dick," Diesel argued back.

Now it was Zero's turn to chuckle.

"Touché. Morning, sexy," he said, leaning forward and giving Diesel a gentle kiss on his neck. Another first for Diesel.

Usually, guys were so focused on sucking his dick that very few wanted to waste time leaning upward and giving him a kiss. When it came down to priorities, most people chose to worship his cock than be intimate with his other body parts.

Diesel closed his eyes and let himself get lost in the euphoric feeling of being cuddled by a sexy, warm man.

"This is nice," Zero whispered. He tightened his arms around Diesel before nestling his face in the crook of his neck.

Usually, when Diesel hooked up with clients, it was rough and impersonal. Clients usually wanted that bad boy, stoner persona—the type who would throw you down on the bed and pound you until you were a blubbering mess of a man. They didn't want sweet or romantic or to cuddle after he painted their faces with his cum. They wanted a high-energy fuck fest that would leave them mindless and thinking of nothing but how much their ass was sore.

But lying here in Zero's arms, he felt an intimacy he had never felt before with another person—man or woman. Yes, he'd cuddled before with Jared, but that was a best friend, comfort thing. There was nothing sexual about it, and he didn't feel any desires or uncontrollable urges when lying next to Jared.

Was he... falling in love?

His brain was screaming for him to get the fuck out of the bed and go hook up with some rando immediately, but his heart was telling him to stay where he was. To lean into the feeling and enjoy the warmth coursing through his body.

He had never felt this way before. The need to be close to someone. Feel their breath on his body. Feel their warm skin against his.

Rolling over, he turned to face Zero.

"Morning, shit for brains," he whispered, giving him a teasing smile.

Zero chuckled and began drawing circles with his thumb against Diesel's naked back. God, he loved that.

"Where's the lube?" Diesel asked, catching Zero off guard.

His eyebrows shot up, appearing excited and confused.

Zero fumbled behind his back, reaching blindly for the bottle of lube sitting on the nightstand by the bed. He shoved it into Diesel's hand, not daring to say a word.

"Condom?"

Eyes going wide, he looked terrified for a moment.

"I... I... sorry, man. My ass is too sore for another pounding," Zero stuttered, looking as though he had just lost first prize in a beer-guzzling challenge.

"It's always about you, you selfish prick," Diesel said, reaching under the covers and gripping Zero's semi. He began tugging on it, loving the feel of the man's cock getting hard and thick in his hand. "This morning is all about me and my prostate getting some one-on-one time with that big dick of yours."

A wicked smile cut across Zero's face. There was also a hint of relief in those eyes. Diesel felt a sense of pride, knowing that he was able to fuck a man so hard that he needed a day to recover between poundings.

"Big dick?" Zero asked, picking up the lube from where Diesel had placed it on the bed. He yanked down the blanket in one swift *ta-da*!

He poured some lube onto his fingers and began applying it to Diesel's ass.

"My dick is normal six-foot-two man dick. You'll still be able to walk after I finish with you. Your dick is freak of nature, porn star dick that should come with its own warning label."

Diesel chuckled as he backed his ass up onto Zero's fingers.

"I'll give you credit. Not many guys are able to take the big guy without some major prep time. But you, you took that hog like a champ!"

Now it was Zero's turn to chuckle.

"So, how do you like it?" Zero asked, adding three fingers to Diesel's hole and working open his tight ass.

Diesel ripped open the condom with his teeth and began rolling the latex down the man's length. Fuck, his dick looked good. It was perfect. A solid eight inches with a nice mushroom head. He pulled the tip of the condom and admired the pulsing thick vein that ran down the length of his shaft and ended at his perfectly trimmed balls.

God, he couldn't wait to lick and suck on those gorgeous nutsacks. But not today. Today, he was going to ride that cock until the man's balls were drained, and his eyes were stuck in the back of his head.

"I told you, this morning is all about me. You're going to lie there and take it while I ride your dick till my ass is good and sore." With that, Diesel threw his leg over Zero's hips and lined his cock up with his hole.

Slowly, he began to sink down onto the man's hard shaft, loving the ache and sting as his ass stretched out around the man's hefty cock.

Smirking down at a lustful Zero, Diesel pressed his palms down against the man's chest and began riding his cock long and deep.

Diesel loved sex, be it with a man or woman, but there was something about being fucked by a man that was always so much hotter for him.

"Jesus, you look so fucking hot, riding my dick," Zero huffed out, gripping Diesel's hips and moving in rhythm with his strokes.

"Yeah? You like watching me work that dick? Taking it nice and deep? Feeling your cock throb inside my hole?"

Zero's eyes dilated. He tightened his grip around Diesel's waist and began pumping his dick up into his ass.

Each brush against his prostate sent a new surge of pleasure shooting through his balls and right to his dick. *God, this man knew how to fuck!*

"I thought I was the one who was supposed to be doing all the work?" Diesel teased.

A carnal growl emerged beneath him seconds before Zero's arm wrapped itself around his waist, flipping them both over on the bed.

Zero thrust his body hard against Diesel's, causing his cock to bury itself deeper inside his ass.

"Fuck!" Diesel shouted as a flood of pleasure shot through his body when Zero's dick slid across his prostate.

Staring up at Zero, his eyes were black, and his tongue was hanging out the side of his mouth. He looked like a sex-starved convict who had just been released from prison and hadn't busted a nut in at least five years.

Diesel loved the carnal look in the man's eyes. He never felt sexier or more desired before in his life.

"Sorry, I need to pound that ass of yours," Zero growled.

"Then take it, big boy," Diesel egged on, hoping he wasn't going to regret it later.

Letting out another growl, like a man possessed, Zero grabbed Diesel by the hips and flipped him over once again so that he was now up on all fours.

"You asked for it," Zero snarled before jamming his dick back inside Diesel's tight hole.

Diesel let out a yelp, more out of surprise than pain. He loved being manhandled and getting fucked by a man who took what he wanted. There was something to be said about sex and aggression. The more aggressive, the more Diesel was on board.

Shoving Diesel's face down into the pillow, Zero snapped his hips and began fucking him hard without mercy.

Gripping the sheets beneath him, Diesel rode out the pleasure exploding from his balls.

Grunting and huffing, Zero pounded his ass like a man fucking for gold at the Olympics.

"Dude, you don't know how fucking sexy your ass cheeks look bouncing up against me while fucking you doggy style."

Diesel smiled into the pillow. He knew. He had watched videos of himself being fucked on previous occasions—for research purposes, of course—and was impressed with how hot his ass looked when being pounded nice and hard.

"Oh yeah, right there." Diesel moaned as Zero's cock assaulted his prostate once again.

The man was quickly becoming his new favorite toy.

His balls tightened as Zero dug his fingers into his hips once again. Diesel reached down between his legs and began jerking his cock, riding the waves of pleasure building in his balls.

"Holy fuck!" Zero shouted, snapping his hips forward and unloading into the condom.

Hearing the sinful sounds coming from Zero's mouth threw Diesel over the edge. He shot his load, not caring where it landed. Sticky, cum-covered sheets were a *later* problem.

Once they both stopped shaking, they fell onto the bed in a pile of sweaty limbs and naked parts.

Slowly, Zero pulled out of Diesel's sore ass and tied off the condom before dropping it on the floor next to the bed. Another one of later's problems.

Barely able to lift his head, Diesel cracked open a lid and smiled at the gasping hunk of man lying on top of him.

"Not too shabby for a man with a broken ass," Diesel joked, grinning like a stupid imbecile.

Zero choked out a laugh, then kissed the top of Diesel's shoulder.

"Thanks. I was highly motivated by a perfect ass offering itself to me for my own pleasure."

Zero chuckled when Diesel smacked his ass from behind.

Yeah, he could definitely get used to mornings like these. He smiled and let the warmth of Zero's arms take him away once again.

31

DIESEL

The ticking from the vintage clock was the only sound that filled the room. Diesel watched as the large hand slowly made its way around the surface.

Thirty more minutes.

He could do it.

They were having another one of their standoffs. Diesel was in his corner, refusing to acknowledge anything that was said. And Dr. Bloom, sitting there motionless, patiently waiting for him to answer her question.

"Mr. Pratt?" she asked, tilting her head slightly to the right while keeping her hands folded neatly in her lap.

"Huh?" Diesel asked, as if he hadn't heard her ask the question three fucking times.

"Do you feel that you are worthy of love?"

And there it was. Time number four.

Sliding his gaze across the room, he shook his head

slowly. "That's a stupid question to ask. What do I give a shit what other people think?"

"I didn't ask you if you cared what other people thought about you. I asked you if you felt that you were worthy of love?" Again, with the tilting of the head. What the fuck was her damage? Did she have an inner ear problem? Was she going to fall over the moment she stood and tried to walk away?

Diesel smirked.

"Is something funny?"

"Nah, just thinking."

"Okay, let me ask you this. Do you believe that Matteo loves you?"

Diesel shrugged his shoulders. "Yeah, of course, he loves me. Just like he loves everyone else at *La Maison*."

"And whose idea was it to come to therapy?" Dr. Bloom asked.

"Matteo's."

"And why did you agree to come?"

Staring down at his fingers, he fidgeted with his palms, praying that the minutes would tick by faster.

"I agreed to come to therapy because I promised Matteo I would."

"And why did you promise him that?"

"Because I could see how much my actions were hurting him."

"So, you did it because of your love and respect for your boss, mentor, and friend."

"I guess." He shrugged. He hated speaking so openly with people.

Opening up only meant that people could see your vulnerabilities and use them against you.

Staring at the clock once more, he thought about Zero and how things had been going between them lately. Was it possible that the ex-Abercrombie model was falling for him? Or was the man simply being friendly, considering how often they worked closely together? These days, sex meant nothing. People hooked up with randos all the time. Hell, ninety percent of the homos in this world were all in open relationships. He really didn't get it. If he loved or cared for someone, there was no fucking way he was letting anybody stick their dick anywhere near his man.

Call him possessive. Call him jealous. He didn't care. When you were his guy (or girl), you belonged to him and only him. No fucking way was he letting his partner go around sucking other people's dicks and shit.

Then a thought occurred to him.

"What does it mean when someone sacrifices their plans to stay home and take care of you while you're sick?" He glanced over at the doc, hoping she wouldn't look too deep into that question.

Of course she did.

"Well, it could mean a lot of things. I guess it depends on the circumstances and the relationship between the two people."

"Say you don't like each other?" Diesel asked, regretting

having asked the question. He was suddenly afraid of what she might say.

The doctor shook her head gently. "No. If a person sticks around to take care of someone, especially when they're all gross and helpless, that is usually a strong indicator that they care for the person."

Butterflies began to take flight in his belly.

What was he? A sixteen-year-old girl? Butterflies? Really? Get a grip. He's a dude. With a dick.

A very nice dick.

And a very nice backside.

Don't forget his sweetness?

And the fact that he cuddles like a champ!

Where the fuck were all these voices coming from? Usually, they just told him how fucking stupid he was being and to go fuck himself, but today they were all ganging up on him, telling him how fucking awesome the guy was and how the man could literally walk on water!

Okay, maybe that was an exaggeration.

"You're smiling." A voice broke through the inner monologue his personalities seem to be having.

"Huh?" Diesel asked, locking eyes with the woman once again.

"Just now. Whatever was going on inside that head of yours had you smiling like I've never seen before. Actually, it was quite frightening. I thought you were about to have a nervous break or something." Her lips turned upward, giving him a playful smile.

Diesel chuckled. He could see why all the other guys at the house liked Dr. Bloom.

"Sure, whatever," Diesel responded, fearing that he might be giving himself away. He turned his attention back toward the window, hoping that she would move on from her inquisition.

"Was it this person? The one who took care of you while you were sick?"

Diesel's eyes dropped to his fingers as his cheeks flushed.

How will you get better if you don't open up? that pesky voice inside his head whispered.

He gave a slight nod with his head.

"His name is Zero, and he's working with us here in London."

Dr. Bloom leaned back in her chair and crossed her fingers under her chin. She appeared to be studying him. Probably reading his body language to figure out if he was being serious or just goofing around.

"I think this young man might be good for you. Clearly, you two have formed some sort of bond and attachment."

If only she knew.

"So, I think you should continue to explore this newfound friendship and see where it leads. The worst that can happen is that this experience has taught you how to smile, no matter how terrifying it is."

Diesel couldn't help but chuckle. *Fuck, this woman was hilarious.*

32

ZERO

Rubbing his eyes with his thumb and index finger, Zero still didn't like what he was seeing. There were too many unknown variables. He didn't like working a job without having all the information he needed.

Even when pulling cons, he always did his research. The area he chose, the flow of traffic, location of exits, whether or not there was police presence, who were his intended targets? The more he knew, the better his chances of success.

Hey, perhaps that's why Marc chose him to be part of his team.

"I still don't like this," Zero said, folding the large floor plans he had been studying for the past hour. "There are too many things we don't know about this job."

Next to him, Jared picked up the floor plans and began scanning them himself like he hadn't been for the past twenty minutes already.

"It is what it is. When I was in the army, we had to go

into buildings and compounds without all the information as well. You do the best that you can with the information that you have. And you need to be able to adapt to the situation as quickly as possible."

"You were in the army?" Zero asked, surprised by this little tidbit of information.

Jared's eyebrows scrunched together as if deep in thought. "Uh-huh. Was kicked out after a few years. Was having difficulty... coping with the environment."

That was code for *pulled out before he went all loco on everyone and started doing things the British frowned upon.* Zero knew better than to continue asking questions.

"Sorry to hear that," Zero responded. "I can't imagine being in a war."

Jared's lips thinned, and his jaw tightened. "I went to some scary dark places when I was released. But Matteo found me and helped me work through some of my darker issues. The man literally saved my life. And now, I have my boy, Isaac, to comfort me and hold me when I have one of my nightmares. That man really is the sweetest."

Zero leaned back on the couch and placed his foot up on the edge of the coffee table.

"You're lucky to have so many people who care about you."

Jared placed the floor plan back down on the table and turned to face him. "Yeah, I really lucked out meeting Matteo and the guys. I couldn't ask for a better family."

The front door jerked open seconds before Diesel's face appeared in the living room doorway.

"Oh, hey, guys. What are you up to?" Diesel asked as he toed off his shoes and took a step into the room.

"Not much. Just trying to come up with a plan for this party the doc's got going on this weekend," Jared answered.

"Any luck?"

"Not yet. Too many unknowns for my liking," Zero answered, running his gaze over Diesel's body.

The man was tall and lean, not in that bodybuilder, hit the gym six days a week type of way, but in an *I keep active to stay in shape* kind of way.

He still wore his black sweater—even though it was fucking hot outside—but at least his hoodie was down around his shoulders, which meant that Diesel was feeling uncomfortable or didn't want to be engaged. So it appeared that Diesel was in a half-decent mood this morning.

Good-mood Diesel was much more pleasant than *stormy-cloud Diesel*. While both were fun to be around, Zero much preferred *good-mood Diesel*—that one gave him blow jobs.

"Well, you guys will figure it out. You're both smart blokes."

Was that a compliment?

"Thanks, man," Jared responded, kicking back his legs and placing his feet on the coffee table as well. "Where have you been?"

Diesel shrugged. "Had my appointment with the head shrink, then stopped for a bite to eat. Here," Diesel said, tossing a brown paper bag to Zero.

"What's this?" Zero asked, opening the bag and pulling out a sandwich.

"Tuna and cucumber. I bought three sandwiches, ate two and didn't want the third. I'm going to go shower." He turned and jogged up the stairs.

"Mmm, my favorite." Zero moaned to himself as he turned the sandwich over in his hands.

"Want half?" Zero asked, turning to face a smirking Jared. "What?"

"Nothing," Jared answered in that teasing tone of his.

"What's with the *jackass* face?"

"Man, you really are dense," Jared said, sitting up and grabbing the floor plan once again.

Zero was so confused. "I don't get it?"

Jared chuckled. "Diesel hates tuna. There's no way he would have bought himself that sandwich if he wasn't intending on giving it to you."

Glancing down at the sandwich, Zero tried to remember if he had ever seen Diesel eating tuna before. Had he ever mentioned to Diesel that he loved tuna and cucumber sandwiches?

Pulling back the wrapper, he opened one half. "Well, that was really nice of him. You sure you don't want some?"

"No thanks." Jared paused and turned his gaze toward him. "You do realize what this means, right?"

Zero shrugged, not sure where Jared was going with his train of thought.

"Diesel buying something for someone else is huge."

"It's just a sandwich," Zero noted, taking a bite and watching Jared's face contort into something that resembled a parent who just realized that their child does not know what a rotary telephone is.

"No. You don't get it. Diesel is one of the most selfish people I know. He doesn't think about anyone but himself."

"He cares about you and the guys at the club," Zero added, finding it really hard to believe that Diesel was that much of an asshole. Yes, he had first-hand experience with that selfish douchebag side Jared was talking about, but the man wasn't all bad all the time.

"Yes, Diesel is nice to me and the other guys, but with people he doesn't know and people he doesn't care about, he is the biggest prick you'll ever meet. His buying you a sandwich is the equivalent of him buying you a commitment ring. It means that he likes you and that he trusts you." Jared smirked and leaned back in his spot. "Guess you're one of us now."

Like? Trust? Was Diesel really warming up to him in such a way?

A small smile tugged at his lips. Perhaps he really was worming his way into the little prick's heart.

He took a bite of his sandwich and let that gooey feeling spread throughout his belly.

Diesel... liking him.

Who would have thought?

Then a thought came to him. He turned toward Jared, hoping he was doing the right thing.

"Do you mind covering for me tonight?"

"Sure thing, man. Why? What are you up to?" Jared asked, eyes asking for confirmation for what he suspected.

"Just something I want to check out." Zero hopped up from the couch, ignoring the cocky smirk Jared had plastered to his face, and bounded up the stairs.

The shower was already running in the bathroom that they shared. Zero gave a knock, hoping Diesel's mood hadn't soured in the ten minutes since he had last seen him.

"Yeah?" Diesel's voice called from behind the closed door.

Zero tried the knob, and to his surprise, it turned. He pushed open the door just a crack.

"D? Can I come in for a sec?"

Diesel's half-shampooed head popped out of the side of the shower curtain. "Yeah, man. What's up?"

He looked worried and concerned, and why wouldn't he? Zero was asking him something that was so urgent, it couldn't wait until after he finished his shower.

Zero felt like an idiot. Why hadn't he waited a few minutes until the man was at least done showering and not standing naked behind a thin layer of plastic?

"I... uh..." Well, this was not off to a good start. "Well, I was wondering."

Get it out, Casanova. Since when did you forget how to English?

Diesel's worried brown eyes locked onto him, making him feel nervous for the first time since they had met.

Why was he nervous? He'd spoken to Diesel a thousand times over the past few weeks. *What the hell was so different about this time?*

This time, you're leaving yourself open to rejection.

Would he get rejected?

Shit. Was this a bad idea? What if Diesel said no? Would their friendship—if that's what you could call two people who enjoyed hanging out together and fucking—get ruined?

"What is it, dude? You look like you're ready to shit a brick," Diesel said with a chuckle.

That relaxed Zero's nerves just a bit.

"Well, there is a fair that just opened in the lower part of the town, and I thought you and I could go check it out tonight. Just the two of us."

Diesel's smile slowly shrank, making Zero wonder if asking Diesel out on a date was such a good idea after all.

"If not, it's cool as well," Zero quickly added. "I can see if one of the other guys wants to go with me some other time." No, he wouldn't. This was his way of trying to take back what he said without it seeming too obvious that he had been asking Diesel out on a date.

Something akin to panic and a bit of confusion quickly cut across Diesel's face.

"No. No. I... yeah, umm, that sounds like fun." Diesel's face seemed to relax, taking on a bit of an unsure look before sliding into a bashful smile. "Tonight. Me and you."

"You sure?"

Now Zero was worried that Diesel was only agreeing to go out with him just to avoid making things awkward between them.

Fuck.

This had been a bad idea.

"Yeah, man." Diesel shot him a more confident, cocky

smile. "I want to see if you got game outside the bedroom as well." He gave Zero a wink which instantly released the butterflies from his stomach and went straight to his dick.

Zero couldn't help but smile. *Thank fuck.*

"If you're a good boy, I might even buy you a hotdog and cotton candy," Zero responded, gaining back some of his confidence and swagger.

"I'm more into the sausage than a hotdog. A bigger piece of meat to fill my mouth."

Fuck. That was a hot image.

Chuckling, Zero pulled the door closed and rested his head against the surface. *Fuck.* He hoped tonight went well. He was really starting to like the selfish little prick, and if Diesel was starting to feel the same way...

He really wasn't sure what that would mean, but for some reason, he really wanted to find out.

33

DIESEL

They decided to take a cab down to the fair. This way, they could both have a few drinks and not have to worry about who would be driving home.

Feeling a tad nervous, Diesel snuck in a few shots of tequila before he left his room for their... date? Yes, he was one of those guys who kept booze hidden in his bedroom. He liked a drink every now and then. There was nothing wrong with drinking alone, in your bedroom, late at night. It was one of his vices, and fuck anyone who tried to judge him for being who he was.

These days, booze was the only thing he kept hidden away in his bedroom. Following his last drug-induced bender, Matteo had the cleaning staff do a deep clean of his bedroom, clearing out all the drugs, pills, and paraphernalia they happened to find hidden in every little crevice.

And boy, were they thorough. Who knew the sweet little

cleaning ladies were so good at finding expertly hidden stashes? But in the end, they found every last reserve he had hidden around his fucking room.

Booze, on the one hand, was the one vice Diesel was allowed to keep. So long as he didn't let it lead him back to drugs. Matteo was closely monitoring that.

"So what do you want to do first?" Zero asked, purchasing two tickets from the lady at the booth.

The woman was dressed in a brightly colored outfit, complete with glittered eyelashes and techno-colored hair that stuck out at all angles. It was kind of like staring at a rainbow-haired porcupine.

The fair itself had been constructed on some cleared farmland about forty-five minutes away from where they were staying. There were rides, games, and food booths scattered throughout. Bulbs had been strung overhead to provide guests with a bit of light to help guide them around the fair.

For midweek, it wasn't too crowded. Diesel guessed the place would be packed come the weekend.

"Umm, how about we go check out a few of those games first?"

"Sweet! I'm awesome at anything that involves shooting."

"Good with a gun, are you?" Diesel asked, walking toward a booth where a little girl was shooting water at a clown's face. The hat on the clown slowly moved upward, steadily approaching the word "winner."

Zero gave him a smirk. "A while back, I used to run with

a crew whose one requirement was that you knew how to use a gun... just in case."

Diesel glanced up at Zero. He wasn't sure if he wanted to know, but the question was eating at him. "You ever killed a man?"

Shaking his head, Zero passed two pounds over to the gaming attendant. "No, I got out before I was ever asked to do something like that. I did put a man in the hospital once though."

Diesel sat down in front of the water gun and waited for Zero to take the seat right next to him.

"Did he deserve it?"

"No. No man ever deserves to be beaten the way that that man was." There appeared to be so much remorse in Zero's voice. He wondered what the whole story was.

Turning back to face his evil smiling clown, Diesel gripped the trigger and waited for the buzzer to go off, beginning their game.

"You'd be surprised," Diesel whispered under his breath, thinking about his mother and stepfather and how much he wanted them to pay for what they had done to him.

The buzzer sounded, and water began shooting out of the guns that they held, drowning the evil clowns where they stood taunting them.

Diesel glanced at Zero from the corner of his eye. He tried not to laugh at the look of concentration plastered on the man's face. With his tongue peeking out slightly from the side of his mouth, Zero's biceps flexed as he squeezed the trigger with all his might.

There was something innocent and sweet about the boyish look of excitement hidden under that veil of concentration. Zero really wanted to win this. It was cute.

Diesel lessened his grip on the trigger, causing the water pressure of his gun to reduce just enough to allow Zero to take the lead. He smiled to himself. He wanted to see that look of excitement when the retired *CK model* realized his goal and won the game.

Above them, a bell dinged, and lights began flashing over the top of Zero's creepy-ass clown face. And people claim that Bruno was creepy? He would rather face a thousand Brunos in a dark room than one creepy-ass wet clown face on its own.

Zero jumped from his seat victoriously, arms raised above his head.

"I won! I won!"

Yes, you won... Diesel forced the smile he felt to remain hidden beneath the surface.

"What do you want? Choose anything. Anything you like!" he heard Zero cheer.

Talk about an excited golden retriever. It appeared that the man had a competitive streak buried deep down... right next to his generous nature.

"What?" Diesel asked, turning to face the happy, gleaming man. He didn't think that the one-night stand would actually be giving him his hard-earned prize.

Could he really refer to Zero as a one-night stand any longer? They had fucked and exchanged orgasms—on multiple occasions, no less. That had to be breaking some kind of one-night-stand sex rule or something.

Had they now crossed over into "fuck buddy" territory?

"What prize do you want? Anything. Pick."

Diesel glanced at the man standing behind the counter gesturing toward the row of stuffed animals.

"But... you won. The prize is yours." He wasn't sure what the proper etiquette was. Should he take the man's offered prize? Was Zero just being polite? Would the dude get offended if he said no?

He kind of wanted the prize now that it was being offered. It was a sign of Zero's triumph but also a symbol of Zero's affection toward him.

"Yeah, and I won the game for you. So pick. Choose. What stuffed animal do you want?"

He won the game for *him*?

Butterflies took flight within Diesel's belly. No one had ever won anything for him before.

Turning back to the row of animals, he quickly skimmed over the selection.

"Umm, how about... the lion with the top hat?"

The man retrieved the prize, then passed it over to Diesel, who took it and stared into the plush animal's eyes. He tried not to tear up. He wasn't used to this kind of kindness from someone he barely knew.

"Great choice," Zero sang, slinging his arm over Diesel's shoulder and leading him toward a row of small boats floating in a makeshift canal of water.

"Hope you're not afraid of water," Zero hummed, holding Diesel's arm and helping him into one of the boats.

"Something tells me that if this boat capsizes, I'll be able to walk back to shore." He rolled his eyes and gave Zero a sarcastic grin.

As Diesel waited for Zero to step into the boat, he wondered how this carnival crew created a canal with water and erected this ride in so little time. The fair was only here for two weeks before it moved on to the next city.

The boat began moving, quickly disappearing into a tunnel of darkness. A gentle, cool breeze brushed against Diesel's face. They must be pumping air into the tunnel, perhaps to keep the machinery cool in the summer heat.

Their boat shifted in the dark, turning an unseen corner. A gasp escaped Diesel's lips as messages of love and hope glowed back at them against the dark backdrop. The tunnel was dimly lit, illuminated by white and pink string lights hanging from the ceiling and walls.

Great, they were in a love tunnel. How roman—

Diesel's heart stopped in his chest when Zero's hand slid over his and gripped it. The gesture was so sudden and gentle that it caught Diesel completely by surprise.

This really was a date.

Diesel swallowed hard.

"Umm, is this alright?" Zero asked, with a hint of insecurity slipping from his lips.

Diesel's eyes lowered to where their hands were connected and rested gently on the surface of his lap. It was sweet how shy and vulnerable Zero was being. He had to admit, he liked feeling special for once. Like someone didn't think that they were worthy enough to be holding his hand.

How could anyone not love that feeling?

Before he was able to chicken out, he covered both their hands with his other free hand.

"Yes, of course it is," Diesel responded.

His natural reaction was to respond with one of his witty, sarcastic comments, but now was not the time to be his usual jackass self. The man was showing his cards. Letting him peek behind the curtain and see what was really behind those guarded brown eyes.

Taking Diesel's hand was clearly something that Zero struggled with. And Diesel totally understood the feeling. It was hard to open up and let people in. Showing feelings left one vulnerable to either ridicule or being taken advantage of. Diesel knew those feelings all too well.

After the debacle with his family, he promised himself that he would never let anyone have power over him again. Even with Matteo, it took a long time to learn to trust and let the man in. It wasn't easy. Matteo worked his ass off to earn his trust and prove to him that he wasn't a threat. That he loved him and only wanted the best for him.

Was he really ready to let another person into his heart? Could he trust the man sitting next to him? He really wanted to. So far, Zero had shown nothing but admirable qualities in spite of all the bullshit Diesel had thrown at him.

Smiling, Zero began drawing circles on Diesel's hand with his thumb, a habit that Diesel was starting to really enjoy.

"So tell me about little Zero?" Diesel asked, leaning his body up against Zero's shoulder.

"My dick?" Zero choked. His voice raised loud enough to capture the attention of the couple in the boat a few feet in front of them.

Chuckling, Diesel shook his head. "No, you idiot. I meant little Zero, as in child Zero. What was it like growing up in the Zero household? Did you get along with your folks? Did you set fire to the family car?"

Zero's grip around Diesel's hand tightened. *Perhaps this wasn't the best conversation topic.*

"There's not much to tell. My father was a conman who used to rip people off for a living. He used to take me on jobs with him cus who would ever suspect that a man with a child would try and rip them off? And my mother? She left my dad and me when I was eleven. She went out to the video store, then never came back."

"Shit. I'm sorry. How do you know that your mother ran off?"

"She emptied all the cash my parents had been saving in a coffee can under the sink and took her toothbrush and makeup from the bathroom. People don't take that shit when they're planning on coming back home."

Feeling his pain, Diesel squeezed his hand a little harder, hoping to force all of his strength into the man sitting next to him. He didn't like seeing Zero down and wished that he could somehow absorb all of his pain and misery into himself.

Not caring what people thought, Diesel leaned his head

against Zero's shoulder. He couldn't help but grin when he felt tender lips press against his head.

Zero was a good man.

They had both been through some pretty rough times in their lives, but sitting here, floating through this dark, peaceful tunnel of love, Diesel couldn't think of a single hateful thing.

34

ZERO

There was something about holding Diesel's hand in the tunnel of love that set off a warm feeling in Zero's belly. It had been a long time since he had that feeling, that need to be close to someone, hold them and care for them, even if the person kept pushing him away.

He got it. He understood that Diesel had some major trust issues. He didn't know much about Diesel's history, but given that Diesel always met kindness with deep suspicion, he knew that the wounds ran deep.

But there was also a hint of gentleness buried deep within that facade of rudeness and selfishness. Every so often, he would get a glimpse of it.

Take the sandwich as an example. Diesel played it off as no big deal, as a simple gesture with no clear thought attached to it. But in actuality, the act was a glimpse into the man he kept hidden and safe behind a wall of indifference and mistrust. Just like Bruno, the barrier was meant to protect him. Keep his feelings and emotions away from those who might harm him.

The fact that Diesel listened, remembered that tuna and cucumber sandwiches were Zero's favorite, and then consciously decided to pick him up one just in case he was hungry, spoke volumes.

Yes, Diesel might act like a prick to the rest of the world, but like Jared said, it was only a way to protect himself.

Jared was right when he said that people had to earn Diesel's trust. He wasn't a man who let people in blindly. One had to prove their worth before he opened that door to them.

Zero hoped that, with time, he would earn that trust and confidence.

"Shall we?" Zero asked, nodding to the Ferris wheel turning behind him.

The sun had set hours ago. The fair was now ablaze with all the bright colors and lights that brought smiles to people's faces.

Behind him, the Ferris wheel danced, calling to all those who were brave enough to take a spin and lose themselves in the magic of the night.

"Sure..." Diesel whispered, staring up at the luminous structure.

There was something in his eyes. An uncertainty that didn't usually appear on a man normally so sure of himself.

Once they were locked in their seat, a strange look fell across Diesel's face.

Was he... scared?

Diesel's knuckles were white as he gripped the bar that sat across their lap.

"You're not afraid of heights, are you?" Zero finally asked, questioning whether he had unknowingly forced the poor guy to confront one of his worst fears.

"No. I... I've just never been on one of these things before," Diesel chattered between clenched teeth. "How high does it get?"

Zero looked around and up, shrugging his shoulders as he wasn't sure exactly how high they were off the ground.

"Not really sure. We're almost at the top, I guess."

"And then what happens?"

Wow, the poor guy sounded so nervous. He found it hard to believe that Diesel had never been on a Ferris wheel before.

"So when was the last time you were at a fair?" Zero asked, sliding his arm around the uncomfortable guy and pulling his body tight against his. Perhaps the feel of his body against his might help to relax him.

"Actually, I've never been," Diesel whispered. The tension in his body seemed to lessen the longer Zero held him close to his body.

Zero's head snapped up. "What? You've never been to a fair? Not even when you were a young boy?"

"Hey, my mother was poor and an alcoholic, and my stepfather was a mean old bastard who didn't give two shits about his kids."

"Oh, so you have siblings?" Zero asked, surprised by this

revelation. "I don't know why I always pictured you as an only child."

Diesel shrugged his shoulders.

"Yeah, my stepfather had a son a few years younger than me."

"That must have been cool having a sibling. I've always wanted one," Zero added, placing his other hand on Diesel's forearm.

"We never really got along."

"How about you and your mom? Were you two close?"

Zero felt Diesel's body begin to tense. It was hard to ignore the way his fingers gripped the bar and squeezed.

This wasn't fear. This was anger.

If the bar had been a throat, the person would be dead by now.

"It's hard to be close with someone who had you arrested for a crime you didn't commit." Diesel's eyes had darkened, and he stared out in front of them.

"Wait! What?" Zero asked, jerking his body forward so that he could turn to face the tattooed man sitting next to him.

The seat they were in swung forward against his sudden movement.

Zero stared into Diesel's sullen face.

He was shutting down again.

No, Zero wasn't going to let that happen. He needed to know. He leaned back and pulled Diesel in against his side once again. He began rubbing circles along the surface of his arm. The smooth touch seemed to calm him.

Slowly, color returned to Diesel's knuckles.

"Sorry, I shouldn't have reacted that way. Please, tell me. What did your mom do?"

The wind whipped against their skin as the wheel continued on its endless journey.

Shrugging his shoulders, Diesel took a deep breath and then proceeded to explain how his mother had betrayed him, allowing his stepfather to pin the robbery on him, causing him to go to jail for two years. It was during those two years that Diesel was introduced to the wonderful world of cocaine. By the time he got out, he was hooked and angry at the world.

"The day I was released, no one met me at the jail. So instead of heading back to that shit hole, I took the few belongings I had in my possession and hopped a bus to London. I was living on the streets for a year before Matteo found me and saved my life."

Zero couldn't believe the shit Diesel's family put him through. His mouth felt dry, and he never wanted to murder a family so badly before.

He pulled Diesel in against his body and rested his head against his.

"I'm so sorry that you went through all that. If I ever meet your folks, they'll be breathing through tubes."

He could almost feel Diesel smile at the threat to his parents' lives.

"If I ever see them again, they won't be breathing at all," Diesel added as well.

Lifting his head, they both locked eyes for what felt like

an eternity. Before he knew what he was doing, Zero leaned in, and their lips found each other.

Time fell away as the wheel continued to spin, and their tongues found themselves new homes.

35

ZERO

*I*t was just after two a.m. when Diesel and Zero finally returned home.

Trying not to wake anyone, Zero carefully unlocked the door and held it open for Diesel to enter.

"Sneaking in after curfew?" a strange voice asked through the darkness.

Diesel jumped back, getting tangled up in Zero's protective arms. Without thinking, Zero pulled Diesel behind him, taking a protective stance in front of him. He didn't realize what he was doing until it was too late.

"Glad to see you still got a set of balls on ya, kid."

The living room light came on, and Zero breathed out a sigh of relief.

"Jesus. You scared the shit out of us, boss. What the fuck are you doing here?"

Giving them both a heavy stare, Marc leaned back on the sofa and crossed one leg over his lap.

"I'm here to get this shit wrapped up. The case has been going on long enough." Marc's eyes shifted to the figure standing behind Zero. "Diesel, was it?"

Diesel stepped around Zero, straightening his hoodie and taking a lean against the wall. He nodded.

"Where are the other guys?" Zero asked, stepping into the living room and taking a seat in the armchair next to the sofa.

Marc was sitting on the couch in a pair of black boxer briefs and a sleeveless Deftones T-shirt. His jeans were folded neatly and resting on the edge of the coffee table, while a small decorative pillow sat at the end of the sofa.

"The muscle stripper boy is downstairs sleeping. Someone needs to tell that meathead that the floors in this place aren't that thick, especially when he's sex-videoing with his boyfriend. Lover? Whatever the fuck he has. Chase, on the other hand, is out meeting a contact to grab some surveillance equipment we'll need," Marc responded.

Diesel snort-chuckled.

It had been a few months since Zero had last seen Marc and his husband, Alex. Marc had recruited him about six months ago to assist Chase with running down the names listed in their *Book of Sin*.

If Marc was here, that meant that he wasn't happy with their progress. *Fuck.* Marc lived in the United States, Brooklyn, to be precise. And if he had come all the way to London... that wasn't a good sign.

"Hope we aren't dropping the case," Zero asked. If the

rumors about this guy were true, he wanted to nail this guy's fuckin' ass.

Marc's eyes narrowed. Sometimes, the guy gave off creepy serial-killer vibes. He was odd, mostly quiet, and only spoke when he really needed to. Most of the time, it was his chatterbox husband, Alex, who kept the airwaves flowing with chatter.

"Do you really think I would let that monster get away with what's he done?" Marc asked, looking at him like he was all kinds of stupid. "I'm here to make sure we nail his ass, then close this fucking case."

Zero nodded. He could live with that. Supposedly, Marc was some kind of genius when it came to strategizing and finding out information.

"You boys should go get some sleep. We got a long day ahead of ourselves tomorrow," Marc commented, glancing over at Diesel, who had already lost interest in the conversation.

The next morning, they all huddled in the living room while Marc played around on his tablet, eyebrows scrunching as he searched for something.

Zero sat in the armchair, popping grapes into his mouth, while Diesel sat with his back against the wall, munching on a roast beef sandwich.

"You boys want a drink?" Chase asked, walking into the room with Jared following behind.

"No thanks," they all mumbled, not bothering to even look up.

Chase plopped himself down on the sofa next to his boss, Marc, while Jared slid in next to his best friend, who was sitting on the floor.

Finally, Marc let out a breath before looking up from his tablet.

"Sorry, guys. If that television wasn't from the nineteen eighties and ready to die, I would have been able to cast my tablet onto the TV and walk you through my notes. So instead, you're all going to have to use your imagination and picture it with that special little brain of yours." Marc growled, seeming annoyed and not happy to be here.

Perhaps he just missed his husband, Alex? For the handful of times Zero had seen them both together, they always seemed attached at the hips.

No. More like he's pissed that you failed at your mission, and he had to come all the way to London to finish the job, that inner voice scolded.

Zero did feel like a failure. He was hired to help with his investigations, yet here he was, unable to take down one fucking awkward scientist.

"So, we know that there are multiple victims, all with similar backstories. They all woke up in various locations across London, each with bruises, cuts, and other sorts of lacerations, with no memory of where they had been or how they got their injuries. All they remember was attending some fancy party but don't remember where the party was or how they got there," Marc began. He swiped at the tablet with his finger. "Victims are both male and female, ranging in age from eighteen to twenty-eight. The only commonality between the victims is that they all like to party. Hard."

The room fell silent, with all eyes falling on Diesel.

"Kind of like you," Marc added.

Diesel's face flushed. "What do you mean, *kind of like me*?" He raised his hoodie, placing it over his head as he continued to glare at the man sitting on their couch.

Seeing Diesel raise his hoodie, Zero immediately knew what that meant—Diesel was uncomfortable with Marc's comment.

Marc wasn't exactly known for his tact. While being a little odd, he was always direct and wasn't afraid to call people out on their bullshit. After a night of drinking, Chase had told him once that Marc kidnapped a client just to prove the man wrong about his strength in security. Apparently, Marc also kidnapped his current husband... but that was a story for another time.

"The victims were all heavy drug and alcohol users, which is also why the police never took their claims seriously. Who would believe that a druggie was kidnapped or assaulted? The police just chalked it up to the victims got high, blacked out, then hurt themselves during their drug-induced hallucinations or shit."

"That's fucking bullshit." Diesel huffed. "The cops should take any complaint seriously, no matter who the person is."

Marc nodded in agreement. "I totally agree. Unfortunately, that's not the reality we live in. Addicts, prostitutes, and other socially disenfranchised individuals are often ignored or turned away because of people's biases and misconceptions." Marc looked back down at his tablet and swiped the surface once again. Apparently, that was enough on that topic for the morning.

"Now, Edwin's journal entry doesn't give us much more information. Just a few details on the doc, some information on his personality, and that he suspected the man of doping his victims and having them assaulted. He doesn't get into details regarding the type of assault or where these acts took place. Zero and Jared were able to snap a photo of an invitation to a private party. We believe that this might be the same party that the victims were all invited to. We will stake out the party and see what goes down. Hopefully, we get enough evidence to confirm our suspicions about the doc."

"And then what?" Jared asked, his hands folded neatly in his lap as he listened intently.

"Then we take him out." There was such coldness in Marc's voice. Like the act of taking someone's life meant nothing to the man.

Zero always knew that Marc was a little different, but was he secretly one of these super smart, high-functioning serial killers who had a basement or cabin full of body parts? *Was he even working for the right side?*

Shifting in his seat, Zero glanced over at Diesel, who was playing with the strings of his hoodie, while glaring at the grumbly American sitting on their couch. Perhaps now,

Diesel would understand what they all went through when dealing with his growly personality. Diesel wasn't exactly Mr. Sunshine.

Or perhaps he is conducting his own threat assessment to determine if the man leading this charge is a deranged psycho who suddenly appeared in their house uninvited.

He hoped Diesel realized that he wouldn't let anything bad happen to him while he was around.

Diesel's eyes shifted toward Zero, and the corner of his lips turned upward ever so slightly. The move was barely noticeable, but Zero noticed. He had been studying Diesel's face these past few weeks and had no trouble catching the slight changes in the sexy man's features.

Slowly, Diesel pulled down his hoodie, warming Zero's heart like never before. The man did trust him. He felt comfortable and safe and didn't need his comfort hoodie when Zero was around.

Somehow, he felt like he'd just won the moon.

Diesel turned his attention back to his sandwich and continued to enjoy his lunch, not giving a shit what the other guys were talking about.

36

DIESEL

The beep in Diesel's ear let him know that his comms had been activated. He shook his head briefly before turning to face his best friend, Jared.

"This is starting to become a way of life for us now," Diesel noted, giving his friend a smirk and a chuckle. "First Isaac's psycho brother, then Ares's crazy old-man stalker, now the mad doctor. Perhaps we should add super spy to our resumes as well."

"We're getting kinda good at this, right, brother?" Jared replied, throwing his arm over Diesel's shoulder.

"Thanks for coming with me to London, Jare. I know you must be missing Isaac like crazy." Diesel tilted his head toward his friend and gave him an appreciative nod.

"I love the little freak like no one else's business, but I've also got your back, bro. And right now, you needed me here by your side while you get your head right. Although, it appears that I might have been replaced by a certain *GQ* tradie beast of a man?" Jared gave him a smirk before leaning forward as if someone might overhear.

Diesel shook his head. "No idea what you're talking about, dude. Protein shakes are getting to your head."

Jared chuckled. "You forget, I know you, dude. You've been fucking your new flatmate on the regular, haven't you?"

Fuck best friends and their abilities to read you. Diesel let his smile attack his face.

"It's more than just the sex, Jare." He couldn't believe he was about to say this. "But I—"

"Hey, dudes? You're speaking over open comms." Zero's voice cut in right before Diesel was about to confess his feelings over an open airwave.

Fuck.

Diesel's heart stopped in his chest, and all the blood drained from his face. Who else was listening in on the comm?

"Shit. Sorry, dude." Jared rushed to apologize, turning beet red as he faced an angry Diesel.

"I'm not. Who would have guessed that deep inside that black hole of a chest, D has feelings and a heart?" Chase chimed in, chuckling uncontrollably.

Diesel's cheeks flushed red once again. He raised his hoodie over his head and glared at his best friend and betrayer.

Jared looked back at him with pain in his eyes. "Sorry, buddy, I didn't realize the comms were on."

Letting out his usual growl, Diesel turned his attention

back to the large metal door they were watching from across the street.

"Whatever. Let's just get back to watching this shit." *Fucking technology. It was good for nothing.*

"Yes, let's," Marc's voice sounded over the comms. He didn't seem too impressed by the topic of conversation.

Seriously. What was with this dude and his constant growly face? His husband was a fucking golden retriever, yet somehow fell in love with a broody panther. Love seriously made no sense.

Back to the door.

They had been huddled outside for the past two hours, first watching men dressed in tight suits and bow ties—looking like porno-grade waiters enter the building. Now they were watching middle-aged men enter with their dates, both male and female, clinging to their arms for dear life.

Marc had checked—the bar was owned by a numbered company, which meant shit to those who really wanted to know. Of course, whoever owned the bar would want to make it as difficult as possible to identify the nature of the business and ultimate beneficial ownership. Marc was pretty convinced that if he kept on pulling back the layers of ownership, he would eventually discover that the doctor owned or co-owned the club. He had tasked his husband with continuing his research.

For now, they relied on Jared's parabolic microphone, hoping to get close enough to pick up voices and sounds coming from inside the bar.

"This is bullshit. How are we supposed to figure

anything out when we have no idea what's going on inside?" Jared huffed in frustration. He dropped his butt onto the ledge of the building next to them.

"Maybe if you morons would shut the fuck up, we could hear what was being said," Marc barked into the comms.

Yeah, the guy was kind of a growly asshole when he wanted to be.

Jared was right. They were wasting this opportunity sitting out here hoping for scraps.

Across the street, Diesel watched as an older gentleman knocked on the door and whispered something to the bouncer before the two of them helped the older man's date into the bar.

Then it hit him.

"All of their dates are wasted. Probably high as fuck, which is why the victims don't remember how they got to the party," Diesel rushed, quickly scanning the street for oncoming traffic.

They had no idea how to gain access to the party. All they kept hearing were random passwords being given by the men approaching the door. Were these passwords then matched against a list of guest names?

Once again, there were too many unknowns.

"Shit. I think the emo stripper is right," Marc grumbled over the comms.

"Use your nice words, or I'm telling your husband, Marc," Chase warned, to Diesel's surprise.

Perhaps Chase really was one of them now.

"We gotta get inside that party." Diesel huffed.

"Yeah, but we have no way in," Zero jumped in.

"Over there. That's my ticket." Diesel pointed at a man helping a wasted dude out of his car. The car was parked in a dark, secluded lot around the corner from the bar.

"No, D, you're not—" Zero began.

Diesel wasn't listening. He didn't care what Zero or any of the others had to say. They needed to get into that party, and he was their best shot at getting in.

"Here, hold this," Diesel said to Jared, passing him his sweater before pulling a small bottle of whiskey out of their equipment bag—what was a stakeout without a little booze and snacks?

He took a swig of the whiskey before pouring a shit ton of it over his skintight tank top before tossing the closed bottle back in his bag.

Next, he reached into the side pocket and pulled out a tiny metal container from which he pulled out a pre-rolled joint. It was a little party favor that he had been saving for later on in the night when he and Jared got bored as fuck.

"D, what the heck are you doing?" Jared asked, watching him light up the end and take two quick tokes. He needed to look believable.

"Here, you can have the rest." He passed the joint to Jared, then took off jogging toward the man who had finally managed to get his date out of the car.

As he approached the man, he wondered if this was the smartest move. But they didn't have any other options. They needed to get inside that party.

"Hey, stud, how's it going?" Diesel asked, sneaking up

beside the man and slipping his arm through the man's left arm.

"What?" the man cried, startled. He stumbled under the weight of his date.

"Looks like your date is done for the night," Diesel said, brushing his firm body up against the man's. "How about you come party with me instead?"

The man looked between Diesel and his date. "No. Umm, my date is fine. He's just had a few too many to drink."

Judging by the fact that his date could barely stand up, he figured that his date had gone well past the limit for personal consent. Men... and women like this asshole were pigs. Taking advantage of people, especially when they were not in control of themselves, made him sick.

"Well, if your date is this drunk on their own, I'm pretty sure he'll be shit at sucking your dick for you later, dude. I, on the other hand," Diesel stepped out in front of the man, grabbing his own cock in the process, "can show you the night of your life."

The man licked his lips as he stared down at Diesel's rapidly thickening cock. Thank God for his ability to pop a boner in any given situation.

"Come on. How about we go do some lines, then you can suck on my hog until you bust a nut?"

Diesel wasn't used to having to work so hard to convince a guy to suck his dick. Maybe he really was losing his dick mojo.

The man's gaze slid up Diesel's lean frame before landing

on his bulge once again.

Smirking, the horny pig released his grip on his date, allowing the poor kid to fall to the ground with a disturbing grunt. The asshole didn't seem to care what became of the boy.

Thankfully, Chase and the other guys were watching, so they would be able to get this kid some help.

"Sure. Why not," the man said, wrapping his arm around Diesel and leading him toward the door to the private party.

This was it. The moment of truth. Would they be granted entrance into the club or rejected the moment they opened their mouth?

"Name?" the doorman asked.

"Mr. Yellow," the man replied, waiting as the doorman scanned the list of names on his clipboard.

Guests must use code names. That would make sense if they didn't want a record of their attendance at this party.

Tapping his finger on the name, the doorman looked up at them.

"Gotcha. You and your guest can go inside."

Diesel took a step to the side, pretending to be high and lose his balance. The man caught him and wrapped his arm around his waist.

"This way," he said before leading Diesel through the doors and into the darkness of the private club.

Inside, another host waited to greet them.

"Welcome, Mr. Yellow; how are you this evening?"

"Great, good. Where's my stuff?" the man asked, seeming

impatient with the interaction. Diesel wasn't sure what that was all about.

The man who greeted them gave him a smile before pulling a small baggy from his suit jacket and handing it to Mr. Yellow.

"If you don't mind," the man said.

"Yeh, no problem."

Diesel felt powerful hands grab him, then spin him around so that he was facing Mr. Yellow.

"Here, take this," Diesel's date growled, shoving a pill into Diesel's open hand.

"What is it?" he heard Zero's voice whisper in his ear. *Oh yeah, the guys were still listening in. His guardian angels.*

"What's with the red pill?" Diesel asked, hoping to answer Zero's question while getting an answer of his own.

"It's ecstasy. Don't worry. It's good. You'll like it," the rough man grumbled.

It wasn't ecstasy.

Diesel had taken many pills and snorted many powders; he knew when he was looking at ecstasy, and that right there was no fucking ecstasy.

"Don't take it," he heard Marc's voice say through his earpiece. "Ecstasy isn't red."

"No shit, Sherlock," he found himself saying out loud before he could stop himself.

"What did you say, boy?" the beastly man next to him asked, looking a little more than pissed off. "Just take the stupid pill, then we can go get you some more dope to sniff."

He wasn't sure what he should do. He knew better than

to take pills from someone he didn't know, but if he didn't take the pill, he was pretty sure that these guys were going to kick him out of the party and probably break a few of his fingers in the process.

Two other bouncers appeared in the wings, looking like they enjoyed eating puppies and souls for breakfast.

Shit, he better handle this now.

Hoping that he didn't die instantly, he popped the pill into his mouth and then swallowed. He wondered how long it would be before he entered another state of consciousness and began questioning his very own existence in this plane of reality.

"There. He took it. Happy now?" his date barked at their host.

The host glanced between Diesel and Mr. Yellow before reaching into his suit jacket and handing the man a beige envelope.

His date peeked inside, then glanced up at the man. "Pleasure doing business. See you again next month."

Again? Next month?

Diesel suddenly got a sinking feeling in his gut. What was going on here?

"Let's go grab a drink," Mr. Yellow barked before grabbing Diesel by the arm and yanking him into the dimly lit club.

They walked across the room and settled onto a rose-colored sofa with black trim and a small coffee table at their feet.

It appeared that they were in an underground lounge of

sorts. It was probably rented by gangsters and rich dudes hosting sex parties and private events they didn't want the general public to know about. The entrance they used was generic and undescriptive, giving nothing away about the happenings occurring just behind its doors.

"What do you see?" Zero's voice whispered into Diesel's ear.

How was he supposed to answer that question without raising suspicion or giving himself away?

"Wow, it's pretty crowded in here. Do all the guys who come in here have to bring a date?" Diesel asked, looking around the room at all the men dancing or making out with their half-conscious dates.

This whole place gave off a very molesty kind of vibe.

"Yeah, everyone brings a date. Most are useless and end up getting turned out by the end of the night."

"And the others?" Diesel asked. He wasn't sure that he wanted to know the answer.

A waiter appeared out of nowhere, dropping off a bottle of champagne in an ice bucket and two glasses.

"Is all this shit free?" Diesel asked, well aware that his "date" still hadn't answered his questions.

"Shut up and drink," Mr. Yellow ordered, pouring Diesel a glass and then passing it to him.

"Remind me to cut out this guy's tongue and shove it up his ass," Chase growled through the earpiece.

Diesel tried not to react to the joke. He lifted his flute and took a sip of his champagne.

Three tables over, Diesel spotted the doc checking on one

of the dates that a gentleman had brought. The girl was passed out, hunched over the table, lying in a puddle of spilled champagne.

"Wow, this place is wild. Half these people look stoned out of their minds." Diesel hoped the guys listening through his earpiece would put two and two together. "A few of them are even passed out."

The doc motioned to a bouncer who retrieved the young woman and carried her through a door at the back of the club. The gentleman she was with downed the last of his drink, then headed to the entrance Diesel and his date had just used to enter the club.

What the fuck was going on?

Slowly, Diesel's head began to feel funny—like he was sleepy and vibrating simultaneously. His palms began to sweat, and his vision began to blur.

"What's... what's... happ..." Diesel stood up, panicked, struggling to maintain his balance.

It was useless.

He fell to one knee, knocking over the bucket of ice in the process.

"Where do you think you're going?" a raspy voice asked in his ear.

Diesel turned his head slightly, trying to identify the owner of the voice, but his head was getting fuzzy and tingly.

"Out... heading... fresh... Zero." That was all he managed to get out before the world around him went black, and his body was suddenly swooped up from the floor beneath him.

Was he flying? Floating up to heaven to join all the other good little boys and girls?

His eyes felt so heavy. He needed some rest. Just a twenty-minute power nap... just enough to get him back on his feet.

The skin on his face felt cold, and a gentle breeze cut across his chest and arms.

His body was floating. Yes, he was floating down a long passageway on his way to see... What was he going to see?

"Stick him in the back with the others. Hurry, and grab the last one."

That was the last thing that Diesel heard before his mind and body got swallowed by the cold, empty dark.

37

ZERO

Somethings wrong! He could feel it in his bones. There was something in the way Diesel was slurring his words that made Zero begin to panic.

He had seen Diesel drunk before, even a tad high, given that he was supposed to be in recovery. But in all those times, he never heard Diesel talk like that.

"We need to get in there. Something's wrong!" Zero shouted from the back cab of the van they were in. "I know it. Something just isn't right."

"I know you're worried, but we need to give Diesel a bit of time to assess the situation before we go storming in and blow his cover," Marc said, turning his head back slightly. He was on his tablet searching for something.

They only got one chance at this. Zero knew the stakes at play. If they ran in and Diesel wasn't in trouble, that would blow their cover. But if Diesel was actually in trouble and Zero did nothing, he would never forgive himself. He

290

hated balancing risk when it came to someone he cared about.

"D? D? Can you hear me? Say something, dammit. Let us at least know that you can hear us," Zero shouted into his mic.

Still no response.

They could hear static and rustling, but that was it.

Zero didn't like this at all.

Had Diesel's earpiece stopped working?

"Someone's coming out," they heard Jared say over the comms.

Their heads snapped toward the door just in time to see Mr. Yellow, Diesel's date, step out. He walked over to the fence dividing the property and began to take a piss.

Where the fuck is Diesel?

"Zero?" Marc called in a stern voice from the front seat of the van. "Don't do anything until we know what happened to Diesel. His comms might have gone out, or perhaps he is in the bathroom taking a piss."

"Taking a piss?" Zero asked, shocked at the bullshit spilling from this man's mouth. "Were you listening to the same feed that I was? That didn't sound like a man who needed to take a piss. That sounded like a man who was on the verge of losing control."

"And if you're wrong? If Diesel is okay and just needed some more time? What then? We will have blown his cover and allowed a monster to walk free. I know it's tough, but you need to be patient and weigh the risks."

Zero didn't like any of what his boss was saying. If there

was one thing that he learned from all his years of pulling cons, it was to always follow your gut instinct. And right now, his gut was going haywire.

The asshole zipped up his fly, then checked the time on his watch. He scratched his ass, then pulled his cell phone out of his back pocket and made a call.

They all sat in silence, listening to Diesel's date call his drug dealer to see if he had any more product up for grabs.

"Okay, I'll see you in fifteen," Mr. Yellow said before ending the call and throwing his phone back into his back pocket.

He'd seen enough. No more wasting time.

"That's it," Zero growled, grabbing the gun from inside his duffel bag and pulling open the side door of the van.

"Where are you..." Chase shouted from the front seat, but Zero was already halfway across the parking lot, headed straight for Mr. Yellow.

"Zero, don't do anything stupid," he heard Marc say over his comms.

Stupid? Him? Never.

Zero reached the man just as he was fishing his keys out of his pocket.

"Where is he?" Zero shouted, punching the asshole right in the face.

The man fell backward, bouncing off the car next to him and landing on one knee.

"What?" the man squeaked, surprised and caught off guard. "Who the fu—" His sentence was cut off when Zero's leg connected with his gut.

The man let out a guttural *oof* that made even Zero's stomach clench in pain.

"Diesel? The man you went into the club with. Where is he?"

Terrified, bloodshot eyes stared up at Zero when the man suddenly realized that the tweaked-out little shit he had picked up in a dark parking lot actually belonged to some other crazed man.

"Shit. Uh—I didn't know. I thought he was single." The man shielded his face as if anticipating another kick to his person.

"Is he still inside? Why did you come out alone?" Zero's anger was taking on a life of its own. He had never felt this angry, this protective over somebody else before.

Footsteps behind him caught his attention, causing the beast inside him to take a step back. He was still there, but he was letting Zero remain in control... for the time being, that was.

Chase and Marc appeared a moment later next to Zero.

The asshole still hadn't answered his question.

"Diesel! Where is he?" Zero shouted, reaching down and yanking the man up to his feet with the strength of a thousand bodybuilders. If he hadn't been seeing red, he might have been impressed by his strength.

"Zero, shit. Calm down," Marc warned. At least he was smart enough not to get between Zero and his wrath.

"S-selected. He was selected," Mr. Yellow spat out, his teeth chattering as his eyes darted between the men surrounding him.

"What? What does that mean?" Zero asked, his grip on the man's shirt tightening with every second that passed.

"The doc. The doc took him. With the others. They were selected."

"Selected for what?" Zero asked again, frustrated. He turned to Marc, hoping that his boss might be able to translate this drunk man's gibberish.

"Perhaps if you put the man down, we can get some actual answers," Marc huffed out, his cold brown eyes burrowing into Zero's chest.

"Fuck, fine." Zero released the man, who was caught by Chase's arms seconds before his ass hit the ground.

"Now. Speak. What do you mean selected?" Marc asked, crossing his arms over his chest, waiting for the bumbling idiot to respond.

Mr. Yellow swallowed hard as he looked back and forth between the strange young men currently crowding him.

"The doc. He throws these parties once a month. He asks us to each bring one junkie, someone we find living on the streets, and he pays us each a thousand pounds and free booze for the night. Then the doc makes his rounds, deciding which junkies he will take with him when he leaves."

Zero's stomach dropped. "What do you mean 'when he leaves'?"

Mr. Yellow looked up at him with sad, concerned eyes.

"He's gone. He took his selection and left for the night."

Time stood still as the gravity of his words suddenly sunk in.

Diesel had been selected.

Diesel had been taken.

Diesel was going to become one of those victims.

Sound rushed back into Zero's ears as his brain and body came back online.

He charged toward the door of the club and began banging on it with the fury of a thousand suns. When the door finally slid open, Zero shoved his gun into the face of the poor unsuspecting doorman.

"If you know what's good for you, you'll let me in," Zero snarled. The man raised his hands in surrender and stepped out of his way.

Blood surging through his veins, Zero charged into the dimly lit room, past the host, who was hollering for him to stop. He dared anyone to try and stop him.

Standing in the middle of the room, Zero held up his gun and fired off a warning shot.

Those sober enough to realize what was happening let out a scream and ducked beneath their tables. That shot triggered a chain reaction.

Men with assault rifles stepped out of the shadows. They glared at Zero, apparently assessing the crazy man who had charged into their club armed with only a single handgun.

Okay, perhaps he didn't think this one totally through before charging in like a dramatic lunatic with a death wish.

But Diesel's life could be on the line.

Fuck this shit!

"D! Where are you?" Zero shouted, desperately scanning the room. His fingers shook as he moved the gun, pointing it at anyone or anything that moved.

"Where is he?" Zero shouted.

A lamp next to him exploded.

Startled, Zero's head whipped around in the direction of the bullet.

Four tables over, a gangster dressed in a black suit that barely contained his steroid-fueled arms held a gun pointed in his direction.

Next, a glass of wine exploded, followed by a pillow and a light overhead.

Man, these guys have bad aim, Zero thought to himself, not registering that perhaps he should fire back or duck behind something to keep from getting unalived.

Just as his mind raced to catch up with his need to survive, blood burst from the side of the steroid man's head. Zero watched as the man fell forward, mouth open as if ready to complain about the hole in his head.

What the?

Stepping into view, Chase gave Zero a friendly nod.

Good, at least someone had his back.

"Kill them!" a deep voice with a thick Russian accent shouted from across the room.

Glass shattered everywhere as the club became a war zone.

Jared grabbed Zero and pulled him down behind an overturned couch.

"Cover me," Jared shouted as he Rambo-style crawled across the floor before tuck-rolling behind a table.

Behind the table, a fight ensued. Shouting and smashing, Zero listened to the commotion as Jared fought an endless number of men, it seemed. Two shots rang out before silence fell behind the table.

"Don't worry. I'm fine," Jared huffed out before throwing his hand up behind the table, essentially signaling to all the bad guys in the room where he was currently hiding.

As expected, a lamp sitting on a table near Jared exploded.

"Shit," Jared squealed before lowering his hand and returning fire.

"Matteo is going to kill me if I return you back to him riddled with holes," Chase shouted at Jared from somewhere along the back wall.

"Isaac might have something to say about it. Can't say there's much boning going on when you're dead," Jared responded, blowing the nose off someone crawling across the floor.

"I hope that was a bad guy," Zero shouted, jumping up from his hiding place and shooting two more men standing off to the left.

"He looked sleazy and shifty. Not really the type of guy to be popular at an underground sex party," Jared shouted back, picking up a full bottle of champagne and whipping it at some angry-looking man gripping a gun. The man gave a grunt before grabbing the back of his head and falling down to his knees.

Bad men were dropping left and right, but there was still no sign of Diesel.

"Fuck!" Chase shouted, capturing Zero's attention

immediately. He was clinging to his arm as blood spread through his fingers.

Shit! He's been shot!

Just before Zero was about to hurdle a table to check on his boss and friend, a thick meaty arm wrapped itself around his throat, capturing him in a choke hold.

Fuck. Zero struggled against the man, holding him in a death grip. Stars flashed before his eyes as oxygen refused to enter his lungs.

Gritting his teeth, Zero jabbed his elbow into the man's side as hard as he could.

The man barely let out a grunt.

More stars.

What the fuck was this guy made of? Zero thought to himself as he stomped down on the foot of the beast currently clinging to him like a desperate ex-boyfriend trying to hold onto his man.

Nothing.

Just when Zero had decided that this was the moment he was going to die, warm wetness splashed across his cheek.

Zero barely had time to register the sound of a trigger being pulled behind him when his body was pulled to the floor under the weight of the dead man still clinging to him.

"Fuck! Did I get you?" Jared rushed, grabbing Zero by the arm and pulling him up from the floor. He desperately searched for injuries, yanking at his arms and grabbing his face with his hands. It was only then, that Zero glanced down at the man missing half his face.

"Damn, you totally exploded that dude's face," Zero noted, disgusted and impressed both at the same time.

"Yeah, well, I figured Diesel would kill me if I let his new favorite toy get killed." Jared smirked.

"I'm going to check the back," Zero said as he cocked his gun and ran off toward the back of the club.

He felt like he was outside his body. His ears felt like they were underwater, and men kept attacking him from all sides. He wasn't sure if it was his skills that kept him alive or if perhaps Chase was covering him as he ran across the room.

Miraculously, he made it to the long hallway leading to the bathrooms and the back door with superficial wounds and scrapes. He was pretty sure he would feel the pain tomorrow, but for now, his adrenaline was working overtime.

When he reached the back door, he was just about to shove it open when he noticed a metal door between the men's room and the back door.

It was an odd location for a door. Perhaps it was a storage closet. Perhaps it was another office. But something about the door screamed, "shady as fuck hidden escape."

Holding the gun at arm level, he pulled on the handle and was surprised when the damn thing moved!

After double-checking his surroundings to make sure no one was lurking in the shadows, he pulled open the door and gasped when he saw a set of stairs leading to the basement.

Now this was the part where he stupidly charged down the stairs, only to be met by a man in a ski mask holding a chainsaw.

What if Diesel is down there? that voice in the back of his mind asked, reminding him that he was supposed to be Diesel's knight in shining armor.

Fuck it. He pulled out his phone and used the flashlight to guide his way.

Once he reached the bottom of the stairs, he was met by a long hallway that disappeared into the darkness at the other end. There didn't appear to be any doors, so at least he didn't have to worry about any killer clowns jumping out at him.

Taking a deep breath, he began charging down the long hallway. Three minutes later, he pushed open the door at the end of the hallway and stepped out into a large, empty parking lot.

What the fuck?

He turned around and took in his surroundings. The lot was empty, save for two lamp posts that barely cast enough light for Zero to see across the street.

And there it was. About a block away, he could see the back entrance that they used to enter the club.

Zero let out a defeated breath.

Parked across the street from the club was the van that they had used to surveil the club.

Was this the lot that the doc had used to kidnap Diesel? Had the doc been aware that Chase and they were watching them from across the street? Jesus. Christ.

Zero's stomach dropped.

He started jogging back toward the van, anger building as he spotted Marc and Chase standing in front of the van discussing something.

"Where is he?" Zero growled at Marc, slamming his fist down on the hood of the van.

Had they gone in when Zero first wanted to, perhaps they could have saved Diesel. If anything happened to him, Marc and the guys were going to pay.

Glancing up at Zero from the corner of his eye, Marc barely acknowledged his presence.

"I asked you a question," Zero barked, not caring if the fucker fired him. This was Diesel's life. He needed to find him and protect him.

Fuck! Why did he waste so much time acting all coy and like he didn't give a shit about Diesel? So much wasted time. Now he might never get a chance to tell the cocky bastard how much he cared for him.

Another side-eye glance.

"Are you done being an asshole?" Marc asked, his hands resting on both sides of the tablet sitting on the van.

Zero glanced down at the lit-up screen.

"What's that?" Zero asked, sucking in a breath of air as he tried to regain control over his emotions. He needed a clear head. He needed to think.

"That's our guy," Marc said, pointing at the screen. A flashing red dot slowly made its way across a map of downtown London.

"What? What do you mean?" Zero gasped, turning the tablet toward himself to try and get a fix on Diesel's location. "I don't get it. How do you know that's him?"

Marc turned to face Chase. "Do you remember that watch Matteo gave Diesel before you guys left the mansion?"

Chase let out a sigh of relief.

"What? What watch?" Zero asked, confused and frustrated.

Marc turned back to Zero.

"Before these guys left the mansion, Matteo gave Diesel a watch with a hidden GPS locator in it. He was worried that Diesel might go on another bender and run off. With this watch, Matteo could track his movements."

"You tagged the guy?" Zero asked, shocked and kind of happy as fuck.

"We like to think of it as showing we care," Chase added, shrugging his shoulders, not seeming offended in the slightest.

"It wasn't until after I finished interrogating Mr. Yellow that I remembered Diesel had been wearing that watch. Then it was just a matter of logging into my app."

Zero was impressed.

He took a step closer to examine something on Marc's cheek.

"Is that... blood?" Zero asked, swiping the crimson fluid from the man's face before wiping it against the back of his jeans. Yup, definitely blood.

Marc shrugged his shoulders. "Hey, we needed answers, and we didn't have a lot of time. I used the quick method."

"What about the pill they had D take when he entered the club? Could that be harmful to him?" Chase asked, reloading his gun like he was heading back into war.

"That was one of the questions I had to ask our perverted friend. Apparently, the red pills are designer drugs that knock out the user, causing them to forget the past six hours. It's convenient when you don't want people remembering where they were or what they were doing. I have a feeling that was what the doc was picking up at that motel the other night. It isn't a drug that you can purchase over the counter."

"So where the fuck are they taking my best friend?" Jared asked, appearing out of nowhere. He squeezed in between Zero and Chase, craning his neck to see the tablet.

His hair was caked in blood, and he had a nasty cut running along his torso.

The important thing was that they all still had their limbs attached, and all were breathing—some heavier than others.

So where was Diesel?

That was the million-dollar question.

They turned back to the screen and watched as the red dot moved south across the London Orbital Motorway. The flashing stopped about eighty kilometers south of where they were currently standing.

"That's it! That's where they've taken him," Zero shouted, relieved and excited. They had a chance at getting him back!

The dot sat there for a few moments before starting to move once again. Chase and Zero exchanged a glance.

Where were they taking him?

They watched in confusion as the moving dot began to dim. *What the heck was happening?* Then it happened. The dot vanished from the screen.

"What the—" Zero gasped, his eyes bulging from his head. "What just happened?"

He snapped his head toward Marc, hoping for some sort of explanation. Marc was the one who created the damn thing, wasn't he?

Marc's eyebrows bunched together, clearly annoyed by whatever the disappearing red dot meant.

"My guess is that Diesel is now inside a lead container."

"What?" Zero screeched a little too high-pitched for even his own liking. "What do you mean 'in a lead container'?"

Was he being buried alive? Was he being trafficked across the border? Was he... He didn't want to think of what other horrifying situation could befall the man who he was falling madly in love with.

Glancing at his watch, Marc scrunched his face before turning his attention back to Zero.

"Judging by how the dot faded slowly before disappearing altogether, that would suggest that the signal was growing weak due to an interference. My guess is that they placed him inside something lead."

Zero couldn't believe this. How could they have lost him once again?

"Wh-why would you build a shitty-ass tracker that can be so easily blocked?" Zero was pissed. Marc was a smart guy; why would he build something so inferior?

Marc's deep-brown eyes darkened—the color in them faded until all that was left were two black orbs glaring back at him.

For the first time since meeting Marc, Zero actually feared for his safety. Sure, Marc had always kind of creeped him out in that sort of Norman Bates, still lives with his mother in a creepy motel kind of way. There was such darkness, such anger, trapped behind those blackened spheres.

They always say to watch out for the quiet ones; well, Marc was the king of the quiet ones.

"First off, that was a prototype that I gave Matteo to test out. Second, I built the device to monitor one's movements, not track a human trafficker and his gang of kidnappers!"

Zero swallowed hard. They couldn't give up. They needed to find Diesel.

"So what do we do? How do we find out where they've taken him?" Zero asked, rubbing his hand over his buzzed hair, hoping a genius idea would pop in his melon.

"We wait until the tracker comes back online. In the meantime, I'm going to see if I can hack into the traffic cams and try and find a location for our boy." Marc swiped his tablet from the hood of the car and made his way around to the passenger-side door. "Oh, and you might want to tell your daddy that his son has been kidnapped. I'm sure Matteo would want to know." Marc was speaking to Chase, no doubt glad that he was not the one to have to tell the big guy that one of his favorite boys had gone missing.

Zero looked at them all like they were crazy. There was no fucking way that he was going to sit around waiting for a tiny red dot to suddenly appear. Not when Diesel needed him.

38

DIESEL

A steady humming overhead brought Diesel's mind back into focus. His head hurt, and his body felt numb. There was a weird sense of sinking, as if his body was in quicksand, and there was nothing he could do to stop himself from being swallowed by the earth. Slowly, he tried to open his eyes.

The room around him was dim, save for the fluorescent lights that kept flickering overhead, providing just enough light to keep the darkness at bay.

A groan beside him made Diesel jump. His body jerked forward but was held in place by straps wrapped around his chest and thighs.

What the fuck?

Panic set in. He glanced to his left.

Beside him, a young woman, groggy and sweaty, was bound to a gurney. The woman let out a groan, eyes still shut but struggling to open just as he had moments before.

Heart pounding in his chest, Diesel glanced to his right. Another man lay strapped to a gurney. This one looked like it had been taken out of a 1980s Frankenstein movie. The side of the gurney was falling apart and looked like it might collapse at any moment.

The man next to him was staring at him, wide-eyed, with a look of fear and confusion on his face.

What was going on?

Diesel struggled against his binds, fear and panic taking hold. There was nothing worse than knowing that you were trapped and not in control. This was one of the reasons that he didn't like doing BDSM with guests. He didn't like giving up control and being at the mercy of someone else. He had trust issues at the best of times; he wasn't about to let some person tie him down and have his way with his junk. If a guest did ask him to partake in a little bondage, he always insisted that the guest be the one to be tied down. That was one of his hard and fast rules.

"What the fuck?" Diesel snapped, kicking and thrashing, trying to break free of his constraints.

"Wh-where am I?" someone to the right asked, his voice scared and shaky.

"Help! Someone, please! Let me go!" the woman to his left cried out.

Shifting himself, Diesel was able to glance around the room.

Three.

Three others were strapped to outdated hospital gurneys, each looking more wrecked than the last.

Where was he? The last thing Diesel remembered was chilling outside the club with Jared, watching the entrance to see who was going inside. He looked down at his arms, which had been strapped to the bars at the side of the bed.

What the fuck was going on?

"Please, help me! I don't want to die," the woman beside him cried in between sobs.

Die? They were going to die?

Panic flooded Diesel's veins as he struggled against the straps to try and free himself. He needed to escape. This was not how his life story was going to end. Tied to an ugly-ass gurney in a cold, dark room, surrounded by strung-out strangers.

"Argh!" They all groaned as the room was suddenly flooded with light.

"Calm your tits. No one's going to die... *yet*," an annoyed voice answered somewhere by their feet. "Welcome, everyone! I trust that you are well-rested and ready for our little adventure!"

Dr. Baasch walked into the center of the room, placed his hands in his dirty lab coat pockets, and smiled at everyone. His greeting was cold and gave everyone chills.

His left eye was a pale, dead blue, while his right eye was a serious, dark brown. His eyes moved together, but only the brown one registered any sight. Diesel had almost forgotten that the doctor only had one functioning eye. The doc refused to wear an eyepatch, Chase had explained to him one day, choosing to show everyone the cruelty and suffering that he had endured since his teens.

According to the doctor's medical files, he lost sight in his left eye when he was seventeen—a horrific act of violence placed upon him by his stepfather and a jug of bleach. Apparently, Diesel wasn't the only one with parents who were assholes.

"First off, I wanted to congratulate you all on being selected! You have all been given the honor of helping to shape mankind as well as providing some much-needed relief and entertainment!" Silent sobs continued as the mad doctor began his spiel. "My name is Dr. Baasch, and you, lucky participants, will be taking part in a little experiment that I have going on."

The doctor made his way around the room, caressing his patient's arms and faces as he passed them by.

Was he examining them? Or was he marveling at the torture that he was inflicting on all of his victims? Some people got off on pain, while others got off on fear. Others, however, got off on watching people suffer. The look of pure terror in their eyes was just enough to give these sick and twisted people mental boners where they stood. Was the doctor one of those people?

"I have two drugs that are currently being developed. Both have military applications, one as an interrogation drug, fueled by the individual's fears and paranoia, the other as a military stimulant, enhancing the individual's aggression and anger. Making them an unstoppable killer."

The room fell silent as they listened in horror at the speech being delivered.

"As many of you may know—or perhaps not—research

and development requires funding. Not many universities are willing to fund a project that can be used for such lethal purposes, so I've had to be... *creative*. What was my solution, you might ask?" His cold, dead eye scanned the faces of those around him.

He reminded Diesel of a demon sent from hell to check out the crop and see which bad seed deserved to bask in an eternity of torment. Diesel had done enough bad shit in his life. Perhaps this was his punishment for a life misled.

Was this how the Diesel Pratt story ends?

The doctor's hand rested on Diesel's bare foot. Like this last part was especially meant for him.

"How do I fund this little project?" the man asked once again as if leading to a dramatic buildup. "By broadcasting our little experiment to a select few billionaires who have a bit of a taste for pain and dismemberment." The doc clasped his hands over his mouth. "Oh, I'm sorry. I meant pain and *experiment*."

The sadistic grin plastered to the man's face told everyone that he had not misspoken. Pain and dismemberment were clearly part of their future.

"Each of you will be given one of the previously mentioned drugs and let loose in the woods surrounding this facility. Hundreds of cameras strategically placed will monitor your progress as you experience the effects of the drug in a highly charged environment. I will be recording the effects of the drugs while my viewers will be watching as you tear each other to pieces." An evil grin spread across the doctor's face. The man really was evil. "The last man... or woman… standing will be returned back to civilization marked as the clear winner of this challenge. Of course, none of you will remember any of this, so it's really pointless sharing any of this with you."

The other three let out terrified cries for help, twisting and turning and fighting against their binds.

Even if they did break free, did they really expect to leave the facility alive? Diesel got the sense that this was a one-way ticket to the man upstairs or, in his case, probably the man downstairs.

The doctor's eyes landed on Diesel. His eyebrows turned downward as if he were addressing an annoying pebble in his shoe.

"So, you must be Mr. Pratt," the man sneered, resting his hand on the bars at the side of the gurney.

Diesel glanced at the others, who were all staring at him with concerned eyes.

Guess he was the first to get axed from the program.

God, even his jokes were inappropriate.

"I heard there was a bit of trouble at the party after we left. Some friends of yours, I presume? One brutish man kept yelling your name." The man stared at Diesel like a vulture circling its prey. "Are they going to be a problem for me?"

This was the first time Diesel was getting such a close-up view of the doctor. He was a rough-looking man with a strong jaw and dark circles under his eyes. Zero had previously mentioned something about the doctor having German and French blood. His father was German, but his mother was French? Or something like that.

Diesel shrugged. "Why are you asking me? I have no idea who you're talking about or what just happened."

An evil smirk cut across the mad doctor's face. "We'll see about that. Guess we know what drug you'll be testing. Can't wait to see you grunt like a dog."

The man stepped away from Diesel, and four men, all dressed in white, stepped forward, each holding a needle in their hand.

Around the room, the other captives squirmed and began to cry out, begging for mercy and to be released. But not Diesel. He was too proud for that. Diesel would never give this asshole the pleasure of seeing him scared.

"Oh, and just in case any of you were thinking of escaping, good luck. We're surrounded by sixty kilometers of forest on either side of this private facility. Even if you do manage to escape, you'll never find your way out of the darkness... especially with your mind belonging to me." The doctor gave them all a sinister smile before breaking out in an evil-villain laugh.

Diesel watched as the doctor left the room without even bothering to give them one last glance. And why would he? They were nothing but lab rats being used to test out his new designer drugs and apparently provide live entertainment to a bunch of bored old rich people.

The woman beside Diesel screamed as one of the men pierced her arm with a needle.

This was it. This was how the Diesel Pratt story came to an end. Alone and in the most painful way imaginable.

It was too bad, really. He would have liked to have seen

what life could have been like having Zero by his side. As much as he hated to admit it, he was really falling hard for the annoying, washed-up CK model.

Yes, the man was arrogant and cocky and way too good for his own liking, but Zero also cared. He had a good heart, and most importantly, he saw Diesel. He understood and always encouraged him to be who he was. That was the type of man that you could be proud to have by your side. The type of man that you could spend your life loving and sharing life with.

Too bad he wasn't going to get the chance to see what could have been. No, this was how his life was always meant to turn out, it seemed. Alone. Sad. And always in darkness.

He couldn't say that he was surprised. He kind of always knew that this was how his life was going to end. No happily ever after, no loving family by his side. Just him, alone, high as fuck, and probably in as violent a way as possible.

Diesel felt a prick in his arm, and then his lids got heavy as the drug slowly entered his system.

It was strange how a drug could make you feel both cool and warm as it spread through your veins.

39

ZERO

*I*f there was one thing that Zero learned these past twenty-four hours, it was that Diesel's family—not his biological one—but his French stripper-club family was crazy. The whole lot of them.

The father, Matteo—the one who tracked his boy—was like some kind of mafioso godfather-type man who apparently lived in a castle and had a team of super assassins at his beck and call.

Ares, the godfather's "husband," who had also been shot by said husband, was apparently wanted by half the world's governments.

Then, of course, there were Diesel's so-called brothers. A pack of emotionally damaged guys who were also apparently undercover stripper-badass heroes who fought crime and rescued their siblings on weekends.

Chase was the unlucky person who got to call Matteo and inform him that one of his favorite sons, a so-called recovering drug addict, even though he didn't seem to be cutting back on all drugs, had been drugged and kidnapped by a deranged doctor who was in the process of transporting him and a few others back to his super-secret villain lair, way out in the middle of nowhere.

After what sounded like a million death threats and more swear words than a drunken sailor with Tourette's, the head of the naked crime family hopped onto his private jet with his stripper guild and league of super-secret assassin commandos and met Chase and crew at the airfield so that they could jump into a fleet of souped-up vans and hunt down and rescue the godfather's missing son.

He couldn't make this shit up even if he tried.

On the plus side, Diesel's tracker had come back online two hours ago and settled on a spot deep in a secluded forested area a few hours outside of London.

Working, yes. But that wasn't to say that the watch was not still working on Diesel's severed arm, which had been buried apart from the rest of his body. Just because the thing was working didn't guarantee that Diesel was alright.

Zero shook his head. What was wrong with him? The guy who he kind of, sort of, maybe perhaps kinda loved was being held captive by a crazy mad doctor guy.

"I fuckin' hate long-ass car rides," one of the guys from the super-secret assassin crew said as his body bounced up and down in sync with the bumps in the road.

They had left the pavement about twenty minutes ago and were now venturing through secondary roads that no doubt led to something evil and sinister.

For a bunch of badass meatheads, this one did a lot of whining and complaining.

"Have some vodka. It will toughen you up and put some hair on those raisins you call balls," Ares yammered, holding out a bottle of vodka he had been drinking.

The guy raised his middle finger as he leaned back against the wall in the back of the van. Ares returned the gesture with a smile. There were six of them huddled in the back of the van—three on one side, three sitting directly across.

Behind them were two other vans also containing a mixture of strippers and super-secret commandos who apparently ate nothing but protein shakes for every meal— the commandos, not the strippers. The strippers apparently ate veggies and cock, according to Levi, who was busy complaining that one of the commandos—a big burly Serbian named Vukan—smelled like fried liver and beans.

They were about thirty minutes away from their destination. They pulled over the vans and began getting themselves ready. They weren't sure what they were going to find, so it was safer if they got dressed, applied their camouflage, and loaded their weapons before they arrived.

The area they were headed to was private land owned by a private corporation Marc was still trying to understand. From what he had been able to gather, the company traded in new, cutting-edge drugs that were only now being approved for use in Europe and Asia. The company was small and relatively unknown, which only meant one thing... they wanted to keep the nature of their experiments a secret and avoid unnecessary attention.

The land that was owned by the mystery company had a large facility built in the center of a deeply wooded area. Land registries noted that the facility was built back in the seventies and used as a research facility, according to records.

Why had the doctor brought Diesel to a facility that was located well off the beaten path? Was he conducting illegal experiments? Ones he didn't want his regular employers finding out about?

"I hear you've been boning our brother," Levi noted as he and Isaac joined Zero, where he sat on a large rock, loading his gun.

Zero's eyes shifted between the two boys. He'd met them once before when they'd stopped by to surprise their boyfriends. They were nice enough to him. And Diesel seemed to really trust them. So what could it hurt to confirm their suspicions?

"Well, we have fucked around a few times, if you must know."

They both looked at each other before the one with the blue hair turned back to ask, "And what's your intention with D?"

"My intention? What are we, in the 1950s?" Zero asked with a smirk on his face. *Were these boys for real?*

They both exchanged glances once again, except this time, the one with the violet eyes decided to take the lead.

"Diesel might come off all tough and badass, but deep down, he's an emotional mess. He needs to be surrounded by people who will love him, support him, and always remind him that he is not alone. That he has people who love him and people who rely on him."

Zero knew exactly what they were talking about. He'd seen it a few times where Diesel pulled back and retreated into himself when he felt that he was not being heard or was made to feel uncomfortable. Zero never wanted him to feel that way again.

"These last few weeks have shown me how special Diesel really is. Just look at how many people have come along on this rescue mission. There wouldn't be this many people if the man weren't special. And as long as he is with me, he will always feel safe and protected," Zero said, eyes shifting between each of Diesel's so-called younger brothers.

"You should have seen the hell this guy rained down at that club the other night. Never seen so much carnage," Chase added, joining the group with Jared as well. "Any guy would be so lucky to have someone lose his shit like that when they're worried about them."

Zero's face heated. He hadn't really thought about it. He just ran into the club and began shooting any asshole holding a gun. He was seeing red and needed to find his guy.

Jared and the other boys smiled. He'd won the battle of the brothers.

"Now you just have to survive the meeting of the dads," Isaac joked, taking another sip of his whiskey.

Apparently, that was what Isaac did. Drink. Whiskey. And have video sex with his boyfriend.

Levi's eyes went wide while Chase suddenly found his shoes so interesting.

Meeting of the dads. How bad could that be?

40

ZERO

They cut the lights once they reached the beginning of the woods so that they could continue to drive undetected. It was dangerous. The night was dark, and the road ahead was barely visible. The only thing guiding them was the faint moonlight that cut through the trees and illuminated parts of their path. As long as they drove slowly and proceeded with caution, they might actually have a chance at making it through the woods unscathed.

"This is as far as we go," the burly man driving growled, setting the van in park and killing the engine.

Everyone jumped out of their vehicles, adjusted their tactical gear—or tight leather pants and crop top in Levi's case—then set along the dark path heading toward the mad doctor's facility.

This part of the operation was led by the league of super-secret assassin commandos. This was a team of eight highly trained ex-armed forces who moved in unison and smelled of protein. One choke hold by any of these guys, and your neck would be flatter than a French crepe at Sunday morning breakfast.

"Over there." Ares pointed to a large sewer grate hidden behind some overgrown bushes. It was well concealed and barely noticeable to the untrained eye.

During their extremely long car ride, Zero learned that in addition to being wanted by several governments worldwide, Ares was also a criminal mastermind, skilled in evasive tactics and traveling under the radar. The man made a great deal of his living smuggling guns and other contraband around the world.

Using hand signals, the *super commando SEAL team* disappeared into the sewer grate to do whatever it was that the testosterone-fueled steroid heads were tasked with doing.

The other, more sane group of people, as Zero liked to think of himself, continued making their way through the dark woods. According to Marc's intel, there was a building located about a kilometer from their current location.

Their current plan was simple. One team was going to locate Diesel and, hopefully, any other victims the mad doctor might be holding. Another team was going to locate the doctor and any other guilty parties. While a third team was going to locate any intel or useful information that could be used to further their cause.

The teams carefully moved through the trees, trying to remain silent and conscious of any traps or dangers too difficult to see in the dark. Throughout the area, torches glowed as if the inhabitants wanted to allow for some light. Was it to provide for safety? Or add to the terror of traveling through the darkness at night?

Zero placed his hand on the trunk of a tree for support as he checked something stuck to the bottom of his boot. A twig. Annoyed, he pulled the offending object from the ridges of his sole, then tossed it to the side so that no one else would step on the offending object.

When he moved his hand, he felt a warm, sticky residue on his fingers. Holding up his hand to one of the nearby torches, he examined the foreign substance.

What the fuck?

Thick red blood stained his fingers and his palm.

"Everything okay?" Ares asked, stopping the row of men who followed him. He glanced over his shoulder with interest.

"I don't know. It looks like blood," Zero answered, holding his fingers closer to the light, struggling to get a better look.

Jared and Chase stepped up next to him, leaning over his shoulder to get a better look for themselves.

"Perhaps it's animal blood?" Jared suggested, glancing over at Chase as he waited for confirmation.

Chase glanced up at Ares. "We need to keep moving. Now."

Jared's face said it all. He didn't like the concern in Chase's voice.

Nodding, Ares rounded up the troops once again and continued their march toward the research facility that was supposedly holding their friend captive.

What was Chase not saying? Chase had worked several years with the Toronto police force in Canada, so when something got him worried, Zero knew it was something serious.

Twenty minutes later, they arrived at a large concrete structure surrounded by a chain-link fence. A sign attached to the fence read "high voltage."

Zero's stomach sank. *How were they going to get around this little snag in their way?*

"I'm on it." Marc hurried to a junction box hidden behind some bushes and began playing around with the wiring. Next, he pulled out his tablet and began entering codes and strings of information Zero had no chance in hell of ever understanding.

"We're in," Marc whispered, shoving his tablet back inside his satchel, then joining Chase and the others near an opening in the fence they were making.

Silently, they squeezed through the cut fencing and moved across the grass, being careful to stick toward the shadows. Given that the facility was in the middle of nowhere, they figured that physical security probably wasn't high on their security list. A few surveillance cameras and a rotating guard or two were probably all this place needed. Marc had already taken care of the surveillance cameras. Now they just had to take care of however many guards there might be roaming the hallways.

The outside of the building was quiet, as if everyone inside had abandoned the place and gone home for the evening.

Zero didn't like it.

Something felt off. Just like that feeling he got when Diesel was in trouble at the club.

"Something doesn't feel right," Zero whispered, huddled behind Chase, who was trying to pick a lock to gain them access to the facility.

"Yeah, I know. It's never this easy. Even gangsters have more guards walking around than this place." Chase glanced around the space before making eye contact with his fiancé. "You better stick to my ass like glue in there," Chase warned.

Levi and Isaac had insisted on coming with them to rescue Diesel. They had spent the better part of two hours threatening their fiancés with castration, murder, and even calling off their weddings if they so much as tried to make them wait in the vans. But it was the threat of withholding sex that finally caused Chase and Jared to break and give in to their demands.

Matteo simply shook his head in disgust, reminding them that their fiancés had now identified their Achilles' heel and would never win another argument again in the future. The look of pure horror on their faces was priceless.

Zero envied the two couples. He wanted that type of love. That playful understanding and support for one another.

"And here I thought that I was the bossy bottom," Levi quipped, slipping past Zero and wrapping his arms around Chase's bulging bicep, tugging it close to him.

Chase rolled his eyes. "I need my arm back, love. People need killing, and someone needs saving."

With an annoyed huff, the violet-eyed dancer released his property and took a step back and out of the way.

With a flick of his wrist, the door unlocked. Chase pulled it open and peered inside.

Empty.

Just like the path they had taken up here, as well as the yard they had cut across.

Strange.

Zero watched as Chase slipped inside, followed by Levi, Matteo, Ares, Jared, the twins, Marc, and finally Zero coming up the rear.

The rest of the super-secret assassin command was off doing God knows what somewhere else on the compound. Zero still wasn't sure what their mission was, but Ares had given his second-in-command very specific instructions.

The inside of the facility resembled any other small laboratory. Hallways led to doors that were passcard-protected. Doors that were unlocked led to thick glass windows that peered out into rooms used for experiments.

"Watch your step," Chase warned Levi as he stepped through a glass door and into a decontamination chamber used to access the lab next door. "Only three are allowed in at a time."

Isaac, Jared, and Chase stepped into the chamber and waited for the door to close behind them before reaching for the latch on the connecting door. Chase gave a tug.

Locked.

Damnit.

"Come back through, and we can find another way

around," Zero suggested, turning to head back the way he came.

A click alerted them to the door being locked from the inside. Zero turned back to the chamber, where a terrified Levi was yanking on the latch of the door that they just walked through.

"It's locked!" he shouted, eyes wide as he banged his fist on the door.

A sinister chuckle seeped in through the overhead speakers strategically placed throughout the room.

"I thought I might run into you boys once again. That was you in my office a few weeks ago, rummaging through my things, wasn't it?"

Zero's head snapped around, searching for the source of their unseen observer. A tiny camera in the corner turned slightly and zoomed in on where Zero was standing.

"My name is Dr. Baasch, and welcome to my research facility."

The sound of the doctor's voice made Zero's skin crawl.

"Where's Diesel?" Zero shouted, looking directly into the camera.

More chuckling. "What, no introductions? How *rude*."

Marc yanked his tablet out of his bag and began typing in words and codes, doing his high-tech wizard thing.

"You know, one of the major concerns any research facility has is the introduction of viruses, bacteria, and other foreign agents into a sterile environment. Luckily, we have several of these nifty little decontamination chambers that help to fight against such risks and exposures."

Chase's eyes went wide when realization set in.

"Want to see how it works?" the voice boomed over the speakers.

"No! Wait!" Zero and the guys inside the chamber screamed.

"It's no trouble at all. It will only take a second to demonstrate," the doctor's voice hissed seconds before the nozzles overhead began spraying a slightly yellow liquid down on Chase, Levi, and Jared.

"Shit! Do something!" Zero yelled, rushing over to the decontamination door. He raised his gun and began shooting bullets into the reinforced glass.

"I'm on it!" Marc shouted, sweat dripping from his forehead.

Inside the chamber, Chase buried Levi's face into his chest, trying his best to shield his lover from the toxic liquid.

"Hurry!" Zero shouted to the sound of the doctor chuckling over the speakers.

Oh, this fucker was dead when he got his hands on him.

"There!" Marc cried just as the jets overhead came to a screeching halt. A second later, the door clicked, releasing the locking mechanism and freeing those trapped inside.

Chase, Levi, and Jared all spilled out, coughing and gasping as they tried to control their breathing.

"Hold still," the twins shouted in unison. They both reached into their backpacks and pulled out their water bottles.

"Shut your eyes," Gunnar ordered, popping the lid off

his bottle. Both he and his brother pointed their bottles at the trio and began spraying their faces and bodies.

Jared threw up an arm, demanding to know what the fuck they were doing.

"It's water. Water neutralizes everything!" Gunnar shouted.

"We're saving your life," Anders cried.

Coughing, Levi and Jared shook their heads. "Is that true?"

Zero shrugged as he helped the guys wipe their faces, hopefully removing any chemicals they may have been exposed to in the decontamination process. "I have no idea. But it's water, so can it really hurt?"

"I've seen it online." Anders huffed.

Wiping the water from his face, Jared glared up at his Scandinavian brothers. "Hey, if it's online, then you know it must be true."

Realizing that the guys were alright, Zero stood and glared up at the camera. "I'm coming for you, asshole."

"I'm counting on it," the doc sneered over the speakers. A door to the left clicked and slowly began to open.

Raising his gun, Zero began moving toward the open door.

Nothing said trap more than an unlocked door and the villain's invitation to enter. Yes, red flags were popping up everywhere.

"Step back," Chase said, sneaking up behind Zero and lobbing something into the hallway.

A loud bang filled their ears, followed by men screaming

and gunfire erupting. Chase peeked around the corner before diving into the hallway and opening fire on all those present.

Moans and shouts were followed by more gunfire and the sound of bodies falling to the floor with a disturbing thud.

The whole thing lasted two minutes but felt like twenty.

"It's safe to come out now," Chase teased from somewhere on the other side of the wall.

They all cautiously stepped into the hallway and took in all the carnage.

Wow, for one man, Chase really did have balls of steel.

"I've never found you more sexy," Levi whimpered, staring up at his man with the biggest heart-shaped eyes Zero had ever seen. "When we get home, I'm sitting on your face for at least an hour."

"Just an hour?" Chase chuckled, staring at his man like the boy hung the moon.

"Long enough for you to stretch out my hole before you abuse it for the next six," Levi returned.

"I should have brought a spray bottle," Marc groaned, rolling his eyes at the love fest exploding right before him. Zero got the sense that Marc wasn't always the most comfortable when it came to public displays of affection or dirty talk, apparently.

"Spray bottle?" Isaac asked next to Zero.

"Dog owners sometimes use them to get their pets to stop doing bad behavior," Zero clarified.

"Well, Levi does love doggy, so it seems appropriate," Isaac added, wincing when Levi punched his arm.

"Let's split up," Marc suggested, breaking them into

smaller groups and sending each group off in a separate direction.

Zero was partnered with Jared. *Go figure.* There was no way that Chase was letting Levi out of his sight. Especially not after their near-death experience.

The two rushed down a corridor, opening fire on anything that moved. More and more men kept popping up, shooting guns and trying to decapitate them with their knives and lead pipes.

Where were all these people hiding when they first arrived?

Rage surged through Zero as they approached a door marked "Communications." With Jared picking the lock, Zero stood guard with his back against the wall. His leg was cut, and his cheek was bleeding. He wasn't sure where he injured his leg, but he didn't have time to think about the pain.

Where the hell was Diesel? Was he still alive? Did he know that they were coming for him?

The lock clicked beneath Jared's fingers. It appeared that Jared and his brothers had more skills than just taking off their clothes and raising their legs above their heads.

"Do I want to know where you learned that?" Zero asked, not sure he wanted to know the answer. In his mind, the *stripper guild* were all angels who never did anything illegal or unsavory.

"Spent a few years in the British Army. I learned a lot of useful skills." There was something unsettling about the way his smile landed. Zero imagined it was probably how Hannibal Lecter looked when speaking directly with Clarice.

Carefully opening the door, Jared listened for any sounds of movement. Silence. But that didn't mean shit when being hunted.

Raising his finger, Zero began counting down from three. Right when he got down to one, an explosion went off inside the room, and gunfire erupted.

What the fuck?

Zero charged into the room, gun drawn and ready to fire. Standing in the center of the room, with his arm holding the doc in a choke hold, was Ares.

Bodies lay scattered and bleeding. One man held his arm, which was dangling at an unnatural angle. Next to him, Matteo stood holding a gun to the man's head.

"Move. I dare you to, asshole," Matteo growled.

Standing there in his tactical gear, perfectly sculpted hair, and shimmering blue eyes, Matteo was sex personified. It was as if the gods of sex and beauty had a child, gave him a loving personality with a dash of a hot temper, and then let him lose on humanity.

The human race stood no chance.

"Let me go, you piece of shit," the doctor spat out.

"Such language from someone who is supposed to be an upstanding member of society," Ares teased.

Zero was still confused as to what just happened.

"Where did you guys come from?" Zero asked, walking over to where the doctor was struggling against the growly-looking man.

"Up there," Ares said, nodding his head upward toward an open air vent dangling from the ceiling.

Perhaps now they could finally get some answers.

"Where's Diesel?" Zero asked, punching the doctor in the gut.

The man barely moved, still trapped in Ares's grip. He let out a laugh.

"That depends."

"Depends on what?" Zero shouted. He was tired of these games and attempts at stalling.

"Umm, guys? You need to see this," Jared called from behind Zero.

"What—" Zero shouted, spinning around and gasping when his eyes landed on the screens Jared was staring at.

The wall was filled with several screens monitoring different sections of the property. Each screen cycled through multiple shots and angles, all capturing different aspects of the area surrounding the facility.

In the center of the wall was one large screen with the word "live" pasted in the top right corner and the number 435 listed just below it.

Zero stepped forward, eyes wide with horror as he watched a man creep up behind a woman who appeared to be hiding behind the trunk of a tree, sobbing.

Zero watched as the number on the screen jumped from 435 to 438.

Were those the number of people watching this live stream?

"Watch this. This is always my favorite part," the doctor said from where he sat, sitting on a chair, gun pointed at his head.

They watched as the scared woman held up her hand in

front of her face, appearing to be transfixed by what she saw. She moved her hand back and forth, smiling as her hand appeared to comfort her.

"This is where the patient gets lost in their hallucination, forgetting that their life is in mortal danger," the doc added, seeming pleased with what he was witnessing.

Zero held his breath as he watched the man stalk toward the woman, his chest heaving as he raised a log above his head. Closing his eyes, Zero listened to the sound of the woman's skull cracking open as the man brought down the weapon in one fell swoop.

The room gasped as the woman's lifeless body fell to the ground, leg twitching as the nerves in her body continued to react.

"Beautiful, isn't it? Seeing how one drug can have a calming effect even when one's life is in imminent danger. The more powerful the hallucination, the more powerful the effects on the body. Can you imagine what that can do for military interrogations? Convincing your prisoner that they are in a safe environment, creating a world in which they feel comfortable enough to tell their enemies their secrets? Think about the power that drug could yield.

"Then, of course, you have the drug that heightens aggression. It dulls all sense of morality—that which makes us human by giving us a conscience—and brings forth the animalistic need to survive. The drug creates such intense fear that the patient becomes overly aggressive in an attempt to protect one's self, that basic need for self-preservation."

The doctor let out another laugh. "Want to know which drug I gave your little friend?"

Zero didn't care. Both drugs were dangerous and could bring about unspeakable horrors if Zero didn't find Diesel quickly.

Checking the rounds in his gun, he picked up a discarded gun and tucked it into the back of his jeans.

"I'm going after him," Zero announced.

"We'll see if there is some sort of a serum that might help counter the effects of the drug," Matteo responded.

Zero took a deep breath, then charged out of the room. He hoped that he wasn't too late.

41

DIESEL

"*F*ocus. You need to stay focused." He wasn't going to turn into a rabid dog and lose all self-control. He was a human being with decency and morals. Okay, some might argue that his morals were questionable, but murder was something he was strongly against.

Concentrate. Remain focused.

That was what he kept telling himself.

He hoped that he had the willpower. Self-control and willpower were not something that he was well known for. Anytime things got tough, he either ran away or gave into the easiest solution. Oftentimes, that easiest solution was drugs. Drugs took away all the pain. Drugs made everything feel better. Drugs always made him... forget.

That's it... relax. Give in. Why fight against all of that pain? You know it's only going to get worse, that pesky voice inside him urged.

He hated that voice sometimes. It always got him into trouble and always left him feeling alone and empty.

Seeing the others freak out and lose control had been terrifying. It was like watching someone flip a switch and suddenly transform into a mindless beast.

Two of them ran screaming in terror—off into the woods with no clear direction in sight.

Diesel and the guy with the crooked nose were given the other drug. The one that made people crazy and angry.

It started off with a bit of discomfort. His face began to flush, and his jaw began to tighten. Then came the feelings of sadness and depression. *Why was he all alone? Why had nobody come to rescue him? Because nobody cared. It was as simple as that.*

That was when he heard the laughing. Male and female voices all making fun of him and snickering at the fact that he didn't have any friends. No family to give a shit whether he lived or died. No boyfriend or girlfriend to wonder where he was or when he would be coming home. No... *nothing*.

That was when the rage began. That buildup started in his gut before rising through his veins. *He would make them all pay. All those who laughed. All those who thought he was worthless. Fuck them all. They were all going to die.*

With anger at his side and determination on his team, he set out into the woods to exact his revenge on all those who hurt him.

It didn't take him long to locate the redheaded guy. He was trying to climb a tree, screaming that the wolves were going to get him and that he needed to get as high as possible so that the beasts couldn't get to him.

Fucking idiot. The wolves were the least of his problems.

Grabbing the redheaded meth addict by his leg, Diesel tugged the tweaked-out fuck down to the ground and straddled his waist. It was so fucking easy. The guy weighed less than a baby koala and had no fucking hand-eye coordination.

Staring into the man's pale-blue eyes, Diesel wrapped his hands around his neck and slowly began to squeeze.

Feeling the man struggle beneath his weight, then clawing at Diesel's arms and chest, only fueled that burning rage, trying to make its escape. He continued to squeeze and watched as the life began to slip from the young man's eyes.

That feeling of power and control. Knowing that the fucker would never laugh at him again. All of it felt so good. So addictive.

And then what happens? When this man stops moving, and the light has been extinguished from his eyes. Then what? Do you think that M and any of the guys at home will ever forgive you? The voice was barely a whisper and sounded a million miles away, but it was just enough to cause him to loosen his grip, then eventually get off of the young man's thighs.

Gasping and sobbing, the man clutched his neck and ran off into the darkness, leaving Diesel alone with the echo of those words and the lingering ache he felt in his heart.

He wasn't an animal.

It was the drugs that were fucking with his mind. No one was laughing. No one was around.

He was alone. Always alone.

He needed to keep his mind focused.

Levi, Isaac, Jared, and the twins. Diesel took a breath in. Chase, Teo, Matteo, hell, even Ares—they all cared for him. *Focus on their voices, their laughter.*

Then another name formed on his lips... *Zero.*

His gentle brown eyes and soft, growly lips. His stupid jokes and quirky smile, and the way he took Diesel's hand when he needed comfort.

Zero was there. Alone in the dark. Keeping him company and reminding him that someone did care. Someone was fighting to get him back. Someone who would not leave him alone to get lost in his rage and become the one thing he feared the most—a mindless shell of rage and hatred.

No. He needed to focus. He needed to fight the effects of the drug.

Placing a hand on the wet dirt, he tried to lift himself up but was knocked back down by a bulldozer on two legs.

Gasping to suck air back into his lungs, Diesel stared up at the stars and wondered what the fuck had just plowed right into him.

Then it rammed him again.

Standing over top of him, the boy with jet-black hair and a mole just under his left eye socket picked up a thick branch and brought it down against Diesel's body as hard as he could.

Throwing his arms up in front of his face, Diesel tried to defend himself and block as many of the blows as he could. But the man's rage and power were too strong.

"I'm going to kill you!" the man shouted, spit flying from his mouth. "You're dead! Fucking dead! You shouldn't have stolen her from me! She was mine! She loved me! She was mine!" the man kept shouting.

Blood began to spill from the open wounds on Diesel's arms. The splinters from the wood cut deep, tearing open his flesh and bringing with it a new stinging sensation.

His attacker had now straddled him and had the advantage of weight and leverage.

"Stop! I—didn't... fuck!" Diesel couldn't get a word in. The pain was too great.

Give in. Let the beast take you. Rip out this fucking guy's throat. Feel his blood as it slides between your fingers... Come on. You know that he deserves it.

That voice was so seductive. So sweet and caring.

Around Diesel, the wind seemed to slow. That rage in his stomach was beginning to build once again. All he had to do was grab the man by the throat and dig his fingers into his flesh. Easy. His fingers would sink in like hot butter.

God, he loved the sound of that.

Eyes narrowing, Diesel reached up and managed to grab the man by the throat with his right hand. With his left, he grabbed hold of the man's branch mid-swing, cringing at the pain that shot through two of his fingers as the solid wood connected the wrong way.

But still, he had achieved his goal. He had the fucker by the throat.

Now, just... squeeze...

"Diesel, no!"

The sound was like a bullet ripping through his skull. It was both painful and alarming both at the same time.

He blinked a few times, causing his grip on the piece of wood to release and the chunk to come barreling down on his skull.

Lights flashed across his eyes seconds before the sound of a gun going off tore through the night sky.

"Argh!" His attacker growled before falling forward and rolling off of him.

Lost in the commotion, Diesel turned to see his attacker writhing around on the ground in pain. He was gripping his hand, which was sleek in his own blood.

Did the guy get his hand shot off? No, all four digits and thumb were still attached, but there was a nasty dark hole in the center of his hand.

The man with the bleeding hand snapped at them both before taking off into the darkness once again.

"D! Are you alright?" Zero's voice shouted, sounding far off in the distance. He felt like he was listening to the world around him while holding his breath underwater.

He felt his body lift and a strong pair of arms wrap themselves around him.

Who the fuck? Diesel's blood began to boil at the thought of someone touching him without his permission. *Whoever the fuck this was...*

"Are you alright?" the man asked, still gripping him in a bear hug.

Who was this fuck?

Unable to control his rage any longer, Diesel shoved the

man hard, causing him to stumble and slam his body into a tree right behind him.

"Don't ever touch me again, asshole!" Diesel barked, reaching down and picking up the log that his attacker had dropped.

That's right, teach this fucker a lesson. Who does he think he is? Going around copping feels whenever he damn well feels like it?

A shimmer of light caught Diesel's eye. Lying next to a bush was a large metal bear trap. Its teeth looked nice and sharp.

Think about how good that would look, attached to the pervert's face, that voice inside his head suggested.

Yes, he was right. It was like the trees were providing him with everything that he needed.

Dropping the log, he stumbled over to where the trap was lying. *This was going to be so epic.*

"D? D, it's me! Zero!"

Diesel's breath caught in his chest.

Zero?

Slowly he turned his head to where Zero lay bloody and huddled up against the tree. *What had he done?*

The pain and anguish came flooding toward him. *How could he?*

He touched you without asking. He grabbed you and tried to beat you into submission, that dark voice inside him said.

"D? It's me. Zero."

Squeezing his eyes shut, Diesel pounded his fists against his head.

Give in.

Fight it!

Just let go. He doesn't really care about you.

He loves you. He came here to rescue you. Are you really going to hurt the only man who ever truly understood you?

With tears flooding his eyes, Diesel turned to face his knight in shining armor.

"I... I can't..." he whimpered, struggling against the rage and feeling so fucking tired. He wasn't sure how much longer his mind could hold on.

Staring into Zero's pleading chestnut eyes, Diesel's heart broke.

Was he strong enough to resist the chemicals flowing through his veins?

It was getting harder and harder to tell what was real and what was a hallucination. Perhaps Zero wasn't even there? Staring up at him like he couldn't believe the monster he was seeing.

No matter whether the man before him was real or fake, there was no way in hell he was going to harm the only man who broke through his defenses and latched onto his heart.

Smiling down at that gorgeous washed-up underwear model's face, Diesel did the one thing he could think of to keep Zero safe.

"I love you," Diesel whispered before stepping into the bear trap and screaming when the sharp metal blades cut into his flesh.

The pain was excruciating.

Anger, rage, sorrow, love. All those emotions came rushing over him.

Staring up at the stars, his mind finally gave in to the rage that possessed him, but not before he saw Zero's loving face staring down at him.

Zero was safe.

42

DIESEL

*G*roaning, Diesel shifted slightly before pain shot up his leg, reminding him that he was injured and that his leg was fucked.

Okay, it wasn't fucked in the way that his life would be drastically changed or altered in any way—it was fucked as in he had to wear a bandage and get his wound cleaned every six to twelve hours. That, and the pain he was in, was excruciating, especially given that he was trying not to take any painkillers. It wasn't that he was addicted to them; he was just trying this new thing where he remained clean and sober... at least until after he recovered. Who knows, perhaps he will enjoy the mundane life and try making it a permanent thing.

He wasn't ready to make any commitments, but hey, you never knew.

Mmm. He could feel the saliva sliding down the side of

his open mouth and pooling on God knows what was pushed up against his face.

He was lying on his back, leg elevated, of course, while his body was curved slightly to the left, cuddling into a large, warm body pillow. One that came with extremely hard nipples and a sarcastic mouth that needed to be plugged at least twice a day whenever possible.

Slowly, he opened an eye and smiled. Lying peacefully next to him, mouth slightly open, was Zero. The man hadn't left his side since he was rescued from the mad doctor and his facility of drugged-up killers.

It had been three days since he and the others were rescued and the mad doctor arrested. Marc had given the drugs to a chemist friend of his who was able to break down the drugs and provide a detailed report about the effects of the drug on the body, including hallucinations and uncontrolled aggression. Seriously, it was a miracle that Diesel hadn't killed Zero or anyone else for that matter.

As it turned out, the winner of each competition was released back on the streets, having no memory of the ordeal or experiment that they had endured. The drug they were given at the party was administered to the participants every six hours to ensure that the winner had no memory of the ordeal they had survived once they were returned. Surviving the murders was the winner's award.

In addition to Dr. Baasch's arrest, Marc was able to pull the IP addresses of all the users who subscribed to the doctor's deranged broadcast. Interpol was currently working on issuing warrants for the arrests of all those individuals.

Sadly, there had been one victim, the woman who had been taken along with Diesel and his two male companions. Her body was recovered, and the police were currently searching the property for the bodies of other victims who had been kidnapped by the mad doctor. It was scary to think how close Diesel had come to becoming one of those markless graves.

Lying with his hand on Zero's bare chest, Diesel ran his fingers gently across his skin.

"Mmm, you can't do that," Zero groaned.

Diesel's eyebrows turned inward.

"Why? Too sleepy?" Since when was Zero not up for a little heavy petting?

"The kids are sleeping."

"What—" Diesel began before he felt something shift toward his foot.

His eyes darted downward to where a sleeping Levi was curled up like a poodle at the foot of their bed.

"What's he—" Another noise cut him off. This one was to the right side of his bed.

Lying in a semi-prone position, with his feet sprawled out over the edge, was Jared, curled up around Isaac, fast asleep. Jared's hand rested gently on the bed next to Diesel with his fingers gently resting on Diesel's side.

Raising his head slightly, Diesel was able to see over Zero's body, where Chase lay on his stomach, with the twins on either side of him, sprawled out on the floor.

"What the heck?" Diesel whispered, staring up into Zero's hypnotic eyes.

"They all wanted to sleep in here with you tonight. They tried to all crawl into bed, but I booted them out when one of them accidentally touched your injured leg. Levi threatened to cut off my balls if I tried to kick him out of bed. I think the guy is a little attached to you."

Diesel smiled. He and Levi had grown close over the years. They weren't best friends like Diesel and Jared or Levi and Isaac, but they had developed a sort of big brother protectiveness about each other.

Taking in all the sprawled-out bodies lying around the room, Diesel couldn't help but feel loved. These guys had risked their own lives to come and rescue him from the mad doctor and were now all camped out in his bedroom while he tried to recover from his near-death battle with a bear trap.

And if anyone asks, yes, having a set of razor-sharp metal teeth closing in around your leg is *very* painful.

Closing his eyes, Diesel rested his head against Zero's side once again.

"Argh, dude, your feet smell." José huffed from somewhere to their left. Even though José was one of Daddy M's newest strays, the Brazilian hunk was quick to join the family ranks.

"You wouldn't be able to smell them if you weren't sticking your nose up my ass," Isaac retorted.

Diesel and Zero began to chuckle, followed by a few others who were apparently awake as well.

The door to Diesel's bedroom creaked open slowly. "I'm telling you, I heard something. I'm just going to check on Diesel and make sure that he doesn't need anything."

"If he needs anything, it's a bit of personal space from you and the rest of your boys with separation issues," Ares growled, following at the heels of his husband.

Diesel let out a groan and tried to burrow his face further into Zero's side.

Zero chuckled. "Hey, that tickles."

"God, they're so embarrassing," Diesel mumbled someplace under Zero's chest muscle. Secretly, he loved knowing that everyone cared.

"See, I told you. Awake, just like I said," Matteo whispered once again as he stepped over arms and legs, making his way over to the bed.

"You guys seriously need to cut the apron strings," Jared mumbled, flipping over and giving the guys a face full of man-cheek.

"This coming from the guy who's practically holding his best friend's hand as he sleeps," Matteo commented, stopping next to Diesel's bed.

"He's got a point," Chase added.

"Worst sleepover ever," the twins groaned in unison.

"Shut your whining, or I'm sending you both back to your rooms," Matteo threatened.

Diesel opened one of his eyes, afraid of what he might see. Yup, there he was. Daddy M, standing next to his bed, with a huge fucking smile plastered to his face.

"God, creeper much?" Diesel groaned, secretly loving all the attention he was getting.

Sitting down on the bed next to him, Matteo began running his hand through Diesel's buzzed hair.

"How are you feeling?"

Turning to face the only real father he had ever known, Diesel gave the man a smile.

"Leg's still a bit sore, but it helps to know you guys are all close by," Diesel answered.

"God, when did our lives become a Hallmark movie?" Isaac groaned. "We work in a goddamn cock palace."

More laughter filled the room.

At this point, all the guys seemed to be awake.

"So, what? You and Daddy A couldn't find an empty spot on the floor?" Diesel teased, loving that everyone was choosing him for once.

Ares snorted. "Please, I had to threaten Daddy M with no dick for a month if he tried to squeeze into that space on your bed."

A black leather shoe went flying by Ares's head, ricocheting off the wall and landing with a loud *clap* on the floor by the door.

Ares looked stunned by the flying weapon. "Fucking Italians. So moody. So violent."

Matteo smirked. "One day, you'll learn to keep that dirty mouth of yours shut."

"And one day, you'll learn to stop trying to kill the one man who loves you," Ares shot back.

Diesel took hold of Matteo's hand and gave it a gentle squeeze. "Have you ever tried seeing a shrink for anger management? I know a great doctor who is very discreet, and she works wonders."

"Now, there's an idea!" Ares added before ducking and surviving the second attempt on his life.

"Okay, we'll let you boys get some sleep." Matteo leaned forward and gave Diesel a kiss on the forehead. "Sleep well, D."

"Night, Daddy M," the group announced in unison before following up with, "Night, Daddy A."

"God, this family is creepy," Ares grumbled before walking out of the room, abandoning his husband at the door.

Diesel just smiled. He loved this crazy and fucked-up family of his.

43

ZERO

One Year Later

"*J*ust shut up and stick it in!" Diesel huffed, sounding frustrated and annoyed.

Zero loved it when his boy got all impatient and needy for his dick. Given that the guy was always so cocky and selfish, it always made him feel so special knowing that the dude couldn't wait any longer to have his ass spread open by his delicious cock.

"Patience, dear. You don't want me shoving it in there before you are ready. I'm not exactly *average* size."

Zero tried not to laugh when Diesel's head whipped around and glared at him.

"And I'm not exactly a virgin. So less talking and more pounding." Diesel bent over further, gripping the shelving unit in front of him, causing his ass cheeks to spread open even wider.

Fuck, seeing that delicious ass of Diesel's on full display, eagerly waiting to be filled, was just too delicious.

Zero slapped his left ass cheek and watched as a bright-pink paw print slowly appeared on its surface. God. He still couldn't believe that this gorgeous ass, this sexy-as-sin man, was all his.

"Seriously, dude. If you don't shove your dick inside me, I'm going to go find one of the other guests to fuck me," Diesel growled, turning his head slightly, promising him an empty threat.

They both knew that Diesel's ass belonged to him. There was no other man or woman who got to touch any surface of Diesel's body. Just Zero. The same rules applied to him. Ever since they declared their undying love for each other—okay, it wasn't so Hallmark-y—more like Diesel strolled into their bedroom naked one night, grabbed Zero's junk in his hand, and declared, "This right here belongs to me. If anyone touches it, they die." Zero had never felt so loved.

"Like, fuck that's ever going to happen," Zero snarled, jamming his cock deep inside Diesel's tight hole and grabbing him around his body so that he couldn't run away.

Diesel gasped as his ass was suddenly invaded.

It only took a moment for Diesel's body to relax and for him to begin moving his ass back along Zero's length. Moaning, he began working his hips back and forth, taking in all of Zero's cock nice and deep.

"Fuck, I love that cock," Diesel whispered as he adjusted his grip on the shelving unit before him.

They were standing in a storage hut, another one of

Diesel's fantastic ideas. He did that a lot. Grab Zero by the hand and pull him into whatever available room or closet or bush he felt provided just enough privacy for them to get their fuck on.

Today's adventure? Levi and Isaac's destination wedding!

Yes, how many guys can say they fucked the best man in the storage closet during his boyfriend's brother's wedding?

Just beyond the door sat fifty of their closest friends and family, totally oblivious to the dicking down that was going on a short walk away.

Zero smirked. He loved how desperate his guy was for him and his dick. That, right there, was true love.

"Open that tight little ass for me," Zero whispered into Diesel's ear as he shoved his cock into Diesel's hole without mercy.

"It's all yours, stud. Fuck me so hard that I limp down the aisle."

"That will give your dads something to talk about," Zero grunted, tightening his grip around Diesel's hips and beginning his assault on Diesel's hole.

He loved it. Knowing that Diesel could take a beating and still want more was such a turn-on. Diesel was tough and mean and always open to trying new things. He wasn't afraid of getting hurt and didn't care what others thought of him. He was who he was, so the rest of the world could go fuck themselves.

God, he loved this man.

"Oh yeah, right there," Diesel groaned, reaching between his legs and gripping his cock. He began jerking his cock furiously. "More. Harder. Oh fuck! I'm so fucking close—"

Zero caught a glimpse of Bruno in a reflection of a tiny mirror that lay perched up against the wall. The fucking demon on Diesel's chest was staring at him. Peeking out from under Diesel's partially opened shirt—most likely judging him for giving his master pleasure. For replacing him as his protector and for loving his master just the way he had for all these long, lonely years.

He and Bruno had come to an understanding. So long as Zero worshiped and cherished Diesel's heart, Bruno would allow him access to Diesel's body, heart, and soul. Zero gladly accepted the arrangement. There was nothing more important to him in the world than Diesel and his heart.

"Can you guys hurry up and finish, Levi is throwing a hissy fit. He wants to get this show on the road so that he and Chase can consummate their marriage."

Diesel froze against Zero's body.

It was Gunnar. Or Anders. One of the twins. They sounded too much alike to ever be able to tell which one was which, especially through the privacy of a door. Well, somewhat private. Do you really have privacy when people on the other side of the door know that you're porking your boyfriend?

"Tell him to hold his horses. I'm getting my prostate massaged by my boyfriend's dick."

Diesel could be so crude at times.

Without missing a beat, Diesel resumed fucking himself on Zero's cock.

Gunnar/Anders chuckled as he walked away from the door.

"D, we need to... Oh, *fuck*, I'm gonna..." A second later, he was unloading into his condom, and Diesel was painting the shelving unit with his own cum.

Pulling off of Zero's dick, Diesel let out a satisfied sigh as he turned to smile at him.

"Man, that feels better." He pulled up his underwear and dress pants that had pooled around his ankles and began tucking in his shirt like he didn't just have his ass rammed and plowed. "Better get out there before Levi has a diva-sized meltdown."

Zero chuckled, tucking in his shirt and doing up his zipper as well.

Once they were all prim and proper and all evidence of their extra-curricular activities had been safely disposed of, they exited the hut and made their way along the stone path, heading toward the dock that led out onto the beach, where all of the guests and wedding party were waiting.

It was Levi and Isaac's joint wedding.

Of course the two best friends decided that they would both get married on the same day. Their husbands, Chase and Jared, had no say in the matter. Not that they were crazy enough to even try going against their lovers' wishes.

Jared smirked, clearly aware of what had just transpired. The twins nodded, similarly showing their support as Zero and Diesel approached.

"About fucking time," Levi huffed out, materializing beside them. "Hope you're still able to walk down the aisle because there's no way that I'm not having my best man standing up there beside me."

Diesel turned and adjusted Levi's collar and silk violet tie. He ran his hand down the front of Levi's suit, making sure that his little brother was perfect for his wedding.

"Don't worry about me. It's your twinky little ass that should be worried when Chase gets his hands on it tonight. I think this 'no sex the day before you guys get married' thing only made him hornier, and now I fear for your safety."

Levi smiled as heart-shaped eyes throbbed in his eye sockets.

"Yeah, the pain is going to be glorious."

All three laughed.

"Okay, I'll meet you at the front. Good luck, little bro." Diesel gave Levi a peck on the cheek before jogging down the aisle to stand next to Gunnar and Anders, who were both Isaac's best men—because, of course, you couldn't have one without the other.

"You better take your seat as well," Matteo said, approaching with Jared by his side.

Matteo was going to be walking both Levi and Isaac down the aisle since he was the closest thing they both had to a father. Levi had insisted that he walk them both down together, and Isaac basically followed suit because he was Levi's best friend.

"You both look amazing," Zero said, admiring Isaac's black-and-white, pin-striped Armani suit and Levi's black-and-purple Valentino.

With that, Zero made his way down the aisle and slid in next to Ares, Matteo's husband. In typical Ares fashion, he grunted and turned his attention back to the cuff links Matteo had, no doubt, forced him to wear.

The ceremony was beautiful. They exchanged vows during sunset on a private beach resort in Fiji. Matteo spared no expense when it came to the marriage of two of the boys he considered his sons.

Like a proud father, Matteo bragged to all of his guests about how happy he was that both his kids had found wonderful men.

Making the event even more special was the fact that two best friends, Levi and Isaac, were able to share their special day together, proving that the bonds we create are stronger than the bonds we are forced into by birth. While this large group of people may not share the same DNA or bloodline, they all came together and chose each other, creating a bond —a family—that was so much stronger than any of the ones that they had been born into.

Watching Diesel up on that altar, standing behind his little brother, supporting him and giving him the biggest smile Zero had ever seen, Zero knew that there was no other man whom he wanted to have by his side.

Diesel was his man. His person. Fate might have brought them together, but it was the love that they shared that kept them together.

Smiling, Zero felt a chill spill over him.

Feeling like he was being watched, he slowly turned to his

right, to where Matteo and Ares both sat next to him, staring at him like he was just about to run off with one of their children.

Well, he did just finish defiling their oldest in the tiny storage hut, not thirty minutes prior. *Could they smell Diesel's sweat on his body?*

"After this ceremony, the three of us are going to talk," Matteo said, eyes narrowing like he was trying to decide on where to dump his body.

"It's time we discussed what your intentions are with our boy and when you plan on making an honest man out of him," Ares added next to Matteo.

Zero swallowed hard. He was hoping that perhaps Diesel's dads had forgotten about this little rite of passage. It was so much scarier when it involved a gun trafficker who had no doubt murdered many men over his lifetime and the rich and powerful *GQ* model who has a reputation for making men disappear.

Fuck, he was so dead.

Turning back to face the ceremony, Diesel's smiling face locked on his.

In pure Diesel fashion, he ran his fingers slowly across his neck before gesturing to his dads sitting right next to him.

Yup, that last pounding in the hut might very well be the last time he ever sticks his dick inside that one-night stand who never left.

Pouting his lips toward Diesel, he gave him a long-distance kiss. Diesel's eyes softened as he took in the gesture.

Yes, the angry, chaotic mess that was Diesel Pratt was his. Always and forever. Till death do them part.

Turning slowly toward the men sitting next to him, he wondered how soon that death might come.

EPILOGUE
DIESEL

Stepping into the cool evening air, Diesel took in a breath and admired the beauty of the *Palais Garnier*. While Diesel would never admit such a thing to another living soul, he found it amazing that something so spectacular even existed.

Matteo continued his ritual of taking the guys out to the opera once a month or on special occasions if there was something that he really wanted to see. Sometimes, the guys went willingly, seeing it as an opportunity to get out of *La Maison* and enjoy some free food, music, and alcohol. Other times, it fell to Ares to perform his husbandly duties—okay, they weren't officially married, but they basically were husbands in every sense of the word, including being fathers to a mansion full of rowdy man-children—and accompany his love to the opera.

But Diesel never minded. He enjoyed stepping into the opulent opera house and admiring the sculptures and architecture. The level of detail applied to each surface, including banisters and staircases, was just incredible. Knowing all the painstakingly hard work that went into the building made the experience so much more powerful. It was like stepping into another time.

"So, how did you enjoy the opera?" Zero asked, stepping up beside him and slipping his hand into his.

They'd been officially dating now for just over a year, and things were still going hot and heavy. Zero basically moved into the mansion—into Diesel's room, to be precise—and they had been playing house for nearly nine months, it seemed. Diesel got the feeling that Zero was edging to pop the question, but he wasn't going to force anything out of him. Not until he was ready. He could be patient. He wasn't going anywhere.

As for dancing and playing with his wiener onstage in front of a sea of horny wealthy gentlemen, Diesel had asked to be taken off the roster. Instead, he decided to join the maintenance crew at *La Maison*, fixing things that needed repairing while still being able to remain close to his family. He still had breakfast with them every morning and even cheered on the boys when they put on a specialty show at the club.

Matteo understood Diesel's hesitance to continue dancing and was pleased to hear that he wanted to continue working and living at *La Maison*. He was family and always would be.

"Talk about snooze fest," Diesel lied, nudging his shoulder into Zero's thick chest.

He glanced up at Zero, wondering how long it would take him to call him out on his bullshit.

It didn't take long.

Zero gave him a pinch on the ass, making him jump with a squeak.

"Try again," Zero ordered.

Letting out a huff, Diesel glanced over at the one-night stand who wouldn't leave. *How did he fall in love with such an annoying ruffian?*

"Fine. I liked it... a lot."

"I thought so," Zero said with a cocky-ass grin plastered to his face. "That's why I suggested it to Matteo."

Diesel's mouth dropped open. "Betrayer."

Zero chuckled while Matteo glanced over in their direction.

Leaning closer to Zero, he added, "You say anything to anyone, and I'll make you watch me ride big red while you sit there tied to the bed." Big red was what they called Diesel's dildo, obviously because of its size and color.

"I don't think that's quite the threat that you think it is," Zero added, throwing his arm around Diesel's shoulder.

"It is when I leave you there all night without giving you any release."

Zero stopped walking, causing Diesel to jerk back under the weight of his arm.

"That's just cruel."

"Glad you finally met the true Diesel," Levi said, walking hand in hand with Chase.

"Yeah, we were wondering when you would take off

those dick-colored glasses and see Diesel for the massive prick that he really is," Isaac added.

"Same," Jared noted.

"I hate you all," Diesel joked, wrapping his arm around Zero's waist as they continued their walk down the opera house steps.

It was a Saturday night, and the streets were buzzing with tourists and street merchants, all doing their best to captivate their audiences and make a quick buck or two.

"Did I mention how much I love seeing you decked out in a suit and bow tie?" Zero whispered, dropping a kiss on Diesel's head as they continued to follow Matteo and the guys. "You're like a hot-as-fuck James Bond, massive dick and all."

"Eww, gross. That's my brother you're talking about," Levi threw over his shoulder.

"Stop your eavesdropping, and you won't be shocked by what you hear," Diesel responded with a smirk. Sometimes, that boy just needed to be put in his place.

"Hold up," Matteo announced, walking back toward Diesel. "I need you two to wait here. Don't do anything. Just wait."

Diesel glanced over at Zero, confused. "I don't get it. Why?"

Ignoring his question, Matteo pulled his cell phone out of his pocket, then began walking along the sidewalk, glancing around as if he were lost.

What the fuck was he doing? Matteo had been roaming

these streets pretty much since he was able to stand on two feet. He knew the place like the undersack of Ares's balls.

Still staring at his phone, Levi and Isaac stepped up beside Matteo and began assisting their father in trying to navigate their location.

"Jesus, I swear, we are not far from the hotel," Matteo noted, his voice dripping with frustration.

"I think it's two blocks over that way." Levi turned, pointing in the direction of their fictitious hotel.

Diesel looked over at Chase and Jared, who were standing over by a lamppost, appearing deep in their own conversation. If he had just spotted the two, he would have guessed that they were simply friends who had just finished watching the opera together. They gave no indication that they were together with the party currently trying to navigate their way through downtown Paris.

This whole thing was getting weird.

"*Pardonne-moi*. Do you speak English?" a woman asked as she approached Matteo and his companions.

Matteo looked up, all flustered and stressed.

"Hi. Yes. Umm, we're American," Matteo responded for some unknown reason.

"You look lost. Can I help you find something?" the Good Samaritan asked, sliding in between Matteo and Isaac. Levi stood in front of Matteo, still struggling to see the map on his phone.

"Yes, we are trying to find our way back to our hotel. It's here," Matteo said, tilting his phone so that the woman could see as well.

The woman smiled.

Diesel's heart stopped in his chest.

"Yes, I know the place you seek," the woman noted, taking Matteo's phone, then snaking her arm through Matteo's. "It's not far from here. I can show you how to get there," the woman offered with a hint of a French accent.

Diesel's grip on Zero's hand tightened as the vein in his neck began to throb. Hundreds of fantasies rushed through his mind. Pain. Dismemberment. Boiling acid. All the many scenarios he had dreamed about and spent hours fine-tuning in his head. Wishing that one day, he would have the opportunity to put one of his many plans into action.

He heard Zero groan beside him as he crushed his hand in his.

"Ooof," Matteo grunted as some asshole bumped into his back.

"*Pardonne-moi, monsieur*," the six-foot brute apologized, straightening himself up and giving Matteo a friendly pat on the back.

The wind was suddenly knocked from Diesel's stomach.

That bastard!

"Hey! Fuck-face!" Diesel shouted, dropping Zero's hand and charging toward the man and woman standing beside Matteo and his brothers.

The man and woman's heads snapped toward Diesel's voice, startled.

Without stopping, Diesel plowed into the man, punching him hard across his jaw. The man fell to the ground with a grunt, and Diesel fell on top of him.

Fifteen years' worth of rage came pouring out of Diesel. The world around him went silent. Nothing seemed to matter except beating the shit out of the man trapped beneath his body.

"Hey, get off of him, you piece of shit!" the woman shouted, bending over and slapping Diesel hard on his back.

Diesel barely felt it.

Pleasure flooded Diesel's system every time his knuckles connected with the moist flesh of the man's face. It was like he had found a new way of getting high. Each punch, each connection, sent a new surge of endorphins into Diesel's brain.

After getting in a few more solid shots, Diesel finally stood, giving the man one last kick to the ribs.

The man stared up at Diesel, lip bleeding, eyes terrified.

Good. He should be scared, Diesel thought to himself.

He felt a steady hand touch his shoulder, knowing immediately that it belonged to the man he loved like a father. Matteo gently pulled Diesel back by his side.

The woman crouched by the man, caressing his face as she checked him over to see what injuries he had sustained.

There was so much love in her touch. So much compassion. It made Diesel sick.

When the woman was convinced that the man would survive, she snapped her head up at Diesel.

"You! Animal! I'm going to—" Her voice suddenly caught in her throat, like an animal that suddenly spotted a predator. "Diesel?" the woman asked, her anger suddenly changing to confusion as she stood guard over the bleeding man lying next to her. "Is that you?"

"Yes, it's me, you fucking bitch," Diesel snarled, wanting to administer so much pain to the woman but not wanting to get more blood on his suit. He figured it was an acceptable loss getting his stepfather's blood on his Tom Ford suit—lord knows the man deserved it—but he drew the line at adding pathetic, alcoholic, piece of shit, mother's blood to the mix.

"But... but, you look all fancy and shit," the woman commented, suddenly losing her French accent and slowly standing up on her feet.

"Yes, I often look fancy... and *shit*," Diesel responded, mimicking his mother's crude speech, "...when I go to the opera with my family."

"He also looks devilishly handsome when attending many of the galas and parties he hosts at the château where we all live," Matteo added, wrapping his arm protectively around Diesel's shoulder.

Diesel had never felt so loved and cared for before in his life.

"Little D? Is that you? Thought you were dead in a gutter somewhere," his stepfather added, sitting up and wiping the blood off his lower lip.

"No. Thanks to you assholes, I now live in a castle, make mad money, and have the most amazing and supportive family a guy could ever ask for." Diesel nodded toward Levi and the other guys. "Not to mention, I have a smoking hot man by my side."

Zero slipped his arm around Diesel's waist, fighting for a position next to him and Matteo.

The two most important men in his life, each standing on either side of him.

His mother's mouth remained open as she tried to comprehend what she was seeing.

"But... I..." She didn't seem to have the words, most likely from years of drinking and bad mothering.

He really hated this fucking woman.

"Is everything okay?" a police officer asked, stepping up next to Isaac.

"No, Officer. These two are thieves. This woman tried to distract my father, while this man bumped into him and stole his wallet."

The officer glared at the two.

"That's bullshit. That fucker just attacked me for no reason," his stepfather argued, holding up his finger smeared with blood.

"Check his pockets, kind sir," Matteo suggested, taking a step back to give the officer room to work.

The officer pulled the man to his feet just as Matteo's wallet fell to the ground.

"Is that your wallet, sir?" the officer asked Matteo. Matteo nodded.

"That's not true. He must have dropped it when this druggy man viciously attacked my husband," Diesel's mother defended. "I've never seen a man so unhinged. He must be on the bath salts or something. You should arrest him and throw him in a mental asylum."

Diesel shook his head. Even after all these years, the woman was still choosing her piece of shit husband over her own flesh and blood.

"Umm, Officer, you might want to take a look at this woman's purse," Ares said, holding up a black leather purse.

Diesel looked over at Matteo, confused. Ares had not come with them to the opera, claiming he had other business to attend to at the mansion.

Matteo's lip turned up slightly in one of his mischievous grins.

The officer took the purse and peered inside. He gave a whistle.

"What's all this?" the officer asked, holding up a large brick of heroin.

Diesel tried not to laugh when his mother's face went white.

"Wh-what? That's not mine," she stuttered. Her eyes shifted to her husband, who also looked terrified.

"This is your purse, isn't it?" the officer asked, holding up the bag and pulling out a second brick.

"Yes... but... no. It's not..."

The officer passed the purse back to Ares.

"You're both under arrest," the officer announced, pulling out his handcuffs and snapping them around the wrists of Diesel's mother.

Revenge was so sweet.

Chase grabbed Diesel's stepfather and held him firmly in place while the officer snapped a second pair of cuffs on the man.

A moment later, a police car arrived, and the two officers placed Diesel's ex-parents into the back, giving Diesel a gentle nod of the head.

Diesel watched as the arresting officer walked up to Matteo and shook his hand. "Always a pleasure to see you, sir."

"Thank you again for all your help. I hope this wasn't too much of an inconvenience for you," Matteo responded.

The officer glanced over at Diesel.

"Never an inconvenience when it comes to getting justice for one of my favorite dancers." The man gave a wink before tilting his cap at the group and making his way back to his car.

Relief settled through Diesel's gut. He felt like a huge weight had been lifted off his chest. Years of anger and rage had finally been soothed as justice had finally been served.

His parents got what they fucking deserved.

"You set this whole thing up?" Diesel asked, turning to face Matteo.

"I spotted your folks pulling this scam a few weeks ago about a block from here. I figured what better way to get you justice than to have your parents thrown in jail on false charges as well."

Ares walked up beside Matteo and wrapped his arm around his shoulders.

"Daddy A procured the heroin, and I called in a favor from Officer Duke. By the way, you remember him, right? He's a member of *La Maison* and often helps me out when things get... sticky."

Diesel nodded. "Yeah, now that I think about it. He had a thing for watching me jerk off on my chest while he licked my feet."

"Yup, that's him." Matteo nodded.

Diesel lost his balance as his body was suddenly pulled into the heaping hunk of man standing next to him.

"No more footsie with *Officer Handsome*. Those little piggies belong to me now." Zero leaned in and gave Diesel a kiss on the cheek.

"Yes... *Robyn*..." Diesel whispered, giving his love a mischievous grin.

Six months ago, he had finally convinced Zero to tell him his real name. Granted, he literally had the man by the balls and his dick in his mouth, refusing to continue to blow him until his boyfriend confessed to his true identity.

Reluctantly, Zero confessed to the hated name, threatening Diesel with a lifetime of topping if he ever shared this knowledge with anyone else in the world, especially the gentlemen gathered around him. Thankfully, no one was paying them much attention.

Zero glared at Diesel, mentally threatening him with every fiber of his being.

Diesel never felt so loved.

"Guess now, we only have to get payback on my asshole stepbrother," Diesel said, glancing over at Matteo.

"No need. Your piece of shit little bro is currently serving time for aggravated assault and fraud. Apparently, he's been ripping off little old ladies by stealing all their savings for the past few years. Don't worry. I've got a guard on the inside that's taking extra special care of him."

Diesel smiled. *How the hell did he get so lucky?*

He looked around at the family standing before him. These guys had his back. They came after him when he was in trouble and needed rescuing. They stood by him when he lost his way and went on his many drug-induced benders. Now they'd all worked together to exact revenge on the so-called family that had him falsely imprisoned for a crime he didn't commit. A sentence that put him on the path of self-destruction, but then ultimately a road that led him to salvation.

That right there was love. That right there was family.

And while he had not felt the need to get high or go on a bender in almost a year—the same amount of time he had been dating Zero—he knew that if he ever felt an itch, he had a solid support system to turn to.

For the first time in his life, Diesel didn't fear the future or being abandoned. He knew that no matter what, he had the love of a fantastic man, the safety and security of a loving family, and of course, a dick that could make any man scream.

Who could ask for a more perfect life?

The End.

ABOUT THE AUTHOR

Matthew Dante is a Canadian author who writes LGBTQ+ Dark Romances and Thrillers. He graduated with a Major in Criminology and has been working in the financial crimes industry for over twenty years. He is an avid reader, world traveler, lover of all things Marvel and DC, and a romantic at heart.

As an author, your reviews are very important as these provide potential readers with a reason to give our books a try. So, if you enjoyed reading this book or others, please consider taking a few moments to leave a review.

To stay up to date on all of Matthew Dante's workings consider joining his newsletter and following him on all his social media platforms. Also, check out his website at matthewdante.com.

ACKNOWLEDGMENTS

I wanted to take a moment to thank you, my amazing readers. Without your love, support, and enthusiasm, none of these stories would ever have been written. You can't imagine how wonderful it feels to read a message from someone who has just finished reading my book and can't wait until the next one is released. These simple words have the most tremendous effect on us fellow authors. It is this excitement and love that drives us to work tirelessly to create the perfect story that we all hope you will love.

I also wanted to take a minute to thank my beta readers, Margaret and Maryanne. Thank you for reading through various versions and providing solid suggestions and input that always help strengthen the story. Your friendship and feedback are greatly appreciated!

Lastly, I wanted to thank my wonderful family. Without your love and support, I would not be the man I am today.

Now, you're all probably wondering where we go from here. I have a few ideas, but let's wait and see what you, the readers, would like to read next. As always, feel free to reach out to me on social media and let me know your thoughts.

ALSO BY MATTHEW DANTE

MM Dark Romance

FRACTURED SERIES

Fractured Love (Book 1)

Fractured Mind (Book 2)

Fractured Soul (Book 3)

ROUGH EDGES

Laying Claim (Book 1)

Protecting His (Book 2)

Devouring Sin (Book 3)

Avenging Des (Book 4)

Defending You (Book 5)

Obeying Orders (Book 6)

BOOK OF SIN

The Collector (Book 1)

The Broker (Book 2)

The Chameleon (Book 3)

The Chemist (Book 4)

As I Say...

The Naughty List (O Deadly Night 3 Charity Anthology)

MM Romance

Love to Hate You

The Devil Wears Pink

A Campfire Confession (Packing: An MM Anthology)

www.ingramcontent.com/pod-product-compliance
Lightning Source LLC
Chambersburg PA
CBHW071159250626
47159CB00001B/142